Praise for Doug Bowman's *Houston*

"The best Texas novel since *Lonesome Dove*."
—Ralph Compton

"With *Houston* Doug Bowman takes his rightful place as one of our great Western novelists."
—Mike Roarke, author of *Silent Drums*

"A pulse-pounding Texas novel, to rank with *Streets of Laredo*."
—Ralph W. Cotton, author of *Cost of Killing*

"An unforgettable book by one of today's best Western writers."
—Porter Wagoner, country music entertainer

By Doug Bowman from Tom Doherty Associates

Gannon
Sam Curtin
The Three Lives of Littleton Blue
The H&R Cattle Company
Houston
The Guns of Billy Free
The Quest of Jubal Kane

THE QUEST
OF
JUBAL KANE

DOUG BOWMAN

A TOM DOHERTY ASSOCIATES BOOK
NEW YORK

This is a work of fiction. All the characters and events portrayed in this book are either products of the author's imagination or are used fictitiously.

THE QUEST FOR JUBAL KANE

Copyright © 1999 by Doug Bowman

A Forge Book
Published by Tom Doherty Associates, LLC
175 Fifth Avenue
New York, NY 10010

www.tor.com

Forge® is a registered trademark of Tom Doherty Associates, LLC.

ISBN: 0-812-54047-6
Library of Congress Catalog Card Number: 99-21178

First edition: May 1999
First mass market edition: August 2000

Printed in the United States of America

0 9 8 7 6 5 4 3 2 1

THE QUEST
OF
JUBAL KANE

I

Jubal Kane rode into the town of Comfort, Texas, on the first day of July, and tied his big roan saddler and his packhorse in front of the first saloon he came to. A dark-haired six-footer who weighed about one-ninety, the young man had been in the saddle almost every day during the past year. Today was his twenty-second birthday, and the urge to wash the dust from his throat with a cold beer was strong.

He might also treat himself to a soft bed in a hotel or boardinghouse. It was not that sleeping on the ground bothered him, for he slept just as well on his bedroll, which consisted of a thick quilt doubled and sewn to a seven-foot section of canvas, as he did on the beds offered by many of the hotels. Most of the time he actually preferred sleeping outside, and as long as he could find a level place to spread the bedroll, preferably on a patch of soft, green grass, he slept warm and dry, even if the ground was wet.

He had been riding about the Hill Country for the past week, and had spent the early part of last night in Fredericksburg. Having gained no useful information there, he had ridden out of town before midnight and camped in a draw a mile or so to the south. He had taken to the saddle at sunup this morning, and had been riding steadily all day.

He stood at the hitching rail for a few moments looking up and down the street. The town bore a striking resemblance to dozens of others that he had already visited this year. He had asked the same questions in all of them, and this place called Comfort would be no exception. Jubal Kane was on a manhunt.

He was hunting three cold-blooded killers, and one of the advantages he had was that he would recognize all of them on sight, while none of them even knew that he existed. He also knew the given name of one, and the surname of another, though that bit of knowledge had as yet been of no help to him.

The three men had murdered his parents on their own property seven years ago, while Jubal himself watched the dastardly deed from only a few yards away.

It had happened one morning during the first week of August, when Bernard Kane and his wife, Tess, were at the barn milking the cow. Fifteen-year-old Jubal had just climbed to the loft to throw some hay down to the horses, when three men burst through the doorway cursing and shouting. "Git away from that damn cow and put your hands up!" a tall, thick-chested man with dirty blond hair shouted, waving a six-gun back and forth as he spoke.

As the Kanes moved away from the cow with their hands above their heads, the same man spoke again: "Hell, we gotta do this anyhow, so there ain't no point in putting it off. These pukes can identify us." That said, he put two bullets in Bernard Kane's chest, killing him instantly. The shooter then pointed to the woman and spoke to one of his companions. "Your turn, Leroy," he said. "That damn female's got a tongue to talk and a finger to point jist like her old man did."

"You're right about that, Mitchell," the man named Leroy said, then raised his Colt and fired.

Jubal lay in the barn loft, mesmerized, as the man pumped two shots into Tess Kane's bosom. She grabbed her chest with both hands and stood swaying for a moment, then fell backward, knocking over the milk bucket. With tears rolling down his cheeks, the young man lay deathly still, watching in horror as his mother kicked out her last breath in a pool of spilled milk.

"Git them horses outta the stables and git saddles on 'em!" Mitchell yelled. "We gotta git moving!"

"You want me to take a look in that loft up there, Mitchell?" the third man asked, speaking for the first time. "It won't take but a minute."

"Ain't nobody in that loft!" Mitchell shouted. "Git saddles on them damn horses and let's git outta here!"

Ten minutes later, Mitchell and the dark-haired man he called Leroy mounted the only two saddle horses the Kanes owned, while the third man stood holding one of the plow horses. Sandy-haired, with a thin beak of a nose and a long lower jaw, he was several inches shorter than either of his companions, and appeared to be in his early twenties. As Mitchell and Leroy rode through the wide doorway, the third man put a bullet of his own into each of the corpses, then mounted the plow horse bareback. "Ain't lettin' you fellows have all the fun!" he yelled in a squeaky voice, then followed the others from the building.

Although the killers had left the barn, Jubal could still hear them laughing and talking as they rode up the hill toward the house. He climbed down the ladder and stood watching through a crack in the wall, as the three men ransacked the house and tied their plunder on the backs of the horses. Though he could not even make a guess as to what all they were taking, it appeared that they were more interested in his father's clothing than anything else. Even as Jubal watched, the man named Mitchell was holding a pair of pants up to his waist in an effort to gauge the size, and Leroy was busy measuring the sleeves of a shirt.

When the killers finally rode out of the yard and down the opposite side of the hill, Jubal was quickly on his knees beside his fallen parents. Though he had never actually seen a dead person before, the pitiful picture he saw now left no doubt in his mind. With their eyes staring glassily at the ceiling and their mouths open wide, he knew that Bernard and Tess Kane had passed on to another world.

He bridled and mounted the remaining plow horse, then headed for his grandfather's farm, which was less than five miles away.

Grandpa Kane sold his dead son's farm two months later, and put the money in a trust fund for young Jubal. Being located in a prime agricultural region of east-central Texas, the place had sold quickly and had brought a good price. Immediately after the deaths of Bernard and Tess Kane, Jubal had moved into the home of his grandparents, where he lived until he turned twenty-one.

Aside from the fact that he had suddenly become a man of his own, his twenty-first birthday also meant that he now had full control over the money in his trust fund. "It's time for me to go hunting, Grandpa," he said after his birthday celebration was over. He took a bite of the frosted cake his grandmother had baked, then continued to speak with his mouth full. "I promised Pa and Ma when they were lying dead in that barn, that I would someday bring their killers to account." He washed the cake down with a sip of coffee, then added, "I've got money to travel on now, and I intend to make good on that promise or die trying."

His silver-haired grandfather nodded, then sat staring into his coffee cup.

"I know it's something that you have to do, Jubal," his grandmother said as she warmed up his coffee. "But you just be careful. You hear?"

"Yes, ma'am."

Jubal rode into Nacogdoches next morning at ten. He first visited the bank and withdrew as much money as he expected to need in the foreseeable future, then bought the small black packhorse that he still led around to this day. An hour later, he pointed the big roan in a south-easterly direction and began his quest. He had sufficient funds on his person and more in the bank, and was prepared to search for his quarry till hell froze over.

Now, standing at a hitching rail in Comfort, Texas, he was busy reminiscing. Tomorrow would be one year since he rode out of Nacogdoches, and though he had visited dozens of towns and at least a hundred watering holes, he had no reason to believe that he was any closer to finding the killers. Nonetheless, he had never even considered giving up the search. Nor would he ever. He took another look at the saloon, then loosened the saddle cinch and headed for the bat-wing doors. His throat was getting drier by the minute.

He stopped just inside the door and stood looking the place over. The saloon was about thirty feet wide and twice as long, with a bar against the west wall that ran half the length of the building. A cast-iron stove that had not been fired in months sat in the middle of the room, with tables and chairs forming a circle around it. The tables had not been rearranged since last winter, leading Kane to suspect that they had not been wiped off since then, either.

There was no stage, no piano, no dance floor. The absence of those three things and the fact that the building had no second story and no cabins in the rear, suggested that if a man wanted a woman he would have to look elsewhere. Mentally taking stock of the saloon's seating capacity, Jubal decided that the establishment could handle close to a hundred men at a time, though he doubted that the small settlement even had that many drinkers. At any rate, he himself was the only customer in the building at the moment. He nodded a greeting to the fat bartender, then walked forward and stood leaning against the bar. "I've been wanting a glass of cold beer all day," he said. "Can I get a small pitcher?"

"Absolutely," the big man answered, then turned and selected a pitcher from a shelf that contained several. He began to chuckle as he drew the beer, his midsection shaking like a bowl of jelly. "I've been needing a little lift all day, too," he said, "but I'm not allowed to drink anything till my shift is over."

Jubal offered a sympathetic smile. "What a shame," he said. He paid for his beer, then picked up the pitcher and a glass and headed for the opposite side of the room, selecting a table that was partially hidden from the front door by the big iron stove. He poured the glass full of the foamy brew and drank it half-empty in a single gulp, for he was very thirsty. He refilled it, then began to sip more slowly as he contemplated his next move.

He had already decided to spend the coming night in or around this town called Comfort. He had seen no hotel or boardinghouse, but neither had he ridden through the town looking for one. He would be needing a refill of his pitcher after a while, and would discuss that matter with the bartender then. Jubal had already noticed the livery stable at the east end of town, and supposed that he could buy a sack of grain for his horses there.

What he needed more than grain, however, was clean clothing. Buying more new duds was out of the question, for his packsaddle was already full. Several months ago he had fallen into the habit of buying something new and putting his dirty clothing on the packhorse whenever he failed to find a laundrywoman easily. Even now, there must be seven or eight changes of clothing in his pack, none of it clean. No more, he decided.

He expected his sackful of duds to be smelling like sunshine and summer breezes when he left this town. Though he had never known one, he had heard that there were also men around who took in laundry. If he could not find a laundrywoman, then maybe a laundryman. Another matter to be discussed with the bartender.

A short while later, a tall man walked through the batwing doors and seated himself at a table on the opposite side of the building. Though the man did not look familiar, Jubal eyed him almost to the point of staring, a habit that he had grown into very quickly after witnessing the carnage in his father's barn. Although he had looked the killers over from his position in the barn loft till their images were indelibly imprinted in his mind, he had no doubt that their appearances had changed over the years. With that in mind, he made it a point nowadays to devote a little more than a casual glance to every stranger he saw.

And though the killers might change, Jubal had burned pictures of all three men into his very being: the way they looked, sounded, and carried themselves. He would recognize them today, tomorrow, or twenty years from now. Sometimes he still dreamed about them at night, and the squeaky voice of the Third Man, the one that he hated most, was the one he heard in his sleep most often. The man had shot both of the Kanes, knowing that they were already dead, and had laughed about it all the while. Jubal had already decided that if the opportunity ever came, he would shoot the Third Man low—very low.

And Kane wore on his right hip a weapon that would guarantee a gut-shot man a slow and agonizing death: the 1873 Colt single-action Army revolver: the celebrated Peacemaker. Jubal had traded in his 1860 model Colt .44 on the new .45-caliber weapon early last year, when the Peacemakers first showed up on the Texas market.

Knowing that he would eventually embark on his present manhunt, young Kane had practiced daily throughout his teen years, and was an exceptional gunhand even before he acquired the new weapon. His speed and marksmanship became even more phenomenal with the acquisition of the Peacemaker, for he immediately doubled the amount of time he spent practicing. And each time he drilled a target dead-center, he would imagine that he was looking into the face of Mitchell, Leroy, or the Third Man.

Jubal had long ago abandoned all hope that the law might someday bring the killers to justice. "Your descriptions of the men are good enough that I'd know 'em all on sight, young man," Nacogdoches County sheriff Pat Patterson had said to Jubal the day after the murders. "Now, you just leave the rest to me. They won't get far, we'll have 'em in no time." Jubal had taken the lawman at his word, and for the next few weeks went about his duties on his grandfather's farm confident that the three men would soon be behind bars.

Not only did that *not* happen, but Sheriff Patterson's attitude took a different turn a month later: Jubal and his grandfather had just tied the wagon team to the hitching rail in front of the general store, which was directly across the street from the lawman's office. As the two made ready to enter the establishment, the young man looked across the street and noticed the sheriff standing on his small porch motioning for him to come over. "The sheriff wants to talk to me, Grandpa," Jubal said to Silas Kane, who was already disappearing into the store. "I'll join you after I find out what he wants."

Patterson did not offer a greeting when Jubal reached the porch, just pointed to the office. "In there," he ordered. Inside the office, the lawman closed the door and dragged a ladder-backed chair to the center of the room. "It's time we quit playing games, boy," he said in a gruff tone of voice. He roughly placed a hand on each of Jubal's shoulders, then slammed him down into the chair hard. "You've had me chasing ghosts for more'n a month now, and I reckon it's about time you told me what really happened in that barn."

"I . . . I already told you what really happened, Sheriff."

"Bullshit!" Patterson said loudly. He grabbed the boy's chin between his thumb and forefinger and began to squeeze as hard as he could, shaking Jubal's head back and forth. "You've been lying to me right down the line, boy! You invented them three men with this same little noggin that I'm trying to shake the truth out of, didn't you? You killed your own ma and pa, then sent me out hunting three men who didn't even exist." He shook Jubal's head harder. "Ain't that the truth, now? Admit it! Admit that you've been lying about what happened from the very first day!"

"No . . . I—"

"Admit it!" The sheriff was shouting now. "You yourself pulled the trigger on your ma and pa, because they made you work and they made you go to school. Then you not only did away with the gun you killed them with, but you've done something with three horses and a lot of stuff from the house. Where's it at, boy? Who'd you sell all that stuff to?" He was squeezing Jubal's chin so hard now that his thumbnail had bitten into the flesh, bringing forth several drops of blood. "Come on, dammit!" he shouted, giving the boy's head another violent shake. "Out with it! Out with it, right now!"

Although Jubal had been involved in many fistfights during his boyhood, and was considered to be an excellent scrapper by his schoolmates, he had never fought a full-grown man. Nonetheless, he could see that he was as tall as the sheriff was nowadays, and believed that he might even be as strong. With those things in mind, he suddenly decided to resist Patterson's shouted accusations and physical badgering.

He seized the sheriff's wrist and jerked the hand free from his own chin, then scooted his chair backward and jumped to his feet. He very quickly picked up the chair and shoved it between himself and Patterson, pointing one of the legs directly at the lawman's face. "I'll use it, Sheriff, or anything else I can get my hands on. You're not gonna run over me anymore." Continuing to hold the chair between them, he circled the sheriff till he himself was standing in front of the door, then opened it with his right hand. He threw the chair across the room so hard that it fell apart against the wall, then he disappeared through the doorway.

An angry Silas Kane appeared in the sheriff's office within minutes. "What the hell do you mean trying to manhandle my grandson, Pat Patterson? I saw the blood on his chin, and all them accusations you made against him are ridiculous. He's a fifteen-year-old boy, Mr. Lawman, and I don't believe that badge gives you the authority to go jerking him around."

Knowing that Silas Kane had a voice to be reckoned with when it came to county politics, the forty-year-old lawman quickly wilted under the older man's reprimand. "I . . . I'm sorry, Silas," he said haltingly. "I was just trying to get to the bottom—"

"Bottom, my ass!" Silas interrupted. "The men who murdered my son and my daughter-in-law are long gone, and they're not ever coming back. You're never gonna find them, either; you lost every chance you had during the first two days." He jabbed his forefinger against the lawman's chest, adding, "It's only six months till election time, Pat Patterson, and I'd bet that I have more friends in this county than you do. Expect me to do everything in my power to see that you're not wearing that damn badge next year." Then he stepped through the doorway, slamming the door behind him as hard as he could.

True to his word, Silas Kane campaigned nonstop against the lawman during the next several months. Nonetheless, Patterson was reelected by a landslide margin, and was still sheriff of Nacogdoches County to this day. He had never touched or even spoken to Jubal again after Silas Kane's tongue-lashing, however. As the years passed and he grew into a man of considerable size, Jubal had even begun to play a little game with the man: On more than one occasion when he saw the sheriff coming down the opposite side of the street, young Kane had crossed over in an effort to assure that a face-to-face meeting occurred. Each time, Patterson had quickly crossed the street to avoid the same.

Now, sitting in the Red Rock Saloon in the town of Comfort, Jubal smiled as he remembered the expression on the sheriff's face as the man scampered across the street to avoid looking him in the eye. It had been young Kane's intention then, as it was now, to even the score for the chin-pinching incident if Patterson ever gave him the slightest excuse. Confident that the lawman would never let that happen, Jubal drained his glass, picked up the pitcher and walked to the bar. "I'll have a refill," he said to the barkeep.

Once he had a full pitcher Jubal did not go back to the table, but took a seat on a barstool. He filled his glass and took a sip, then spoke to the bartender. "Do you know of anyplace where I can get some clothing washed?" he asked.

"Sure do," the man answered. "The Wilson House takes in washing. Mizz Ophelia'll wash up your clothes all right, but if she has to fire up the washpot just for you, she'll probably charge you double." He pointed over Jubal's shoulder toward the window. "The Wilson House is the only boardinghouse within twenty miles of here. You can't miss it, 'cause it sits damn near in the middle of the road about a quarter mile south of town." He drummed his fingers against the bar for a moment, then began to shake his head. "Guess I mighta been talking out my ass when I said Mizz Ophelia'd probably charge you double if you were her only customer. The truth of the matter is that I don't know what she charges, but if you rent a room and buy a meal or two from her, I believe you'll get your clothes hung out to dry a hell of a lot cheaper."

Jubal nodded, and wiped his mouth on his sleeve. "Makes sense," he said. He sat sipping his brew quietly for the next several minutes. When the man who had been sitting on the west side of the room left his table and walked through the front door, Kane was once again the only customer in the building. "I'm trying to locate three men that I ran into a few years back," he said to the bartender, "and I was wondering if maybe you can help me."

Smiling, the fat man placed his elbows on the bar and cradled his chin with his interlocked fingers. "Well, bygosh I guess we just won't know till you tell me who they are, will we?"

Jubal chuckled softly. "I'm not sure I can do that," he said. "At least, not very well. One of 'em is a very muscular man about thirty years old, whose last name is Mitchell. He's about the same height as me, and has blond hair. One of the others is dark-haired, about the same height and age as Mitchell, and answers to the name of Leroy.

"The third one is about five-seven, with sandy hair, a long lower jaw, and a smeller that looks more like a beak than a nose. I never did hear his name, but he'd be in his late twenties now, and his squeaky voice is so unusual that anybody who ever hears it is pretty likely to remember it."

The man backed away from the bar and stood with his arms crossed against his chest. "So you intend to kill all three of them as soon as you find them, right?"

"I didn't say that."

"You didn't have to. A fellow don't go looking for men he can't even name unless he's got his dander up. Yessir, I'd bet a week's pay that you ain't hunting 'em just to say hello." He stood shaking his head for a moment. "Don't make no difference, though, 'cause I ain't seen none of 'em nohow."

Jubal nodded, then slid off the stool and changed the subject. "This Wilson House you mentioned, do they have a place to put up horses?"

"Yessir. Mizz Ophelia's got at least a dozen stalls and a good-sized corral. Matter of fact, the barn looks to be bigger than the boardinghouse, and that's saying something. Just tell the lady that the bartender at the Red Rock Saloon sent you. She'll take good care of you, and her hired man'll do the same for your horse."

Kane was already headed toward the front door. "Good luck to you," he said over his shoulder, "and I appreciate the information." Outside, he stood on the boardwalk looking up and down the street for a moment, but saw no movement in either direction. Though the afternoon sun hung no more than two hours above the western horizon, the day was still hot enough to discourage people who might otherwise be roaming the streets. During the hot days of summer, most townfolk took care of business in the cool of the morning, then waited till after sunset to visit with one another.

Jubal took one last look around him, then stepped into the street and tightened the saddle cinch. Moments later, he mounted the roan and led the black packhorse down the hill toward the Wilson House.

2

The Wilson House had a wide porch that ran all the way across the front and down its west side, and as the bartender had indicated, was situated only a few feet from the road. The hitching rails were located at the end of the porch on the east side of the house, so that the rumps of the hitched animals would be out of the traffic.

The bottom portion of the huge, two-story building was built of thick logs and appeared to be at least fifty years old, while the much smaller and much newer upper portion was made of smooth lumber and painted white. Both the lower and the upper portions had numerous windows of various sizes, all of which were fitted with glass panes and bordered by an assortment of bright-colored curtains.

Jubal had just dismounted and tied his animals to the hitching rail, when he heard the lady speak.

"Can I help you, young man?" She was standing above him at the end of the porch. A tall, gray-haired woman who appeared to be about sixty years old, she obviously liked her own cooking, for she probably weighed at least two hundred pounds. She continued to stand with her arms folded, a big smile on her face.

"Yes, ma'am," Jubal said, flashing two rows of perfect teeth. "If you can put myself and my horses up and feed us all, you can help me a whole lot."

"That's what I'm in business for," she said, her smile constant. She motioned toward the steps that led to the porch. "Come on through the front door, and I'll send Wesley around for your horses. He'll feed 'em, water 'em and take care of 'em just like they were his own."

"Yes, ma'am." He slid his Winchester out of the boot, threw his saddlebags across his shoulder and headed for the porch. He paused at the top step and pointed to his packhorse. "I've got two bags of dirty clothing tied on that packsaddle," he said. "The bartender up at the Red Rock told me that I could get it washed here at your place."

She nodded. "The bartender's name is Lanny, and he told you right. It's a little late in the day to fire up the washpot now, though. Wesley does the washing to earn a little extra money, and I let him keep every penny of it. He'll wash up your things and hang 'em on the line bright and early in the morning. In this kinda weather it won't take 'em more 'n two or three hours to dry, then he'll roll 'em up and put 'em right back on your packhorse."

Jubal smiled. "That'll be fine, ma'am. He won't have any problem finding my dirty clothes, he'll probably be able to smell them."

She chuckled, and held the front door open. "Your room is the second one on the right," she said, pointing down the hall. "Supper is at six o'clock, and it works out a whole lot better when everybody gets to the table on time. You got a watch?"

"Yes, ma'am."

"Very well, then." She stood quietly for a moment, then added, "My rate is a dollar a day for a room and three meals, and thirty cents a day for each horse. In your case that'll come to a dollar-sixty a day. Is that agreeable?"

"Yes, ma'am," he said, beginning to fish around in his pocket. "I'll pay you for two days right now."

"No, no," she said. "You pay when you get ready to leave, and I hope you'll be staying longer than two days."

Jubal nodded, and turned to walk down the hall. "I'll tell Wesley to take care of your laundry," the lady called after him. "Getting your clothes done up is gonna be between the two of you, so you can settle with him in private."

"Yes, ma'am."

The room was at least as nice as most of the hotels Kane had slept in, and he stood in the doorway looking for only a moment. He crossed the room and seated himself on the wide, firm bed, which appeared to be several inches longer than his six-foot frame. Resting against the wall near the head of the bed was a small table which supported a washpan, a towel, a pitcher of water, and two glasses. A small mirror hung on the wall above the table.

Sitting on the bed and looking around him, it crossed his mind that someone, most likely a woman using a stepladder, had put in a great deal of time and hard work decorating the room. All four walls and even the ceiling had been plastered with wallpaper of many different colors and floral designs, and try as he might, Jubal could not see a seam where one sheet ended and another began. No, sir, he quickly decided, a man did not hang that wallpaper. Only a woman would possess the patience and the dexterity of hand necessary to perform such a meticulous job.

Kane walked to the east side of the room and pulled the curtains aside, then raised the window. A man who appeared to be at least fifty years old had just untied Jubal's animals from the hitching rail and was now leading them toward the barn. Apparently hearing the squeaking sound of the window being raised, the man made eye contact with Kane, then waved hello. Jubal returned the greeting with a nod of his head, and the man walked on.

A glance at his watch told Kane that he had more than enough time to shave his face before supper. He took his soap, mug, and brush from the saddlebag, then the wooden box containing the razor that had belonged to his father. It was the only razor Bernard Kane had ever owned, and likewise the only one his son Jubal had ever used. Though the blade had worn thinner over the years, it still held an edge, and Jubal would use it as long as he could. When and if the time came when he couldn't, he would store it away somewhere, for he intended to keep it as long as he lived.

He took the leather strop from his saddlebag and put his foot on one end, then ran the razor up and down it at least a dozen times. Then, testing it with his thumb, he decided that it was plenty sharp enough to handle his heavy beard. A few minutes later, he left the room with a clean shave.

He looked at his watch just before he walked into the dining room. The time was two minutes to six. "You're right on time, young man," Ophelia Wilson said with a chuckle. "If I hadn't seen which direction you came from, I'm not sure I would have recognized you."

Jubal smiled. "I've been wearing that beard for five days," he said. "First good chance I've had to get rid of it."

Several men were already seated at the table, and the

lady stood at the far end. She continued to talk to Kane: "Well, you must have had a mighty hard time scraping that bunch of thick whiskers off. Why didn't you say something? I'd have brought you a pan of hot water."

"You shore never brought me no hot water!" an old man seated at the near end of the table said loudly. "Is he paying you more money, or is it just because he's better looking than the rest of us?"

She laughed aloud. "I couldn't help noticing that he's a mighty handsome man, Mr. Winfrey, but the truth of the matter is that I'd have brought you some hot water, too, if you'd ever asked me for it."

"Well, that's good to hear," Winfrey said. "I'll remember it the next time I need something."

Several of the boarders began to mumble and nod their heads in agreement with the old man.

"All right, all right!" the lady said loudly. "From now on, all anybody has to do to get hot water is speak up!"

Old man Winfrey led the others in a short round of applause.

Mrs. Wilson spoke to Jubal again: "Take this seat right here at the end of the table, young man." She pointed to the chair that she had been leaning against. "You've got long arms, so you can pretty well reach whatever you want to eat."

Kane pulled out the chair and, without speaking to anyone, stood leaning over the table as he began to fill his plate. The table held a variety of food the likes of which he had not seen since the last time he ate Christmas dinner at his grandmother's house: pork chops swimming in thick gravy, fried chicken, mashed potatoes, red beans, cornbread, hot biscuits, fried okra, and thick slices of garden-fresh tomatoes. Cakes of three different colors waited in the middle of the table. When his plate would hold no more, Jubal poured his cup full of coffee, then seated himself in the chair and dug in.

Though there were seven men besides Kane seated at the table, the meal was for the most part eaten in silence. All of which was fine with Jubal, for he had never been one for small talk. It had always seemed to him that when a group of men got together, regardless of their number, it was usually only one or two who did all of the talking, and the topic seldom varied. The talk was almost always about weather, cattle, grass, and water.

Of course, on occasion the conversation was about men who had become famous or infamous for one reason or another, usually well-known lawmen or outlaws. When the talk turned to gunfighters, there were always several men in any crowd who were personally acquainted with the fastest and deadliest gunman of all time. Seldom did any two of the storytellers name the same man.

As was the case at most boardinghouses, the residents of the Wilson House usually gathered on the front porch to exchange bits of wisdom or humor during the hour between supper and bedtime. Tonight was no exception, and after a trip to the outhouse, Jubal joined them. As he seated himself on the top step, the conversation going on around him concerned the relationship between fathers and sons. "I was always afraid of my pa when I was growing up," one man was saying. "He never did hurt me or nothing, but I was afraid of him anyhow."

Old man Winfrey, who was seated in a cane-bottom rocking chair, leaned forward and addressed the speaker: "A boy's s'posed to be scared o' his pa," he said. "It's the most natural thing in the world. Even the animals in the woods understand it. A boy'll usually mind his ma 'cause he loves and respects her, but he's got to be sorta leery o' his pa." He was quiet for a moment, then added, "Now that same boy might grow up to be six feet tall and weigh two hundred pounds. He might have a ten-inch dick and a bucketful of balls, but he's still gonna be a little bit scared o' his old man."

A few men chuckled, but nobody disagreed with Winfrey.

Jubal sat listening to the others talk for the large part of an hour, but except for an occasional grunt or a nod of his head, did not join in the conversation. When the sun finally dropped behind the horizon, he got to his feet. "I hope all of you fellows get a good night's sleep," he said. "I'm certainly ready to give it a try." Without another word, he walked through the doorway and down the hall to his room.

A few minutes later, he was lying on his bed enjoying the evening breeze from the open window. He had not retired to his room because he was sleepy, but because he was bored by the monotonous prattle of the boarders. Actually, he was wide-awake and, as usual, thinking about his quarry.

When Jubal's parents were killed, Sheriff Patterson had persuaded the man who ran the local newspaper to withhold some of the details concerning the murders. Consequently, the fact that there had been an eyewitness in the barn loft never appeared in print, even after several other newspapers across Texas picked up the story.

Had the sheriff withheld the details because he had disbelieved young Kane's story right from the start? Or was it because he did not want the outlaws to know that they had been seen? There was no way of knowing at this late date, but regardless of the lawman's reasoning, Jubal was convinced that it had been handled correctly. Otherwise, knowing that he had witnessed their actions, the outlaws might have ambushed and killed him years ago.

While still in his teens, Jubal got the idea that the killers might have been escaped convicts, though he had never discussed it with the sheriff. If the same thought had ever occurred to Patterson, the lawman had obviously not followed through on it. Jubal had tried for several years to remember what kind of clothing the men wore, but finally faced the fact that he had simply been too frightened to notice. He did remember, however, that the sleeves of the shirt worn by the man named Leroy were several inches too short.

Adding the matter of the ill-fitting shirt to the big to-do that the outlaws had made over his father's clothing, then considering that all three had been horseless and that each man had a gun but no gunbelt, the idea that they might have been prison escapees had occurred to the youngster early on. He had even said as much to his grandfather. "Maybe they stole their guns the same place they stole their clothes, Grandpa." When it became obvious that Silas Kane did not think much of his grandson's idea, Jubal had eventually dismissed it from his own mind.

Tonight the idea dominated his thoughts again, however, and this time there was nobody around to dissuade him from his way of thinking. This time he would follow up on his suspicions. A few days from now he would be on his way to Huntsville, hoping he could get in to see the warden at the state penitentiary.

After thinking on the matter for a while longer, he decided that getting the warden to listen to his story might not be easy, for the man was most likely one of the busiest people in Texas.

Jubal fluffed up his pillow and turned on his side, all the while trying to think of a way to gain an audience with the head man at the state pen. What if he presented an introduction written by a prominent law official? Wouldn't the warden devote a few minutes to him then? Most likely, he decided quickly. And where better to find a prominent law official than San Antonio? The sheriff of

Bexar County no doubt delivered a large number of convicts to Huntsville Prison every year, and it was highly possible that he was personally acquainted with the warden. Just before he dozed off, Kane made a decision to head for San Antonio the day after tomorrow. He would have a talk with Sheriff Randy Bacon, a man whose name and reputation were known throughout Texas and beyond.

Leaving his animals in the corral to rest the next morning, Jubal walked to town and spent most of the day there. He bought a few things that he needed, then visited the bartender at the Red Rock Saloon long enough to drink a pitcher of beer. At dinnertime he ate a bowl of red beans and rice at a small restaurant, then walked to the livery stable, where he talked with the friendly hostler till late in the afternoon. Before leaving, he bought a sack of oats from the man, saying that he would return for it in the morning about sunup. Then he headed for the Wilson House. He had had his exercise for the day, and it was very near suppertime.

He rode out of Comfort and headed southeast an hour after sunup next morning, leading a packhorse laden with sixty pounds of oats and seven changes of clean clothing for its master. He expected to be at the twin springs a few miles northwest of San Antonio by nightfall, and would spend the night there. He had camped there twice last year, and even now remembered the exact spot on which he had spread his bedroll.

It was possible that there would be no grass left near the springs this time, however, for it was getting on into the summer. Lots of people and their animals were traveling nowadays, and the grass nearest the waterholes was the first to go. If there was no suitable graze near the springs, Jubal would sleep as far away as he had to, for he had always insisted on bedding down close to his animals.

He traveled steadily throughout the day, and reached the springs when the sun was still two hours high. Not high enough that he had the campsite to himself, however. In fact, three covered wagons and several people were crowded around the springs, and Jubal counted nine horses grazing close by. He stopped only long enough to fill his coffeepot with water and let his horses drink, then remounted. He rode out of sight, holding the coffeepot off to his side almost at arm's length, for his attempts to balance it so the water did not slosh out on his leg and into his saddle had been unsuccessful.

A quarter mile farther on, he came to a grassy meadow bordered by small clusters of evergreens. He dismounted and tied his animals, then unburdened both. He dragged his saddle and his packsaddle into a bunch of short junipers, then tied nosebags filled with oats on his horses. While the animals ate, he began to gather fuel for a fire. Dead grass, twigs, and sticks were all close to hand, and he soon had a healthy blaze going.

He chopped up a few potatoes and dropped the pieces into a small boiler, then added half of the water from the coffeepot. Then, after pouring a handful of grounds into the coffeepot, he set both the pot and the boiler on the fire. Supper, consisting of potato soup, Bologna sausage, cheddar cheese, leftover Wilson House biscuits, and strong coffee, would be ready shortly. He selected a smooth patch of grass and spread his bedroll, then picketed his horses on good grass about forty yards away.

When he returned to his campsite he pulled the boiler and the coffeepot off the fire, then seated himself on a folded blanket. He sliced off several chunks of Bologna sausage and cheese with his pocketknife, then retrieved his ever-present soup spoon from his saddlebag. Moments later, he was eating a meal that was far superior to the average trail fare.

After eating, he drained the boiler and wiped it as clean as he could with handfuls of grass, then put it back in his pack. He set the coffeepot aside, for it still contained enough coffee to open his eyes in the morning. It would certainly not be the first time he had drunk warmed-over coffee for breakfast.

He extinguished his fire with handfuls of dirt, then sat thinking of nothing in particular as he waited for daylight to disappear. Just before dark, he walked to the meadow and moved his horses to new grass. Then, as the moonless night closed in, he pulled off his boots and stretched out on his bedroll fully clothed, his Peacemaker and his Winchester close to hand.

Shortly after noon next day he tied his horses in front of the Menger Hotel in San Antonio. Though the establishment was widely known as one of the best hotels in the West, it had yet another claim to fame: General Robert E. Lee had once ridden his great horse Traveler right into the lobby, explaining later that he had performed the feat "just for the hell of it." Though it was well known to most Texans, and few doubted that Lee had been drunk when it occurred, the hotel management, knowing that drunken cowboys would be tempted to duplicate the general's actions, had over the years refrained from publicizing the incident.

Jubal eased the saddle girth, then, with his saddlebags across his shoulder and his Winchester cradled in the crook of his arm, walked into the hotel. When the silver-haired desk clerk informed him that a room would cost him four dollars, Kane knew that he would spend only one night at the Menger. Though he was not exactly short of funds, he nonetheless considered the price to be extravagant. Besides, the last thing he needed or wanted was a fancy hotel room. He had chosen the expensive establishment only because he hoped it might favorably impress Sheriff Bacon, and he fully intended to be off the premises tomorrow.

Kane walked down the hall to number sixteen and unlocked the door. The room was impressive, all right, with tall, curtained windows, a thick carpet on the floor, and a bathtub in the corner. Though the clerk had said that a bath was included in the price of the room, and that hot water would be brought to him for the asking, Jubal had no need for it. He had shaved, bathed, and changed into clean clothing at a creek five miles out of town.

He locked his rifle and his saddlebags in the room and returned to the front desk. "Which way to the livery stable?" he asked the clerk.

The old man appeared not to hear for a few moments, but finally spoke. "Well, now," he said, "I reckon that would depend on which one you're huntin'. There's six of 'em in Santone, you know."

"No, I didn't know," Jubal said quickly, raising his voice a little. "I need a place to put up my horses, and since I just rented a room from you, I'd naturally be interested in the stable closest to the hotel."

The old man pointed south. "Go to the corner and turn east," he said. "Two blocks later you'll run right into it."

At the hitching rail, Jubal neither tightened the saddle cinch nor mounted the roan, but simply untied both animals and led them down the crowded street. Following the directions he had been given, he learned very quickly that the clerk had greatly underestimated the distance.

When he finally reached the stable he knew that he had walked at least a quarter mile. He had for all practical purposes left the town behind, for the busy street became an uninhabited road long before it reached the livery.

The huge building's large doors were open wide, creating enough room for two or even three wagons to pass through the doorway at the same time. Jubal decided that the overhead clearance was also excessive. He gauged the distance from the ground to the ceiling to be at least fifteen feet, and doubted that anyone would ever load a wagon that high with anything. And the tall, wide, and deep loft would hold enough hay to feed a small herd of horses for a year. He shrugged, then read the sign proclaiming that the establishment was the combination of a livery stable and a blacksmith shop, that the owner and operator was a man named Roscoe Nemecek.

"Can I help you, mister?" The question had come from someone with an exceptionally deep voice, who was well back within the darkened building. When the speaker walked into the lighted doorway, Jubal was somewhat astounded. Standing six and a half feet tall and weighing at least three hundred pounds, the middle-aged man was even bigger than his voice. Shirtless, and wearing pants that had been cut off above the knees, he was quite possibly the most muscular man Kane had ever seen. The thick shock of black hair that he wore was by no means limited to his head. His shoulders, chest, arms, and even the backs of his hands were almost as hairy as an ape. "I'm Roscoe," he said, then repeated the question: "Can I help you?"

"Yes, sir," Jubal said, indicating his pack animal with a jerk of his head. "I believe you can. I intended to leave both of my horses with you, but it's farther out here than I thought. If you'll lock up my pack and take care of the packhorse, I'll bring the roan back to you later."

The big man stepped forward and took hold of the black's reins. "It'll be a pleasure, young fellow, and I appreciate your business." He motioned to a small room off to his left. "I sleep there in the office at night, so if anybody steals your pack they're gonna have to take me, too."

"That'll be just fine, sir." Kane looked the giant over again out of the corner of his eye, then chuckled softly. "I doubt very seriously that anybody would consider trying to walk over you in order to get to my pack." He turned to the roan, tightened the cinch and mounted. "I've got some business to take care of," he said, "then I'll bring the saddler back to you." He pointed the animal's head toward town, then rode away at a trot.

"You do that," Roscoe shouted after him. The big man locked Jubal's pack up in the office, then led the packhorse down the hall to a trough full of oats.

3

★

A short time later, Kane tied the roan at one of the several hitching rails in front of the sheriff's office, which was located on the ground floor of the county courthouse. Inside the huge court building, a sign identified the first room on the right-hand side of the hallway as the lawman's headquarters. Jubal stepped to the office and stood in the open doorway. Two deputies were bent over a desk with their heads together. With a large map spread out before them, and talking in low tones, it appeared that one of the men might be pointing out a particular area of the county to the other.

After his presence had gone unnoticed for what he considered to be a reasonable length of time, Kane rapped his knuckles lightly against the doorjamb. "Is Sheriff Bacon around?" he asked.

The youngest and skinniest of the two walked to the doorway. "Looks like you oughta be able to see that the sheriff ain't here," he said, then looked over his shoulder at the older man for approval. Both deputies chuckled, then the skinny one continued, "Now, don'tcha think you could see the sheriff if he was in this office?"

Jubal stood staring coldly into the deputy's eyes, a granite expression on his face. "I didn't come here to be insulted, fellow, and I damn sure don't like your idea of humor. Now, where the hell is Sheriff Bacon?"

The older deputy stepped away from the desk and answered the question. "Don't neither one of us know exactly where he is, young man." He walked across the room to the doorway. "Truth is, he seldom tells us anything about where he's going, just goes wandering around the town whenever he takes a good notion. Sometimes he walks, sometimes he rides. This time he's riding a big dapple-gray."

The younger deputy, a blond-haired six-footer who appeared to be about twenty-one years old, spoke again: "What is it that you want to see the sheriff about?"

Kane was slow to answer. "I'll wait and discuss my business with Mister Bacon," he said finally. "Then it'll be up to him whether he wants to tell you about it or not."

"Well, I ain't no little kid, mister," the deputy said indignantly, looking at his older partner as if seeking confirmation. He grabbed the left side of his shirt with his thumb and forefinger and pushed it forward so Jubal could not miss the badge, then raised his voice almost to a shout. "I'm an officer of the law, you know!"

"Yeah," Kane said, turning toward the front door. "I know."

He rode up and down the streets of San Antonio for the next hour, inspecting horses at the various hitching rails. He had seen a few dapple-grays, but with the exception of one, all were hitched to buggies. He had given no more than a passing glance to the single gray that wore a saddle, for it had been a mare, and a much smaller animal than the sheriff of the county could be expected to choose.

Jubal had just about decided to give up the hunt, when he halted at a corner and looked down a narrow street that ran toward the river. There, halfway down the block, at the hitching rail of an establishment that a tall sign identified as Trader Paul's, stood a dapple-gray that was at least sixteen hands high. With no hesitation, Kane turned the corner and tied his mount at the same rail a few moments later. He stepped onto the boardwalk, then entered the building.

Before he even cleared the doorway, he decided that the place sold a little bit of everything. Looking down the first aisle he could see saddles, harnesses, and bridles, along with axes, saws, plows, and other tools. The second aisle held racks and shelves containing a wide assortment of shoes, boots, and clothing for both men and women, and shelves along both walls were stacked with canned goods. And though the establishment could hardly be classified as a saloon, there was nonetheless a wide shelf behind the counter that held dozens of whiskey bottles of different sizes. A dark-haired man who appeared to be about thirty years old stood behind the counter. He greeted Jubal with a nod. "Can I help you, sir?"

"Maybe," Kane said, offering a broad smile. "I'm looking for Sheriff Bacon."

The man pointed across the room to a table where two men sat in straight-backed chairs. "Well, I reckon you've found him," he said. "That's him over there playing dominoes with Paul."

Kane thanked the man and moved off. As he neared the table he could easily see one of the reasons for Bacon's reputation as a tough lawman. Not only did he sit high in his chair, but his long legs took up most of the room beneath the table. Obviously several inches taller than Kane himself, the thick-chested, broad-shouldered man presented a near-perfect picture of physical strength. A thick shock of brown hair crowned his hatless head, and he appeared to be in his late thirties.

When Jubal approached the table, the lawman looked at him questioningly, then laid his dominoes facedown on the table. "Is there something I can do for you?" he asked.

"My name is Jubal Kane, Sheriff, and I'm sorry if I interrupted your game. I need to have a talk with you, but there's nothing urgent about it. Do you think you'll be back in your office later on?"

The lawman nodded. "Within the hour," he answered. "I guess you'd like to talk in private, huh?"

"Yes, sir."

The sheriff studied the long line of dominoes lying faceup on the table, then chose one from his own hand to play. He motioned to the man across the table, then spoke to Jubal again: "I'll be back up there as soon as I beat Paul out of some more money with these dominoes, Mister Kane. Truth is, I'm a little anxious to find out what you want to talk about."

"Thank you," Jubal said, turning toward the front door. "I'll see you in your office."

Back at the courthouse, Kane tied his mount and loosened the cinch, then seated himself on the long wooden bench beside the main doorway. He would do his waiting outside, for he wanted nothing else to do with the sheriff's skinny deputy. Sitting on the end of the ten-foot bench with his shoulders leaning against the wall, he was comfortable enough.

During the next hour several men joined him on the bench for short durations, making small talk for a few minutes, then disappearing down the street or back into the courthouse. Jubal soon decided that San Antonians must be the friendliest people in Texas, for every man who had passed in or out of the building had either smiled and nodded to him or spoken a greeting.

Finally, after a glance at his watch told him that he had been sitting on the bench for an hour and twenty minutes, he got to his feet. It was then that he saw the sheriff approaching the courthouse from a different direction than he had been expecting. Maybe like many other politicians, the man had deliberately taken a circuitous route for the purpose of being seen by as many of the county's voters as possible, Kane was thinking.

The lawman dismounted and tied his animal, then stood looking down the street. He was an imposing figure to say the least, and the bulging muscles of his upper body could be seen even through his shirt. Kane gauged the man's weight to be at least two-forty, and his height about six-five. The high-crown Stetson that he was now wearing made him appear to be even taller. He doffed the hat and wiped the sweatband with his hand, then ran his shirt-sleeve along his forehead. He nodded to Jubal, then pointed to the bench. "Nobody on the street," he said. "I guess we can do our talking out here."

After both men had seated themselves, the sheriff crossed his long legs and hung his hat on his knee. "You said you wanted to talk," he said with a smile. "I'm listening."

Jubal cleared his throat. "Well, Sheriff," he began, "it all started back in the summer of eighteen sixty-eight . . ."

During the next twenty minutes Jubal told the story and told it well, with hardly an interruption by Sheriff Bacon. Finally, the lawman leaned his shoulders against the building and closed his eyes, as if trying to picture the grisly deed in his mind. "I remember reading about the murders," he said after a while. "The San Antonio papers carried the story, but they also informed us that they didn't have many of the specifics."

"Sheriff Patterson withheld some of the details," Kane said, "especially the fact that I had witnessed it all from the barn loft. I like to think that he sat on that information because he feared for my safety, but I sure wouldn't bet on it."

Bacon shook his head a few times. "He probably believed that he stood a better chance of catching them if they didn't know they had been seen," he said. "I've known Pat Patterson for years, but I've never known him to worry too much about somebody else's health. I'd bet the idea that the killers might decide to hunt you up and eliminate the only eyewitness never crossed his mind."

"That sounds about right to me, Sheriff," Jubal said. "He let me know pretty quick that he didn't believe my story; even accused me of being the killer."

Bacon nodded, then sat thoughtful for a few moments. "You say you think they might have been escaped convicts. Well, since they were all afoot, and the clothes they had on didn't fit, that assumption seems reasonable to me, too. And I can understand you not being able to recall exactly what they were wearing. What you witnessed from that barn loft should be enough to shock most any young man right out of his mind, and I'm a little bit surprised that you remember anything at all about how they looked."

"I remember, all right," Kane said quickly. "One reason I didn't pay much attention to their clothing might have been because I was so busy studying their faces. I knew even then that if I came out of that loft alive, I would someday meet all of them face-to-face.

"I'd recognize every one of them instantly," he continued. "It's like their facial features have been burned into my brain, right down to the color of their eyes and the splotchy freckles on the sandy-haired man's beak of a nose. I still see them in my sleep sometimes, and I can recall the sound of their voices even when I'm awake."

The sheriff nodded. He wiped the sweatband of his hat again, then placed it on his head. "Your idea of having a talk with the warden of the state pen is more'n likely a good one, and you're probably right in thinking that I might be of some help to you there.

"The warden's name is Jack Brady, and we've known each other since we were kids. Jack's a year older than me, and we must have played together for at least five years while we were growing up in Houston." He slapped his leg and chuckled at a memory, then explained: "I remember one day when we went swimming in Buffalo Bayou—I reckon I was about ten years old at the time.

"Anyway, when we got tired of swimming, Jack decided we ought to fish for a while. He had a ball of heavy line, and a big hook like his daddy used for saltwater fishing. He cut a limb off a pecan sapling and tied the line to it, then caught a green lizard and hooked it through the tail. Then he threw the line into the water and sat down for a wait that turned out to be mighty short. That lizard hadn't been swimming for more than ten seconds, when it suddenly disappeared in a big splash.

"Now, that line was strong and the hook was big, and neither one of 'em was gonna break. Whatever was on the other end of that line wasn't gonna give in, either. When I saw that the limb was almost bent double, I decided to give Jack a hand." He chuckled again. "My decision to help out didn't change a damn thing, Mr. Kane. Whatever that critter was, he dragged both of us down the bank and almost into the water before we let go of the limb. I thought it was probably a big old carp, but nobody else did. Jack's pa said it was an alligator, and that he'd bust our asses if he ever heard of us going swimming in Buffalo Bayou again."

Jubal laughed along with the lawman, then asked, "Did you? I mean, did you ever go swimming in the bayou again?"

Bacon nodded. "Of course," he said. "Many times."

Neither of them spoke again for quite some time. Jubal had told his story and asked the sheriff for the letter; now he could do nothing but wait for the man's answer. Bacon finally turned the conversation back to the request. "I don't mind writing that letter for you," he said, "and I believe Jack'll help you any way he can. I do know that the prison has pictures of most of the men who serve time there—maybe not all of them, but most of them. I'll ask him to let you look at pictures of inmates both past and present. If you recognize the men you're hunting, not only can Jack give you their names, but he can tell you where they came from. Then you'll know where to begin your search."

Jubal nodded. "Thank you for listening, Sheriff. I'm sure your letter'll get me inside the warden's door, and I'll hand it to him just as quick as I can make the trip to Huntsville."

Bacon got to his feet and took a step toward the courthouse door, then turned. "I suppose you intend to kill all three of 'em when you find 'em. Is that right?"

Jubal looked the lawman in the eye for a few moments, then folded his arms and fastened his gaze on the boardwalk between his own two feet. He did not answer the question.

"All right," the sheriff said after a while. "I reckon I understand." He turned toward the door again. "I'll fix up a letter of introduction for you, then you can be on your way." When Kane got to his feet to follow, Bacon added, "No, no, just keep your seat. I'll bring it out here to you."

*   *   *

When Jubal headed back to the livery stable half an hour later, the sheriff's letter to Warden Brady was riding in his hip pocket. Once he reached the stable, he turned his saddler over to Nemecek with a minimum of conversation. Though Roscoe obviously liked the sound of his own voice, he seemed to realize that Jubal was not one for small talk. The big man simply reached for the reins and led the roan down the hall. "You can get your animals anytime you want to in the morning," he said over his shoulder. "I'm usually up at the first hint of daybreak."

Kane spun on his heel and began the walk back toward town at a fast clip. He had a glass of beer in the first saloon he came to, then continued on. When he reached the Menger he avoided the main entrance, entering the hotel's combination bar and restaurant through a separate door that opened directly off the street. One glance around the huge room told him that he was standing in the fanciest eating-and-drinking establishment he had ever seen, and that he would pay dearly for the slightest amount of either that he consumed.

He smiled at the thought, then headed for one of the leather-bound booths that lined the south wall. He had scarcely seated himself, when a Mexican waiter arrived with the bill of fare. "Can I get you something to drink from the bar, sir?" he asked in perfect English.

Jubal nodded. "I'll have a glass of whiskey and water," he said, then began to study the menu.

The waiter placed Kane's drink in front of him two minutes later, motioning toward the bill of fare. "Today's special is still on, sir. You get sirloin steak, green beans, mashed potatoes and a large slice of egg custard for only two dollars."

Knowing that he could have bought the same meal somewhere down the street for thirty-five cents, Jubal smiled and pecked the menu with his forefinger. "All right," he said. "I'll have the special."

He slid deeper into the booth and leaned against the wall while he waited for his food. After taking a closer look at his surroundings, he began to wonder if the hotel actually made a profit off the restaurant and the saloon. Probably not, he quickly decided. Though their prices were outlandishly high, he believed that it would take many years to pay for the useless luxuriousness that he saw about him.

Even the bar was bordered with highly-polished leather, and the high-backed stools were covered with the same. All four of the walls sported murals that had obviously been painted by someone whose services did not come cheap. The only opulent things he could see that actually served a worthwhile purpose were the decorative chandeliers that hung from the ceiling. They created an abundance of light throughout the room.

The meal Jubal was later served turned out to be the best one he had eaten in a long time, and he mentioned that fact when the waiter came for his empty plate. "Best food I've eaten this year," he said, pushing his glass across the table. "Would you bring me another drink?"

"Yes, sir," the waiter said, then pushed the empty glass to the other side of the table. "We never serve a second drink in the same glass, sir. Hotel policy."

A few minutes later, Kane leaned his shoulders against the wall again and began to sip his drink very slowly. He had been paying close attention to the two bartenders behind the bar, and had already noted that one of them had not even moved since he himself had entered the room. Business would surely pick up after dark, Kane was thinking, but at the moment, he could see only three customers in the building besides himself.

He had already decided that he would go to bed early and get a good night's sleep, for he had a long, hot trip ahead. He saw no reason to even question the bartenders across the room, for unless the circumstances of the men he was hunting had improved greatly, it was highly unlikely that they would ever patronize such an expensive establishment as the Menger Hotel. Nor would they be likely to visit its adjacent restaurant and saloon.

When the meager amount of light shining through the windows told him that it was past sunset, he inhaled the last of his drink and got to his feet. He left a quarter on the table for the waiter, then paid his exorbitant exit fee to the head bartender. When he stepped through the side door of the saloon and into the hotel lobby, he almost ran into Sheriff Bacon. "Pardon me, Sheriff," he said, after stopping just short of the man's nose. "I guess I need to look where I'm going."

"No problem, my boy," the big man said, patting Jubal on the back. "My own mind was a thousand miles from here." He took a few steps down the hall, then turned around, continuing to walk backward as he spoke: "I don't envy you none on that ride you gotta make, Mr. Kane. It can get downright miserable anytime, but right here in the middle of July? No, sir, I don't envy you at all." He turned and walked on down the hall shaking his head.

Jubal stepped into his room a short time later, and began to undress the same moment he finished locking the door. He leaned a straight-backed chair under the doorknob, then was soon stretched out on the comfortable bed, the cooling breeze created by opposing windows blowing across his naked body. It was, in fact, the only time he had been cool enough to be comfortable since early morning.

He lay thinking about what Sheriff Bacon had said. The trip to Huntsville would be a hot one, all right, and it was well over two hundred miles. One of the good things about it, however, was that most or maybe all of that distance he would be using a good wagon road. With such a well-defined path already in existence, he could very easily do his traveling at night if the hot sun began to take a heavy toll on his animals.

He would put his horses on good grass during the hottest portion of the day, and limit his travel to early morning, late afternoon, and, occasionally, nighttime. He had long ago learned that most animals prefer about the same temperature as humans, so if he kept himself as comfortable as possible, his horses would be just fine. With that thought in mind, he fluffed up his pillow and went to sleep.

4

★

Though he had awakened several times during the night, and had trouble dozing off again, he was sleeping soundly when the heavy footfalls outside his door woke him next morning. With his eyes closed, he lay listening as the noisy steps progressed farther down the hall and out the front door. Finally, opening one eye, he was happy to see that daylight was creeping through the window.

He used the washcloth and the pan of water on the night table to wash the sleep from his eyes, then dressed himself and gathered up his saddlebags and his rifle. He was out on the street a few minutes later, and was immediately surprised at the number of men moving about. Maybe he had temporarily forgotten how normal people lived, he was thinking, but with the day being no more than ten minutes old, he had expected to see a deserted street.

He leaned against the building for a few moments looking up and down the main thoroughfare. Though it was not full daylight yet, he could see movement in every direction, and his eyes finally came to rest on a cluster of men standing in front of a lighted building that was probably a restaurant. And since he would have to pass right by it on his way to the livery stable, he would eat his breakfast there. He stepped out on the boardwalk and headed toward the light.

Three men still stood outside when Kane reached the building. Addressing no one in particular, he pointed toward the window with the barrel of his rifle.

"Can a fellow get breakfast in there?"

"Reckon so," one of the men answered. "The place don't never close."

Jubal smiled and nodded his appreciation, then stepped inside. A handful of men were seated at tables, but the majority of the customers sat on stools along a two-sided counter. When Kane saw that three of the people seated at the counter were painted women, he had no doubt as to what their profession might be. It could be that their comings and goings were what had awakened him several times during the night, he was thinking. When one of them caught his eye and began to smile flirtatiously, he gazed at her stonily for a moment, then walked to a table near the wall and took a seat. A waitress was there quickly.

Within the next half hour he ate an order of ham, eggs, buttered biscuits and jelly, and drank three cups of the best coffee he had tasted lately. The look he had given the painted woman must have done the trick, for she had not looked his way again. Long before he had finished eating his breakfast, she had walked through the doorway and out onto the street, her female companions close behind.

The sun was an hour high and shining directly in Kane's eyes, when he rode out of the livery barn and headed east. He expected to reach the town of Seguin by late afternoon, but did not intend to stop there. He would skirt the settlement on the north, then spend the night somewhere between there and Luling. He knew that he would come upon both the Guadalupe and the San Marcos Rivers within the next two days, but even though he had traveled this same road and crossed both rivers before, he could not remember which of the two was closest to his present position.

He thought on it a while longer, then shrugged. What difference did it make? The first one he came to would be the first one he crossed. He did remember that the San Marcos had the clearest water of any river he had ever seen. He even remembered standing on the bank and watching the fishes prowl along the bottom in places where he believed the water was more than ten feet deep.

He traveled in an easterly direction all morning, nooning at a boarded-up spring at the side of the road. A sign stating that the water was clean and pure had been attached to a nearby pecan tree, and some thoughtful soul had even left a tin cup hanging on a nail. Jubal built no fire for coffee, but washed his dinner down with cool water from the spring. Then, after allowing his animals to graze for an hour, he was back in the saddle. A look at his pocket compass showed that he was headed due east.

While his horses had been cropping grass near the spring, he had spent a few minutes studying his map, which indicated that he was at least two hundred miles from his destination. He would be traveling northeast sometime tomorrow, for he would take the road leading from Luling to Giddings. According to the map, which was the most up-to-date one he had been able to find, the relatively new settlement of Giddings was roughly the halfway point between San Antonio and Huntsville.

The July sun bore down through a cloudless sky. Kane continued to hold his animals to a walking gait, for he believed that the temperature was at least a hundred degrees. Though he had purposely bought no grain in San Antonio, so as to lighten the packhorse's load, the coal-black animal had nonetheless become so lathered during the heat of the afternoon that it looked almost white.

And although Jubal had brought the animals to a halt several times and allowed them to stand in the shade for a few minutes, the act had amounted to nothing more than a small remedy for a large problem. At this particular time it was simply too hot for traveling, and he knew that he would make an early camp at the first sign of water. He was too big a lover of horseflesh to allow their punishment to continue. From now on he would allow his animals to loaf during the heat of the day, and travel only during the morning and late afternoon. And maybe he would do some night riding as long as he was on an established road, or in an area that he knew well.

When he topped the next rise, he saw a small creek at the bottom of the hill, shaded by the usual cluster of tall pecans. His horses were also aware of the water, and voluntarily quickened their pace. Although the sun was still three hours high, the creek would be tonight's campsite. Jubal spoke to his animals as if they were human, informing each of them that the day's work was almost done.

He would feed them the last few pounds of grain that the packhorse carried, more to lighten its load than for any other reason. With the exception of the extreme western portions of the state, there was plenty of green grass all over Texas at this time of the year, and even a working animal with time to graze should remain in good condition. Of course, Kane would continue to treat his horses to a feed of oats when they were lodged at a livery stable, but he probably would not carry grain on the trail again until early fall.

When he reached the creek he dismounted and watered the horses, then led them downstream to a suitable campsite, about fifty yards from the road. He unburdened the animals and tied on their nosebags, then raked up several handfuls of dry grass, bark, and twigs. He kindled a small blaze, then walked up and down the creek till he had gathered an armload of wood.

He first fed the flame with several of the smaller pieces, then broke the larger limbs over his knee and placed them over the fire in the form of a pyramid. Half an hour later, when the pyramid collapsed, he would have a bed of coals over which to prepare his supper and boil his coffee.

He found good grass in plain view of his campsite and staked out his horses. A few moments later, he filled both his coffeepot and his boiler with water from the creek. Then he sat down on his bedroll and began to peel Irish potatoes with his pocketknife. That done, he sliced them into small pieces and dropped them into the blackened boiler, which was half full of water. He poured a handful of grounds into the coffeepot, then deliberately crashed his burning pyramid into the flames. He would wait a few more minutes, then put both the boiler and the coffeepot on the red-hot coals.

As had been the case many times in recent memory, his supper would consist of boiled potatoes, Bologna sausage, cheese, and handfuls of oatmeal cookies that had by now crumbled so badly that they had almost turned into powder. Powdery though they might be, they nonetheless tasted just as good as ever, and Jubal would buy some more as soon as he ate the last of these. His horses liked the cookies just as well as he did, and he had fed them a full bag about a week ago.

He had eaten his supper, washed up his potato pot, and was sitting a few feet from the dying campfire sipping coffee, when he spotted two riders coming down the road from the east. They watered their animals at the ford, then sat their saddles looking toward his campsite, carrying on a conversation that Jubal could hear but not understand. When they finally crossed the creek, pointed their horses south, and began to ride in his direction, Kane got to his feet.

The men, one past forty and the other half that age, rode their black horses right into Jubal's camp, halting less than twenty feet away. The older of the two wore a heavy salt-and-pepper beard, and carried no visible weapon. The younger man was dark-haired and clean-shaven, and wore a Colt Peacemaker with well-worn grips on his right hip. The bearded man spoke: "Weren't no use'n ya gittin' up, young feller, ya oughta jist kep' yer seat. Me'n my friend here jist wanted ta see if we could trouble ya fer a cup o' that coffee."

Jubal pointed to the coffeepot. "Get down and help yourselves," he said. "I think there's at least two cups left."

They dismounted simultaneously, and each man took a tin cup from his saddlebag. Kane stood watching as they filled their cups, then seated themselves on the ground. It had long been his policy to be courteous to all men but to trust none. So ingrained was that policy that his next move was almost automatic. He took a few steps sideways and leaned his back against the big pecan, never taking his eyes off the uninvited visitors.

Nobody spoke for the next several minutes. When they had finally drunk the coffeepot dry, the two men got to their feet and returned their cups to their saddlebags. Finally, the younger man spoke. "I don't reckon we could find a better camping spot than this'n right here, Fuzzy," he said to the older man. He pointed to a level place a few feet from the campfire. "I'm gonna throw my bedroll down right there."

"I intend to put my own bedroll there," Jubal said, speaking a little louder than usual. "You folks can find your own campsite real easy, there's plenty of room along the creek in either direction."

"Why, there's plenty of room right here!" the young man said loudly, then turned to face Jubal. "This happens to be a free country, fella."

Kane waved his left arm about to indicate the immediate area, then began to shake his head. "Nope!" he said, matching the young man's gruff tone. "This particular part of it ain't free! It was free when I got here, but it ain't free now!"

"This whole damn country's free!" the young man said, almost yelling now. "Who in the hell do you think you are, trying to tell me where to sleep?"

Jubal stood quietly for a moment, particles of fire seeming to creep into his green eyes. "I'm not telling you where to sleep, fellow; I'm telling you where you can't sleep. It just happens that I'm a loner; I travel alone, and I camp alone. I was here first, so you're gonna have to keep moving." He pointed to the level place the man had selected for his bedroll. "I'm gonna tell you something else, too, and you'd be wise to pay attention: If you spread your bedroll right there by my fire, you're gonna sleep a hell of a lot longer than usual."

They were still staring at each other with hands close to gun butts, when the man called Fuzzy stepped between them. "Weren't no use'n this argyment ever startin'," he said, addressing his comments to the younger man. "O' course it's a free country, but it ain't free after somebody settles on it. Now, this feller settled on this spot 'fore we got here, so it's his'n fer th' night." He paused for a deep breath, then continued. "I ask ya now, Scooter, weren't he nice enough ta give us some o' his coffee?" Without waiting for an answer, he put his hand on the young man's shoulder and pointed him toward his horse. "Now, mount up and let's git outta here. If we don't let our shirttails touch us, we can make it ta Clear Sprangs 'fore nightfall."

Scooter stared at Kane sullenly for a moment, then, giving the older man no argument whatsoever, walked to his horse and threw a leg over the saddle. Fuzzy nodded to Kane, then mounted his own animal. He led off in a westerly direction, and a few minutes later, the two men rode out of sight. Neither of them ever looked back.

Kane refilled his coffeepot with water from the creek, then began to gather up the kindling he would need to start his fire in the morning. When he decided that he had raked together as much dead grass, leaves, twigs, and bark as he would need, he dragged the corner of his canvas tarp over the pile. A man learned such tricks very quickly on the trail, for the weather was the most unpredictable thing about living in Texas. An overnight rainstorm or even a heavy dew could render a camper's kindling useless, and he very well might have to drink creek water for breakfast instead of coffee.

Jubal continued to cast his eyes occasionally to the west, for he trusted neither of the men that he had just ushered out of his camp. Though the one called Scooter had obviously wanted to fight, it appeared he had lost his nerve once he saw that Kane could not be buffaloed. He might, however, be considerably braver under the cover of darkness, Jubal was thinking.

And the man called Fuzzy—had the little speech he made to the younger man actually been designed for Jubal's ears rather than Scooter's? Possibly, Kane decided. Jubal had been unable to read the man's facial expressions, for he had seen none. The thicket of heavy beard left nothing to read except his eyes, and indeed they had seemed a little shifty.

Kane knew one thing for certain: There was no way in the world that he was going to spread his bedroll on the same spot that he had pointed out to the man called Scooter. He would move his animals to new grass just before darkness settled in, and at the same time cast his eyes around for a place of concealment. He would wait for total darkness to move his bedroll, for one of the men might be carrying a spyglass in his saddlebag.

At sunset, Jubal crouched behind the trunk of the big pecan with his own telescope in his hand. He glassed the road and the distant ridges to the west for several minutes, but saw no signs of life. He pushed the sliding tubes together to condense the length of the instrument, then returned it to his saddlebag. A moment later, he was headed across the meadow to move his horses.

He watered the animals again, then led them a hundred yards farther down the creek and picketed them on good grass. As he walked back toward his campsite, he spotted a much better place for his bedroll. The creek was only a few inches deep here, but the cutbanks were about four feet high, with clumps of leafy bushes growing between them and the water. Several large rocks, some as big as a covered wagon, were scattered along the west bank.

Jubal selected his sleeping place without even breaking his stride, and a few moments later, reseated himself beside the ashes of his campfire. He was confident that if he was being watched with a telescope his actions would seem perfectly normal; that it would appear to the watcher that he intended to spread his bedroll right where he was sitting.

When it became obvious that daylight was finally about to give up the fight, Jubal decided that it was time to move to his new roosting place. It was now the period between twilight and full dark; the time when daylight was disappearing faster than the eye could adjust to its absence, and he knew that his movement could not be detected from any appreciable distance, even with a spyglass. Later on, when it became as dark as pitch, the stars would provide a little more light, and moving around could be dangerous.

With his Winchester in one hand and his bedroll in the other, he very quickly covered the distance to the sleeping place he had selected. A short while later, he was lying fully clothed and with his boots still on, in one of the many clusters of bushes about forty yards from his campsite. The cutbank and the large rocks were close by in case he needed either of them for cover. As the night grew darker and the stars came out, he could make out the shape of the big pecan. His saddle, bridles, and packsaddle still lay under the big tree's canopy, along with his cooking and eating utensils and all of his food.

For the next two hours, he lay on his stomach with his chin resting on his forearms, his eyes trained on the area around the big pecan. He also kept watch on the area to the west, for although he could not see very clearly in that direction, he felt that he would at least be able to distinguish a man on horseback, and possibly a man on foot.

He continued his vigil hour after hour. Even after he was sure that it was past midnight, he remained alert, for he was expecting company before the night was over. The longer he thought about it, the more convinced he became that either of his recent visitors would cut a man's throat for a dollar, and had probably been riding around the country looking for a chance to do exactly that.

Otherwise, why would they be traveling together? It was quite common for men with a wide discrepancy in their ages to ride together, but they were usually kinfolk, and most often, father and son. These men had made no attempt to pass themselves off as being related to each other. In fact, the older man had referred to the much younger Scooter as his friend.

So, what did the two have in common? What they had in common, Kane believed, was the fact that both were thieves, and quite possibly murderers. Scooter would be the hotheaded and quick-handed gunman, while the forty- or fiftyish Fuzzy considered himself to be the thinker for both men. Maybe Scooter himself thought that the old man was brainy, or at least idolized him for some other reason, for he had meekly accepted the mild ass-chewing Fuzzy had given him at the campsite, and had mounted his horse with no argument when he was ordered to.

It was getting on toward daybreak now, well past the time when Jubal should have been on the road in keeping with the new schedule he had set for himself. He had just swept the area around the big tree with his tiring eyes, when he spotted two dark objects about fifty yards west of his position. He had not noticed them before. Had they been there all along? He stared at them for a long time, blinking occasionally in an effort clear his eyes. No, he decided finally, they had not been there before, but had somehow crept into his peripheral vision undetected.

Since the objects appeared to be about as tall and about as long as a horse, Jubal finally came to the conclusion that he was looking at two riderless horses. And they were standing right beside a twenty-foot juniper, no doubt tied to a low-hanging limb. Had Fuzzy and Scooter come to pay him another visit? If so, where in the hell were they, and how had they managed to cross that fifty yards of open meadow without attracting his attention?

After racking his brain for a few seconds, Jubal had his answer: He had not seen them cross the meadow be-

cause they had not crossed it. One of them, most likely
Scooter, had tied the horses there to hold Kane's attention
on the off chance that he should awaken and spot them,
then had backtracked to join his partner. The two had
then made a wide circle on foot, intending to cross the
creek and approach Kane's camp from the east. Since they
knew that he had watched them ride out of sight toward
the west long before sunset, it was logical for them to
believe that he would not expect them to reappear from
the opposite direction.

He thought about his conclusion for only a moment
before accepting it completely. They had crossed the creek,
all right; the only remaining question was whether they
had crossed it north, or south, of his present position. He
had no way of knowing, but he was convinced that they
would be here soon. Or were they already here? He answered that question the same moment it entered his
mind. No, they were not here yet, for he was positive that
the horses had not been tied to the juniper long enough
for their riders to make the circle on foot.

Hatless, and clutching his Winchester in his left hand,
he eased himself over the cutbank and waded the few
inches of water to reach the east side. The cavity that the
creek had carved because of heavy rains and flooding over
the years was several yards wider than the stream itself,
and was lined on both sides by bushes and sparse undergrowth. Though the vegetation was not thick enough to
provide complete cover, the creekbanks themselves were
high enough in most places to shield his movements.

Shortly after sunset, he had jacked a shell into the fir-
ing chamber of his Winchester and added a sixth to the
cylinder of his Colt. Both weapons were ready for instant
action. Now, bent over at the waist, he began to ease himself toward his campsite, taking one step, then waiting
two. He paid no attention to the west bank, for he was

convinced that the men had crossed the creek.

The east side of the stream received a much closer inspection, however. Each time he came to a new bush, he parted the leafy branches and gave the area to the east the once-over, then moved on to the next one.

He hit pay dirt twenty yards from his campsite. He had just parted two branches to get a clear look, when he saw one of the men move. He froze in his tracks and squinted, trying to strain his eyes for a better view. Eventually, he was able to make out what appeared to be the forms of two men standing under the dark canopy of a medium-sized pecan. Even as Kane watched, one of the figures bent over at the waist and took a few steps toward the campsite, then seemed to think better of the idea, for he suddenly whirled and returned to the tree hurriedly.

Now that he knew where the men were, Jubal bent one of the branches so that he could see over it, then seated himself on the creekbank, his feet hanging over the edge. He had an open field of fire in every direction. He also had a lot more time than his visitors did, for daylight would be along soon. He would simply wait them out, for they would have to show their hand within the next few minutes. Even now, the skyline in the east was beginning to take on a pinkish hue.

Five minutes later, they made their move. They walked out of the shadows side by side, which was exactly what Jubal had been hoping for. The coming dawn now provided enough light for him to see that each of the men carried a pistol in his right hand. Bent over as close to the ground as possible, they began to creep toward his campsite, moving at an oblique angle to his present position.

Knowing that the men were playing a dangerous and stupid game, and that the odds had suddenly shifted in his own favor, Jubal waited no longer. He laid the rifle on the ground, then stepped up on the bank and drew his

Peacemaker. "Are you sons of bitches looking for me?" he asked loudly. As they whirled around toward the sound of his voice, he shot Scooter, then Fuzzy, in the chest, then repeated the process before either man hit the ground.

Both of the intruders died quickly, and only Scooter moved after falling to the ground. He kicked his right leg spasmodically for a moment, then lay still.

Kane stood his ground for several minutes waiting for the dawn to provide more light, then he walked forward. Although their glassy eyes told him that neither man would ever rob anyone else, he nonetheless toed each of the corpses with his boot. He ejected the four spent shells from his Colt, then pushed in three new ones. As was the case with every other man that Kane knew, it had long been his habit to carry only five shells in his six-shot revolver. With no cartridge under the hammer, the gun could not fire accidentally.

Moving at a fast clip, he walked to the juniper and untied the thieves' horses, then brought them back to the campsite. He loaded each of the dead men on one of the horses, then led the animals a hundred yards downstream. At a thick cluster of willows, he halted and pushed the bodies over the edge of the creekbank. A few moments later, he threw their guns, saddlebags, saddles and bridles on top of them. Each of the horses had headed south at a gallop as soon as Kane slipped its bridle off. Jubal was happy to see them head for the hills, for he knew that horses running loose on the road would surely attract attention quickly.

At the campsite, he kicked dirt over the blood, then decided that the area looked just as it had the day before. He then headed for the meadow and his own animals. Breakfast would be several hours late this morning, for he intended to put many miles behind him before he built another campfire.

Half an hour later, after mounting the roan and taking up the slack in his packhorse's lead rope, he made a final sweep of the area with his eyes. It would be purely accidental if anyone found those bodies before the buzzards pointed them out tomorrow or the next day, he decided. With that thought in mind, he guided his animals onto the road and continued his northeasterly journey.

5

Although he did not push his animals, Jubal traveled
steadily, sometimes riding for most of the night. Two days
later, he rode into the town of Giddings at midafternoon.

Giddings had been established on the H&TC Railroad
in 1871, when track was laid from Brenham to Austin.
The community had been settled chiefly by Wendish im-
migrants who moved to the railroad from the Serbian
Community six miles to the south, and evidence of
German architecture could easily be seen in any direction.
The town began to prosper right from the start, and was
soon selected to be the seat of Lee County. And although
area criminals discovered the new town early on, its in-
habitants were quick to let the rowdy element know that
their shenanigans would not be tolerated. Notorious out-
law Bill Longley would later be hanged there, on October
11, 1878.

There was no movement whatsoever on the street as Jubal rode into town, which he attributed to the fact that the temperature was probably somewhere around a hundred degrees. As he passed the hotel he nodded to two men who were sitting on a bench beside the doorway, and his greeting was returned. Since the hotel had a wooden awning, and was located on the corner, Kane supposed that the bench on the north side of the doorway might be one of the coolest places in town. He intended to find out as soon as he could stable his horses and make arrangements for his own lodging.

A few minutes later, he turned his animals over to a liveryman only a few years older than himself. That in itself was a rarity, for travelers were almost always met at livery stable doors by men too old to work as blacksmiths or ranchhands. This time, however, the hostler was a muscular blond with shoulder-length hair, and appeared to be about twenty-five years old. "I'll be staying in town overnight if I can find a vacant room," Jubal said, handing over the reins of his horses. "Give 'em a good feed of oats now, and again when you wake up in the morning. I won't be needing them till after sunup."

The man nodded, and loosened the cinch on the roan's belly. "I'll do exactly that," he said, then pointed back up the street to the hotel. "You ain't gonna have no problem getting a room, either. Their business ain't no better'n mine, which has been off all year. Way off."

"I'm sorry to hear that," Jubal said. "I don't guess—"

"It don't matter one bit," the hostler interrupted, then slid the saddle off and placed it on a rack built especially for that purpose. "It'll all balance out in the long run; business just runs in cycles, mine and everybody else's." Without speaking another word, he led the packhorse forward and began to unbuckle the packsaddle. Moments

THE QUEST OF JUBAL KANE

later, he put the packsaddle in the office and locked the door, then led the animals down the hall toward the stables, leaving Jubal standing holding his Winchester and his saddlebags.

Kane had liked the hostler immediately. Like himself, the young man was obviously not inclined to indulge in small talk. And unlike most liverymen, who were sometimes such incessant talkers that a man might have to walk away while they were still rattling, this man had more or less passed the time of day, then proceeded to take care of business quietly. Jubal smiled, spun on his heel, and headed up the street.

By the time he reached the hotel, one of the men had departed the bench. Kane nodded to the one remaining. "Is that seat as cool as it looks?" he asked.

The middle-aged, sandy-haired man chuckled. "Probably not," he said, "but it's the coolest place I've been able to find today." He pointed east with one of his thumbs, and north with the other, adding, "You get a little bit of breeze from both directions."

Jubal jerked his head toward the lobby. "As soon as I get through taking care of business, I might join you if you don't mind."

The man patted the plank. "Plenty of room here," he said. "And it wouldn't make no difference whether I minded or not—this here's a public bench."

The desk clerk rented him a first-floor room for seventy-five cents, and Jubal was gone down the hall only long enough to lock his saddlebags and his rifle inside. Then he returned to the bench outside the front door and took a seat. "Hello again," he said to the man beside him, his right hand extended. "My name's Jubal Kane."

The man grasped the hand, gripping it much harder than was necessary. "I answer to the name of Henry Thomas," he said. "I could tell by the way you were looking everything over when you rode into town, that you ain't never been here before. Either that or you're hunting somebody."

Jubal pulled his hand away. "My first trip to Giddings," he said.

"Well, I reckon everybody ought to come here at least once," Thomas said, unbuttoning the pocket on the bib of his overalls. He handed Kane a half pint bottle that was still half full of whiskey. "Ain't gonna claim that this stuff'll cool you off none, but a few snorts of it'll sure make you worry about the heat a whole lot less."

The label claimed that the whiskey came from Bourbon County, Kentucky, and that it was six years old. Kane twisted the stopper from the neck and wet his lips. "That ain't no way to drink whiskey, Jubal!" Henry Thomas said loudly. "Turn that bottle up and kill it!"

Kane drank it all, then handed over the empty bottle.

"That's more like it," Thomas said. "About twenty minutes from now you might even be a little hotter, but you ain't gonna notice it near as much."

They sat talking for half an hour, and just as Thomas had predicted, the heat seemed to bother Jubal a little less. The whiskey had made him hungry, however, and he said as much. "I haven't eaten since breakfast, Henry, and I'm about ready to put on the feed bag." He pointed down the block and across the street. "Which one of those restaurants over there is the best?"

"One's probably about as good as the other," Thomas said. "Same man owns both of 'em. Of course, he don't do the cooking in either one, so there might be a little difference in the taste of things."

Jubal pointed again. "Well, which one do you eat in?"

"Don't eat in either one of 'em," Thomas answered. "Never have. Ain't paying nobody to feed me when I can do it myself. Do it better, too." He jerked his head in a northerly direction. "I live by myself about a quarter mile from here. I don't eat but twice a day, but I fix my food exactly the way I want it."

Jubal was on his feet now. "Well, I don't even have a house to do my cooking in," he said, motioning across the street. "I'll have a bite to eat over there, then I'd like to buy you a drink in the hotel saloon."

Thomas shook his head. "I don't go in saloons, either," he said. "I like a nip now and then just as much as the next man does, but I can buy a bottle without going in one of them places, taking a chance on getting my head stomped in by some bully who can't handle his liquor."

Jubal glanced at the hotel saloon, then back at Thomas. "Well, let me step in there and buy you a bottle, so you—"

"Nope," Thomas interrupted. "I've got plenty of whiskey at home, and I'm headed there right now." Without another word, he got to his feet and disappeared around the corner.

Kane stood smiling for a few moments, then began to walk across the street, shaking his head and wondering if he would meet any more people in this town who were as strange as Henry Thomas.

He ate beef stew and a bowl of lima beans in a small restaurant that appeared to have no name. The sign out front had simply stated that eats could be found inside. He contemplated asking the waiter if the place had a name, but thought better of it. Instead, he asked the young man what time the establishment opened for breakfast in the morning. "Six o'clock sharp," was the answer. "All the pancakes and sausage you can eat, for only thirty cents."

"I'll be here," Kane said. While the waiter stood by smiling, Jubal laid an extra dime between his two empty bowls, then walked to the counter and paid his bill.

He recrossed the street and went into the hotel saloon. The only talking he did was to the bartender, and then only to order a pitcher of beer. With the pitcher in one hand and a glass in the other, he seated himself at a small table along the east wall, hanging his hat on the back of the second chair to discourage company. With an unobstructed view of the entire room, he paid close attention to every man coming or going during the next two hours, but saw no one resembling any of the men he was searching for.

Finally deciding that it was bedtime, he carried the glass and the empty pitcher back to the bar, then stepped into the hotel lobby through the adjoining doorway. An expensively dressed, middle-aged man stood at the counter, and the hotel clerk was nowhere in sight. The man spoke to Jubal with an accent that was decidedly Northern. "Is it always this hard to find someone with which to conduct business in this hotel?" he asked.

"Don't know," Kane said, turning the corner and stepping into the hall. "This is my first time here, too." He unlocked the door to his room, and half an hour later, was sleeping soundly.

He ate the pancake-and-sausage special at the restaurant next morning, then headed for the livery stable at sunup. He could see smoke coming from the flue protruding from the roof of the hostler's office, and supposed that the man was cooking his breakfast, or at least heating his morning coffee. But maybe he isn't, Jubal quickly said to himself, for as Kane neared the building, the man stepped from the office and into the wide doorway. "Good morning," he said. "I guess you're ready to ride."

Jubal nodded. "I need to get a few miles behind me before it gets too hot." He pointed to an expensive vehicle in front of the building that he had not seen the day before. "Is that your buggy out there?"

The hostler shook his head. "Nope," he said. "A fellow drove it in here about sunset yesterday. Said he was gonna hunt up something to eat, then rent a room at the hotel. Judging from the way he talked, I'd say he was a Northerner. Had on what looked to be a wool suit, coat and all. Had his shirt collar buttoned and a damn tie on. Can you imagine a man dressing like that in this kind of weather?" Not waiting for an answer, he headed down the hall shaking his head. "Gotta be a damn Yankee," he muttered, as if talking to himself.

When he returned with Kane's horses, the liveryman, who had never offered his name, loaded the packsaddle on the packhorse expertly, then a few minutes later, cinched the saddle down on the roan. Jubal stood by idly and allowed the man to perform the chores unassisted, for he knew that many hostlers considered it part of their job. The act of performing above and beyond the call of duty was also designed to put a traveler in a gratuitous mood, Jubal was thinking. He fought back a chuckle, for he knew that he was about to give this man an extra quarter.

He rode out of the barn a few minutes later and took the road to Bryan. From there it would be no more than a two-day ride to Huntsville.

He pulled his hat brim low, for the bright sunlight was shining directly in his eyes. When he looked over his shoulder he felt like he should wave good-bye to Giddings, for he had run into two characters here that he would not soon forget. Henry Thomas, though strange, was probably no stranger than the liveryman, who had shaken hands with Jubal twice, but had not offered his name either time. Kane smiled, and kicked the roan to a trot. Neither had he spoken his own name to the liveryman.

6

★

The town of Huntsville was founded as an Indian trading post in 1836, the year of Texas independence, and Sam Houston was among the many prominent settlers who lived there. The Texas state prison, built in 1847, was also located there, and received its first convict on October 1, 1849.

Men convicted of murder, robbery, rape, cattle-rustling, and a myriad of lesser crimes served their sentences there. Those sentenced to pay the supreme penalty sometimes kicked out the last few seconds of their lives at the end of a rope behind the thick gray walls—walls that were claimed to be escapeproof by the prison's designers and builders. Jubal Kane doubted that the boast was true, for he had certainly heard of men escaping from the Huntsville prison.

Jubal rode into Huntsville at noon, four days after leaving the town of Giddings. He knew that he stood little chance of getting an audience with Warden Jack Brady on this day, however, for he had arrived in town on a Sunday. Even as he rode down the street he could hear church bells ringing, one close by, another from a good distance away.

He found a livery stable easily, right at the end of the street that had brought him into town. He left his pack-horse with the liveryman, then rode away on the roan, saying that he would return with the saddler at a later hour. He rented a room at a hotel two blocks from the stable, then began to ride around the town. He was anxious to get a look at the Texas State Penitentiary, an institution that he had heard about all his life.

The prison was not hard to find. He had only to ride up the hill for a short distance, then look to his right. He sat his saddle, gazing at the massive concrete structure for a while. Had the men who killed his parents ever been incarcerated there? Were they there now? He hoped to have the answer soon. Finally, he turned the roan back toward town, deciding that he had seen enough. Even in the bright sunlight, the fortress had given off a dark and dismal look of depression.

As he rode down the hill he began to wonder how many innocent men might be existing behind those gray walls. He had no doubt that some of them had been sent there on scant or even manufactured evidence. And he knew that even the testimony of eyewitnesses could sometimes be totally unreliable. He had seen that fact demonstrated during his last year of high school, when his teacher introduced her pupils to what she called a "perception differential" test: With no warning, a man had burst through the schoolhouse door, yelling at the top of his lungs, then ran around the room jumping up and down and waving his arms. He stopped twice during his act and turned completely around, giving everyone in the room a good look. Then, pulling at his hair and screaming like a madman, he ran from the room.

Once he had disappeared, the teacher explained to the students that the man's actions had been designed to test their abilities of perception. She then asked that each student write down a full description of the man, and give an account of his actions. When the youngsters had complied, the teacher copied several of the descriptions on the chalkboard. The particulars were so varied that it appeared that no two of the students had even seen the same man.

After listening to her pupils argue back and forth among themselves for a few moments, the teacher invited the man back into the classroom. A hush fell over the students immediately, for none of them had even come close. Some had described the man as being tall and fat, while others had seen him as tall and skinny. One girl said she thought that he had only one arm. Two of the youngsters said that he was black-haired, while others claimed that his hair was brown. One girl said that she had been unable to tell what color his hair was, because it had been hidden under his floppy hat.

In truth, the man was a redhead, and had come into the room hatless. He was neither fat nor skinny, nor was he tall. He stood five-foot-eight, and weighed a hundred and fifty pounds.

The teacher's demonstration had stuck with Jubal Kane over the years. He had been just as wrong about what he had seen in the classroom as his fellow students had been, and for a long time afterward he sometimes lay in bed at night thinking about the morning he had witnessed the murders of his parents from the barn loft. Had his perception of the killers been as far off the mark as his description of the happenings in the classroom? His immediate answer to that question was an emphatic no.

He had studied the face of every man carefully, even committed the sound of their voices to memory, for he knew even then that he would someday embark on his present mission.

He rode on down the hill at a walking gait and turned the roan over to the liveryman when he reached the stable. Then, with his Winchester and a change of clothing in the crook of his left arm, and his saddlebags lying across his shoulder, he began to walk up the street, pausing occasionally to peek through the window of one business establishment or another. SCOTTY'S BARBER SHOP, read the sign above the door of a small building near the hotel. The shop was closed today, of course, but Kane would certainly check it out early in the morning. Maybe he would get a more favorable reaction from Warden Brady if he had a bath, a shave, and a haircut. He bought two magazines from a streetside vendor, then continued on up the street.

His room, on the second floor of the two-story Doran Hotel, had everything a man might be needing: a large clothes closet, a chest of drawers, a nightstand, and a table with two chairs. Two towels, a washpan, and a large pitcher of water were on the table, along with two glasses and a tin cup. The room was in the corner on the back side of the building, and Jubal created a draft strong enough to tousle his hair when he raised the two perpendicular windows.

He took off his shirt and sat on the side of the bed, enjoying the breeze for a while, looking through the front window and watching the traffic on the street below. When half an hour had passed without a single female coming by, he piled the pillows one on top of the other and stretched out on the bed with a magazine. A few minutes later, he was sound asleep.

He was on the street again two hours later, looking for a likely place to eat his supper. He walked around the town for half an hour, then ended up right back where he started from. He had decided to eat in the hotel restaurant.

After eating an order of pork chops and applesauce, he flirted with his dark-haired waitress for a while, then climbed the stairs to his room just as darkness settled in. He would not be making the rounds of the saloons tonight, for he did not believe that his men would even slow down in this town. Not unless they were locked behind those walls up yonder.

He lit the lamp and pulled the nightstand closer to his bed, then stripped off his clothing and stretched out in the cooling breeze. He needed a good night's sleep, for he wanted to be at his very best when he spoke with the warden tomorrow. A few minutes later, using the same magazine that had put him to sleep earlier, he dozed off and dropped it to the floor.

He awoke at daybreak, but deliberately stayed in his room for a while. He washed the sleep out of his eyes, then sat beside the window watching the town come to life. When he had finally decided that everybody else was awake, he walked to the lobby and paid his room rent for another night. Then he headed for the hotel restaurant and breakfast.

After eating ham, eggs, and several doughnuts, he returned to his room for the change of clothing, then he was out on the street. He had already decided that his first order of the day was a trip to a barber. Once he had a shave and a haircut he would take a hot bath, and put on the clean jeans and his favorite blue shirt.

A few moments later, he stepped into the shop, his clean duds tucked under his arm. A dark-haired, middle-aged man who was obviously the barber sat in the shop's only chair, no doubt waiting for a customer. A six-footer, who looked as if he had been eating well and often, he was on his feet quickly. "Come right in," he said, popping a large cloth to rid it of any hair left behind by a previous customer. "What'll it be this morning?"

"I suppose I'd better get the works," Kane said, pointing toward the rear of the building with his thumb. "Have you got a bath back there?"

"You bet," the man answered quickly. "The water'll be hot by the time you're done up here." He cupped his hands around his mouth and called to someone in the back room. "Bather coming, Harry!" Then he motioned to the chair. "Have a seat. I'm sure he's already putting a fire under your water."

Jubal slid into the chair, and the man spread the cloth over the front portion of his body, pinning it behind his neck. "My name's Scotty Greer," the barber said, beginning to run a comb through Kane's hair, "and I've had this same shop since back before the war. I don't recall ever seeing you around here before, so you must be a newcomer."

"Newcomer's the right word," Jubal said. "I just rode into town yesterday and I'll probably ride out tomorrow. Depends on how long my business takes."

"Well, I won't ask you what that business is. I always figured that if a man wanted everybody to know what he was doing, he'd take out an ad in the paper." He whacked off a handful of hair with a scissors. "What do you think about the job Mr. Ulysses Simpson Grant is doing in Washington?" he asked, making no attempt to hide the sarcasm in his voice.

"I don't spend much time thinking about him," Jubal answered.

"Well, I sure do. I voted against Grant both times, but of course he won anyway. I just don't think a drunk should be holding the nation's highest office, and I lay the blame for this depression right on his head." He worked quietly for a while, then continued. "I'll tell you who could straighten this country out, and I'll vote for him if he runs in the next election. I'm talking about Rutherford B. Hayes.

"Hayes is not only a well-respected Harvard lawyer. He served four years in the House of Representatives and he's been governor of Ohio twice, so I reckon he ought to know what makes things tick by now. From what I read, he's a decent, God-fearing man, and he's already let it be known that he'll pull all of the Yankee troops out of the South and put an end to all this so-called Reconstruction."

"Well, I'm sure that would please a lot of people," Jubal said. "The troops never have messed with me, though, so I just ignore 'em and go on about my business."

"That's the only way," the barber said, leaning the chair back and beginning to whet his razor on a leather strop. "If you let their presence bother you, it'll eat you up."

When Jubal left Greer's shop he not only looked better, but felt better. A few minutes later, he was at the livery stable. "Come for your horses?" asked the aging liveryman, who had identified himself the day before as Ben Yates.

Kane shook his head. "I'll walk today, 'cause I need the exercise. I just came by to put these dirty clothes in my pack."

The hostler motioned toward his office, and Kane stepped through the doorway. He first extracted a small writing tablet and a pencil from his pack, then stuffed his soiled clothing inside. "Might need to write something down," he said to Yates, then got to his feet and walked to the door. "I don't expect to need my horses today, but I might be needing 'em early tomorrow."

"That's fine," Yates said, nodding. "They're in good hands."

Jubal shoved the writing tablet inside his shirt and began to walk up the hill at a leisurely pace. When he reached the prison he climbed the concrete steps and spoke to the gatekeeper, who was clearly visible inside the iron bars. "My name is Jubal Kane," he said, "and I'm here to see Warden Brady."

There was no answer for a few moments, then the man finally spoke. "Is the warden expecting you?" he asked, using a tone of voice that was decidedly gruff.

"No," Jubal answered, and added quickly, "Sheriff Randy Bacon, from San Antonio, sent me." He patted his hip pocket. "I've got a letter here that the sheriff sent to Warden Brady."

The tall man poked his nose between the bars. "You got a weapon on you besides the one hanging on your hip?"

Jubal shook his head. "No, sir."

"Well, you'll have to hand over that Colt and the cartridge belt before you come through this gate. You can't come in nohow till after the warden says you can." He poked his hand between the bars. "Give me the letter and I'll take it to him, then we'll see what he says after he reads it."

Kane produced the letter, and the man disappeared. When he returned several minutes later his tone of voice had softened considerably, and his commands sounded more like requests. "Hand me your gunbelt, please, then I can open the gate. The warden says to send you right in."

Jubal complied, then when the big gate swung open, stepped inside. "Now, I ain't the one who makes these rules," the man said after he had closed the gate, "and I hate to submit a grown man to this kind of stuff. But they say that I have to frisk you for a weapon before you go any farther. I hate—"

"Go ahead," Kane interrupted, taking the tablet from inside his shirt and raising his hands. He held his arms over his head while the man conducted a feeble search, then stood waiting for directions.

"Down the hall there on the right," the gatekeeper said, "all the way to the end. The warden's door's always open."

A few seconds later, Jubal framed himself in the doorway and knocked on the jamb lightly. "Come in, come in," Brady said. He rose from his chair and met Kane halfway across the room. "I'm Jack Brady," he said, offering a handshake. "I reckon you must be Jubal Kane."

Jubal grasped the extended hand. "Yes, sir."

The warden was a round-shouldered man who stood a little less than six feet tall. He was dark-complected, with coal-black hair, and if he was really the same age as Sheriff Bacon, the years had certainly treated him well. He pointed Kane to a heavily cushioned chair, then seated himself behind his desk. "I've read the letter from Sheriff Bacon," he said, "and he speaks well of you." He lit a cigarette from a prerolled stack, and offered one to Jubal, who shook his head and turned the palms of his hands forward.

The warden smiled and nodded, then spoke again. "How is Randy these days?" he asked.

"He sure looks healthy to me," Jubal said, then chuckled. "He's about as big as a horse, and it's easy to see that he don't miss many meals."

"Never did," Brady said. "Even when we were kids he had something to eat in his hand about half of the time." He chuckled at the memory. "Randy was a big boy even then, and he took up for me more than once when somebody wanted to jump me."

Jubal had already decided that he liked the warden. "Sheriff Bacon didn't tell me about fighting any of your battles," he said. "He did tell me that the two of you grew up together, and he told me about the day an alligator almost dragged both of you into Buffalo Bayou."

Brady slapped his knee and began to laugh loudly. "It had to be a damn alligator. Of course, we never did see it, but there ain't no fish in Buffalo Bayou big enough to drag two half-grown boys around." He chuckled a couple more times, then turned serious. "Randy says in his letter that you've got a story I ought to listen to."

"Yes, sir," Jubal said. Then, speaking a little softer than usual, he began his narrative.

The warden sat with his elbows on his desk and his chin resting in his hands while he listened to the story. Only a few times did he himself speak, and then only to ask a question or clarify a point. When Jubal had finished, Brady crossed his arms and leaned back in his chair. He fired another cigarette, then spoke through a cloud of smoke. "So you got the idea that the men might be escaped convicts because they didn't have any horses and their clothes didn't fit, huh?"

Kane nodded. "I guess that's it," he said. "Anyway, it seemed worth a try, so I finally decided to come see you."

The warden sat quietly for a while, staring at his desk. "You heard the surname of Mitchell and the given name of Leroy in the barn that day, huh?" he asked without looking up.

"Yes, sir."

"Well, there ain't no telling how many Mitchells and Leroys have passed through this place," Brady said. "Probably several of 'em back there right now. I wasn't here in 'sixty-eight, but we've got pictures of inmates that date back a lot farther than that."

"That's what I was hoping," Kane said. "I'd recognize every last one of 'em if I saw his picture."

The warden nodded. "Well, I'll try to help you there, Jubal. Going through all the pictures we've got is gonna be a long, tiring process. It might take you several days to find out whether the other two have ever been here or not, but we can find out about the man named Mitchell in a matter of minutes. If you had surnames on the others, we could check them out mighty quick, too. Everything's filed alphabetically, you know."

Brady walked to the door and called to someone across the hall named Fry, then reseated himself at his desk. A few moments later, a man appeared in the doorway, then walked to the desk with raised eyebrows. "Yes, sir?" he asked.

The warden got to his feet. "I want you to let this young man named Jubal Kane look at every picture we've got in the record room, Mr. Fry. That task might take several days, but what I want you to do right now is pull the record of every man we've ever had here with the surname of Mitchell. Spread 'em all out on that long table in there and just let him take his time."

"Yes, sir," Fry said. Then he turned and spoke to Jubal. "If you'll follow me, we can get started right away."

Kane followed Fry, who was at least as tall as himself, up a flight of stairs and down two different halls to a large room in the southeast corner of the building. With the shades up on all of the windows, Jubal thought there was plenty of light in the room for reading. Nonetheless, Fry lit one lamp, then another, and set them both on the table.

Then he pointed to a chair. "Just make yourself comfort-able right there," he said. "I'll have the criminal history of a whole bunch of men named Mitchell in front of you mighty quick." He spun on his heel and moved toward several large filing cabinets along the opposite wall.

The search was a short one. When Jubal opened the third folder, he almost sprang out of his chair, then leaned forward with a short, audible intake of breath. There, at the top of the page, was a picture of the man who had gunned down his father. There was no doubt about it, Jubal was thinking. He held the folder closer to his eyes, the scene from that hot August morning in the barn run-ning through his mind once again. The man in that picture was the same man who had pumped two shots into the chest of the defenseless Bernard Kane. Positively!

Jubal spoke to Fry, who was standing beside the filing cabinets. "I don't need any more folders, sir, I've already found what I was looking for."

Fry was there quickly, looking over Kane's shoulder and reading aloud from the record: "Calvin C. Mitchell," he began, "born in Kentucky in eighteen forty-three. Moved to Texas with his parents in the mid-fifties and spent all of his teen years in Bandera County." Then, sens-ing that Jubal preferred reading the record for himself, Fry began to gather up the extra folders. Since they would not be needed, he would return them to their proper places in the filing cabinet, he said.

Then Kane began to read from the file, copying every word in his tablet. Calvin Mitchell had been a headache for Bandera County authorities throughout his growing-up years, and had finally received a five-year prison sen-tence in 1866 for burglary of the Bandera County Courthouse. His partner in the burglary, who had also received a five-year sentence, was a second cousin of the same age named Leroy Lively.

Leroy Lively! Jubal stared at the name for a few moments, then called to the man across the room. "Mr. Fry, would you please look up another name for me?"

Fry was there quickly. "Of course," he said.

Kane pecked the folder with a forefinger. "I'm reading about a prisoner named Leroy Lively," he said. "I'd like to see what he looks like."

Fry nodded, and returned to the filing cabinets. A couple minutes later, he laid another folder on the table.

Just as Jubal had expected, he was soon looking at a picture of his mother's killer. And as was the case with Mitchell, there could be no doubt. Leroy Lively was definitely the man who had put two shots into Tess Kane's bosom.

Jubal leaned back in his chair for a few moments with his arms folded. It had all been so easy, he was thinking. Why had Pat Patterson not done this years ago? Being a county sheriff, he could have gained access to these same records if he had just asked. Patterson did not give a damn, Kane decided, and Patterson also believed that Jubal had murdered his own parents.

Within the next two hours, Kane studied the criminal history of the two men, writing it all down in his tablet. Lively also was born in Kentucky. His family had eventually joined their kinfolk in Texas, however, and Leroy had grown up with his cousin Calvin. The two had indulged in petty crime throughout their teen years, and local authorities had done them no favor by overlooking one offense after another, usually taking them home to their parents with no more than a mild reprimand.

The year they were seventeen, and old enough to know better, they had stolen three calves from a neighboring rancher and tried to sell them to the rancher's own brother, who lived only a few miles down the road. A lenient judge had sentenced them to a year's probation. A few years later, however, when they were caught inside the courthouse at midnight rifling drawers, each of them drew a five-year sentence in the state penitentiary.

If ever there had been any doubt in Jubal's mind, it would have been erased when he read that on July 30, 1868, both Mitchell and Lively had escaped from custody. Kane repeated the date to himself. July 30! Just three days before his parents were murdered!

The file went on to explain that prison personnel, who considered Mitchell and Lively to be minimum-risk prisoners because they were "short-termers," had designated both men "trusties," and had begun to allow them outside the walls without supervision. On the day of their escape, they had been ordered to clean out a long ditch that ran along the edge of prison property. Several hours later their picks and shovels were found hidden in a cluster of bushes, but both men were long gone.

On September 1, 1868, the escapees were recaptured in Houston, where they had gotten involved in a drunken brawl. They were returned to the prison a week later, and had both served out the remainder of their sentences. They were released together in the fall of 1871.

When Jubal finished copying the information, he dropped the pencil on the tablet and sat thinking. The escapees had been free for only one month, just long enough to snuff out the lives of the relatively young and hardworking Kanes. Knowing that the killers had been sitting right here in this prison at the same time the sheriff had been shaking Jubal's chin and accusing him of killing his own parents, created a hard knot in the young man's stomach, and he fully intended to discuss it with Pat Patterson someday.

Fry had long since departed the room, no doubt needing to attend to some of the numerous other duties that were part of his job. Jubal closed the files he had copied, then shoved the pencil into his pocket and picked up his tablet. He was soon back in the warden's office. "We found Calvin Mitchell's file right away, sir, and it led us to the man named Leroy. He's Leroy Lively, Mitchell's cousin."

The warden nodded. "I don't have near as good a memory for names and faces as a man really needs for this job, but Mr. Fry tells me that I was here long before those men were released." He reached for a cigarette. "He's bound to be right, because I took this job in eighteen seventy. I do try to limit my personal contact with the inmates, though, so that's probably the reason I don't remember those two." He struck a match on a paperweight, then lit up and blew smoke through his nostrils. "Did you find out anything about the fellow you call the Third Man?"

"No, sir. It might take more than one day, but I'll look at every picture in that room, if you give me permission."

"Permission granted," Brady said. "Do you want to look over some more of them today?"

"No, sir, I'd like to get an early start in the morning and look through the files alphabetically." He chuckled softly. "I'll stay with it however long it takes, but I'm hoping that the man I'm looking for is named Adams."

The warden nodded, then took a small, square cardboard pass from his desk drawer. He wrote Jubal's name on it in ink, then handed it over. "This'll get you through the gate in the morning, and you can show it to anybody else who questions your presence in the building. I'll assign a trusty to help you in the record room. With him digging out and replacing the files for you, all you'll have to do is glance at each picture as he puts it in front of your nose. You can move a lot faster that way."

"Yes, sir," Jubal said. "That'll certainly work."

"Very well," Brady said. "The trusty will be waiting for you just inside the gate at eight o'clock in the morning."

Jubal thanked the warden again, and was out the front gate two minutes later.

7

Jubal rode out of Huntsville at sunup three days later, headed west. He had just spent all of one day and part of another looking at pictures and reading descriptions of convicts. The files that did not have pictures took up the most time, for he sometimes had to read half a page in order to get a full description of a man.

The prison trusty had met Kane at the front gate each morning. He seemed to be highly educated, and had been a tremendous help. After the first few hours of searching each day, when he sensed that Jubal was beginning to tire, he would seat himself at the long table and read aloud the descriptions from those files that bore no pictures. By noon of the second day they had gone through every file in the cabinet. The prison had no picture or description of the Third Man.

This morning Jubal was retracing his steps on the same road that he had traveled a few days ago. He would not follow the road all the way to San Antonio, however, nor would he pass the campsite where he had last seen Scooter and Fuzzy. When he reached Giddings, he would take the road to San Marcos. From there, Bandera County was almost a straight shot to the west.

Jubal knew very well that he was literally riding in circles. Hell, he had almost been in Bandera County a few days ago, for the county line was only a few miles north-west of San Antonio. He also knew that the information he had gained was well worth the long, hot ride, however, for now he had a starting place. With any luck he might even run into someone who not only knew both Mitchell and Lively, but also knew the identity of the Third Man.

The town of Bandera was founded in 1852 as a cypress-shingle camp. A Mormon colony was established there in 1854, and a year later the area became the site of one of the earliest Polish communities in the United States. Many of the settlers planted crops for sustenance, but soon most turned to cattle, for the surrounding Hill Country area was an ideal habitat for longhorns.

Jubal Kane rode into Bandera ten days after leaving Huntsville. He quickly learned that the six-room hotel had six vacant rooms, and that he could take his pick. He chose the front room on the west corner, for it was directly across the narrow hall from the office. There was no lobby or even a desk, only a sign nailed to the outside wall stating that anyone seeking lodging should knock on the first door to the right after entering the building. Jubal did so, and made arrangements for a three-night stay.

The middle-aged man, whose hair had obviously turned gray prematurely, had opened the door wide at Jubal's knock. It was easy to see that his office was also his living quarters, for even from where Kane stood he had seen the man's bed, cookstove, and a table containing several pots and pans. The man's red nose and bloodshot eyes suggested that he might be a heavy drinker, and Jubal intended to find out before the night was over. Kane knew that liquor loosened tongues and that, poured in the right man's glass, it was by far the cheapest means of getting information that might otherwise be difficult or impossible to come by.

Seeing that the man was in the process of preparing his evening meal, Jubal made no attempt at conversation, nor did he mention his name. And although he had only to glance at his rent receipt to know that he was talking with one Barney C. Witt, he refrained from calling the man by name. That would come later in the evening, when Kane had a quart of liquor in his hand.

Leaving his rifle, saddlebags, and a change of clothing in the room, Jubal untied his animals from the hitching rail and led them to the livery stable, which was located at the west end of the street. "Gonna be around for a while?" the hostler asked, as Kane dismounted in the doorway. He was a hunchbacked man who appeared to be past the age of sixty, and the absence of a hat revealed the fact that he was bald, with only a small patch of gray hair above each ear.

"I paid my rent at the hotel for three nights," Jubal said. "Unless something happens to bring about a change in my plans, I'll be in town for at least that long." He motioned toward his animals with his thumb. "I guess they need the rest more than I do; this kind of weather is mighty hard on 'em."

"We're probably gonna get somewhere between four and six more weeks of this," the hostler said, beginning to unbuckle the packsaddle. "We got about five inches of rain a week ago and it cooled things off for a day or two, but then she shot right back up to a hunnerd degrees."

Jubal watched quietly for a while, then pointed toward the office, which sported a thick hardwood door. "Will you be keeping my packsaddle in there?"

The hostler nodded. "That door stays padlocked. I lock it even when I walk back to the corral, since my brother ain't around no more to help keep an eye on it. His rheumatiz' keeps him close to his own front porch nowadays, so I just fell into the habit of locking the office everytime I walk out the door." He dragged the packsaddle a few feet in the direction of the office, then added, "Of course, it ain't locked right now, 'cause I just stepped out the door when I saw you coming. I'd sure have locked it, though, if I hadn't known that I was gonna be standing right here in front of it."

Jubal nodded, then smiled. The man had convinced him that his belongings would be under lock and key, all right. Kane bade him good day, then began to walk back up the street. He paused at a small building in the middle of the block. The lettering on the window identified the cubbyhole as the office of an attorney named Winthrop J. Clayton. With the window shade drawn and a lock hanging on the door, the place appeared to have been abandoned.

Kane doubted that such was the case, however. He supposed that the lawyer might live most anywhere in the county, and probably showed himself in Bandera only when he knew there was money to be made. Jubal would keep the man's name in mind, however, for if he had been doing business in the town for a long period of time, he would most likely be acquainted with both Mitchell and Lively.

A few minutes later, Jubal was seated at a table in Sally's Restaurant, which was located across the street from the hotel. "The beef stew's still simmering on the stove," the dark-haired waitress said. "I ate a bowl of it myself for dinner, and it was very good."

Having already noticed the absence of a wedding band on the young lady's finger, Jubal raised his eyes from the menu and looked her over approvingly. "If that stew's good enough for somebody like you," he said, smiling flirtatiously, "it's plenty good enough for me."

Her face suddenly flushed, then took on a rosy tint. "You have a choice of cornbread or warmed-over biscuits."

"Cornbread."

Without another word, she picked up the bill of fare and headed for the kitchen. Less than five minutes later, she placed his food and a steaming cup of coffee on his table, then was gone again.

He sat staring after her till she disappeared into the kitchen, then he began to concentrate on his supper. One bite told him that the girl knew what she was talking about. The stew was excellent; seasoned perfectly, with just enough hot pepper to tingle the mouth. He ate the concoction hungrily, then regained the girl's attention by waving at her and holding up his empty bowl. She was there quickly, a knowing expression on her face. "Refill?" she asked.

"Please," he answered. "And you can warm up my coffee, too."

He continued to sit at the table long after he finished his meal, sipping coffee and hoping for an opportunity to talk to the girl. Each time she delivered hot coffee to his table, however, she made herself scarce immediately thereafter. When Jubal finally decided that she was deliberately avoiding him, he got to his feet. He laid a quarter beside his empty bowl, then walked to the counter and paid for his supper.

When he reached the front door, he turned and waved good-bye to the pretty waitress, who appeared not to no-

tice. He walked on up the street, smiling. She would remember him, all right, he was thinking. After finding that
quarter on the table she would most certainly not forget
the man who had left it there.

A man standing in front of the hotel pointed over his
shoulder with his thumb, when Jubal asked directions to
the county courthouse. "It's over on Back Street," he said,
then quickly walked away.

Back Street had no identifying marker on the corner,
but after Kane had walked north for a block, he saw the
courthouse off to his right. It was a one-story brick building that was much longer than it was wide, and was one
of only three buildings on the block. The street ran past
a hardware store and ended in front of a large warehouse.
Beyond, there was nothing but large clusters of bushes,
weeds, and undergrowth. Kane supposed that the street
actually had no official name, but was called Back Street
by the locals because it was on the backside of Main.

Jubal could see that the courthouse was closed for the
day, so he reversed his direction. Back on Main Street, he
stood in front of the Cypress Saloon for a few moments,
then pushed his way through the bat-wing doors. The establishment was no different than hundreds of other saloons in Texas, with the usual thirty-foot-long bar running
along the wall, the familiar cast-iron stove in the middle
of the room, and the usual number of tables and chairs
scattered around in no particular order.

Kane took a stool on the far side of the bar. "Have
you got cold beer?" he asked the red-haired bartender,
who appeared to be no more than a few years older than
himself.

"Pretty cold," the man said. "We make our own ice,
you know."

"No," Jubal said, "I didn't know." He smiled, then
nodded. "I'll have a beer."

He was served promptly. He took one sip from the foamy mug, then quickly took another. "This is the best-tasting beer I've had in a long time," he said to the bartender. "A man might accidentally drink a lot more of this than he planned to."

The redhead chuckled. "That happens pretty often," he said. "Especially on weekends. As for the beer, we don't make it on the premises like some of our competitors do. It's brewed and delivered to us by a company in San Antonio."

As the day wore on and more drinkers came into the saloon, the redhead was suddenly a busy man, and Jubal saw less of him. A second bartender, who was short and fat, showed up at sunset. He refilled Jubal's mug without being asked, then scooped up a coin from the bar.

By the time darkness closed in, the place was half full of men, and Kane had looked them all over well. None resembled Mitchell or Lively, or even looked enough like either of them to be kinfolk. Jubal had not expected to find either of the men in Bandera, for he believed that the last place they would want to live would be a town where every inhabitant already knew they were thieves. It was also possible, and maybe even probable, that all of their relatives had left the area long ago out of embarrassment. However, it should not be too hard to find someone who knew, or had at least heard of, both Mitchell and Lively, Kane was thinking. He spoke to the redhead. "Give me a quart of the best whiskey on the premises," he said.

A short time later he walked from the saloon, carrying a quart of liquor that the label claimed had been distilled and bottled in Bourbon County, Kentucky.

Barney C. Witt was standing in the hall when Jubal stepped through the front door of the hotel. Kane held up the bottle, making sure that Witt could see the label. "You want to help me with this, Barney?" he asked.

The man pointed to Kane's room. "You mean in there?" he asked.

Jubal nodded. "In there."

Witt motioned toward his living quarters. "Let me get some glasses and a pitcher of water, then I'll be right with you."

Kane nodded and walked into his own room, leaving the door open wide.

8

"Win Clayton is probably somebody you ought to talk to," Barney Witt was saying, as he poured his fourth drink from Jubal's bottle. "He knew Mitchell and Lively very well, 'cause he's the man who prosecuted them for breaking into the courthouse. He's into private practice now, but back then he was the county's prosecuting attorney. Win's a pretty steady fellow, I reckon, always seems to know you when he sees you. His full name is Winthrop J. Clayton, you know."

Jubal nodded. "I read it on the window of his office."

"Well, I don't think he messes with that Main Street office much nowadays, probably just keeps a lot of stuff in there. He moved into a new place over in the county building a good while back. Now all he has to do is walk down the hall a few steps and he's in the courtroom."

While asking only a few questions, and never revealing

the reason for his interest in Mitchell and Lively, Jubal had been listening to the man talk for the better part of an hour. He himself had been sipping lightly, but had let Witt know right from the start that he was welcome to drink as much of the whiskey as he wanted. Kane's main concern now was to get as much information as possible before the man lost his memory for the night.

"You're sure that no relatives of either man still live in this county, Barney?" he asked.

Witt took another sip. "Of course I'm sure," he answered. "Old Harlan Mitchell and his wife pulled out of this county the same week their son Calvin got carted off to the penitentiary. That's a damn crying shame, too. I've been told that his poor old mother cried all week long. The day she left, she told a few people that she just couldn't hold her head up in this town anymore. Wouldn't tell a soul where she was going, either." He upended his drink, then continued to talk while he mixed another. "Any son of a bitch who would put his own mammy through all that shit ain't worth killing."

Jubal nodded in agreement, then raised his glass and wet his lips. "Lively's folks left the county, too?" he asked.

"Lively's pa and ma both died before he ever got into any serious trouble. He didn't have anybody to look out for but himself, and he did a piss-poor job of that. I've been told that, instead of trying to think for himself, he just followed Mitchell around, letting him call all the shots. I reckon that, for some strange reason, he thought Mitchell was smarter'n other folks."

Witt inhaled the next drink quickly, and its effect was almost instantaneous. He began to slur his words so badly that they were indistinguishable, and he seemed to have a problem holding his head up.

Finally, when he had lifted the man's head off his chest for the third time, Jubal spoke his mind. "I guess we'd better get you back to your own quarters, Barney. We can continue our conversation later."

Witt got to his feet without assistance, and once standing, seemed to sober up somewhat. "The man who owns this hotel ain't gonna catch me drinking," he said, then made his way across the room unsteadily. He leaned against the doorjamb, adding, "He lives in Dallas, ha-ha." He eased himself through the doorway and crossed the hall to his own quarters.

Kane slept so late that the sun was already shining around the edges of the window shade when he awoke next morning. He sat on the edge of his bed for a while, then picked up his pants to get at his watch. Seeing that it was already past seven o'clock, he let the pants fall back to the floor and crossed the room in his underwear. He would bathe himself as well as he could from the washpan, then shave his face and change into clean clothing. Today he would be calling on Mr. Winthrop J. Clayton.

He had breakfast at the same restaurant in which he had eaten the day before. He had been hoping for another look at the little dark-haired waitress, but she was nowhere to be seen. His platter of sausage and eggs was served by a Mexican waiter who was well over six feet tall. No use asking him for information, Jubal very quickly decided, for even making the young man understand what he wanted for breakfast had been a little difficult. Besides, the waiter was too young to know the answers to any of Kane's questions.

A few minutes before nine, Jubal stood in front of the courthouse, watching people as they showed up for work. Even with no description to guide him, Kane believed he had spotted the lawyer right away. As the man stood fidgeting nervously outside the front door, waiting for it to be unlocked from the inside, Jubal decided that he looked just like a man who would answer to the name of Winthrop. He was short, fat, and white as a ghost, and appeared to be about fifty years old. He carried a thick leather pouch in a pale right hand that looked as if it had never known a callus. Yessir, Kane said to himself. That would be none other than Winthrop J. Clayton.

Jubal's suspicion proved to be correct a few minutes later. When the front door finally opened, the fat man walked briskly down the hall and disappeared into an office that bore his name above the doorway in capital letters. Jubal Kane was right on his heels. "Pardon me, sir," he said, before the man could even seat himself. "Would you be Mr. Win Clayton?"

The lawyer turned quickly. "I certainly would, my boy." He seated himself behind the desk and pointed to a chair on the near side. "Have a seat right there."

Jubal continued to stand. "Well, I don't mean to barge in here and take up a lot of your time. You see, I'm not really a client, I'm . . . well, I just wondered if maybe sometime I could have a talk with you, man to man."

Clayton sat biting his lower lip for a moment, then got to his feet. He walked around Jubal and closed the office door, then returned to his chair. "Now," he said. "This is man to man."

"I guess so," Kane said, finally taking the seat he had been offered. He took a newspaper clipping that was yellowing with age from his pocket, and handed it across the desk. "Maybe you should read this before I say anything else."

Clayton accepted the two-column article, which had been published in 1868. He took a pair of eyeglasses from his desk drawer and slipped them on his nose, then began to read. When he had finished, he handed the clipping back, asking, "Am I to assume that you're related to the folks who were killed in that barn?"

Jubal nodded. "They were my parents."

The lawyer sat quietly for a while. "I see," he said finally, then leaned forward on his elbows. "I'm sorry to learn that such a terrible thing took place, but I sure can't think of anything that I can do about it, especially at such a late date."

Jubal shook his head. "I didn't expect you to do anything about it, Mr. Clayton, I was just hoping that you might be able to give me a lead on the whereabouts of Calvin Mitchell and Leroy Lively." He pointed to the newspaper article. "What this clipping does not say is that a fifteen-year-old boy hiding in the barn loft was a witness to the murders. Sheriff Pat Patterson kept that information out of the papers, because he was concerned about the boy's safety.

"I was that fifteen-year-old boy, Mr. Clayton. I saw Calvin Mitchell put two bullets in my pa's chest, then watched Leroy Lively do the same to my ma."

"Well, I'll be damned!" Clayton said loudly. Then he leaned back in his chair and began to speak softly. "I guess you're sure about who did the shooting, but I'd be interested in hearing how you came to know their names."

Jubal told the man the whole story, including the fact that he had spent a full year searching for the men before finally deciding to check out the state prison. "After Warden Brady read the letter from Sheriff Bacon, he gave me free access to the prison files and pictures. I spotted Mitchell right away. The information in his file pointed out Leroy Lively, so we dug out his file, too. I studied the pictures of both men for a long time, just like I studied their faces that day in the barn. A mistaken identity is completely out of the question."

"Them sons of bitches!" Clayton bellowed. Then, a little softer, he added, "I sent their sorry asses to the penitentiary once, but of course, they'd be out now. You can't keep a man in there but just so long on a little old burglary charge."

Jubal nodded. "I was just hoping you'd remember something Mitchell or some of his folks might have said back then that would give me an idea about where to go looking for him."

"That's what I've been sitting here racking my brain about, but nothing like that ever happened. Old Harlan Mitchell hated my guts because I was prosecuting his son, so I don't think he ever spoke to me at all. His wife did, though. She did everything but get on her knees and beg me to let her son off, but I told her that was the biggest part of the problem: he'd been let off too many times already.

"I don't think she ever spoke to me again after that day. Neither Mitchell nor Lively ever spoke directly to me, either, but both of them stuck out their tongues at me after the judge sentenced their asses to five years in the state pen."

Kane nodded. "I can imagine that," he said. Getting to his feet now, he nodded again. "I appreciate your time, Mr. Clayton, and I've enjoyed talking with you. I'll be in town for at least two more days, in case you happen to think of something else. I'm in the room just inside the front door at the hotel. If they were numbered, I guess it would be number one."

Clayton followed Jubal halfway to the door, then suddenly stopped and put a forefinger to his temple. "Just a minute," he said. "I think I just got an idea. There's a man living over on Pipe Creek named Clifford Shaw, and I believe he was pretty tight with the Mitchells.

"I represented Shaw in a little land squabble a few years back." He chuckled softly. "I won the case for him and he paid me for it, but it's possible that he still thinks he owes me a favor." He turned back to his desk and wrote on a pad for a while, then tore out the sheet. He handed it to Jubal, saying, "Now, this little note says that your pa is a longtime friend of the Mitchells', so you're gonna have to play the part. I believe the old man will spill his guts if he knows anything."

Kane reached for the note. "Just give me directions to Shaw's place, then I'll go find out what all I can make him believe." Moments later, he was out the door.

He ate a piece of apple pie and drank a cup of coffee at the restaurant, then headed for the livery stable. A few minutes later, he rode the roan out of the barn and headed east toward Pipe Creek. He had crossed the creek the day before on his way to Bandera, and knew that it was about a two-hour ride. "When you reach the creek, just follow it north for about a mile," Clayton had said. "Shaw raises Holsteins for the dairy farms around San Antonio, does mighty well at it, too. You won't have any problem finding his place, just keep going till you see a lot of black-and-white milch cows that look like they'd rather be back home in Holland."

Kane reached the creek at one o'clock in the afternoon. He watered the roan, then pointed the animal north alongside the shallow stream. He had traveled no more than a quarter mile when he began to see the grazing cattle. Although there were a few cows with calves about, most of the animals he saw were year-old heifers. Not a single bull could be seen, which led Jubal to believe that Shaw knew exactly what he was doing. The rancher himself determined which cows were bred to which bulls, rather than allowing the cattle themselves to choose.

At the top of the next rise, Kane rode past two tall barns with large corrals, then on to the white, two-story house. At the hitching rail, two large collies met him noisily, prompting him to remain in the saddle. "They're all bluff!" a deep voice shouted. Jubal turned to see a tall, slim, white-haired man walking from the nearest corral, a small basket under his arm. "Get down and tie up," he said. "The dogs are harmless."

Jubal dismounted, but held on to the reins. "Good afternoon," he said. "My name is Jubal Kane, and I've been admiring your cattle as I rode up the hill. I've got to admit that they're considerably better-looking than any longhorns I ever saw." The man pumped Kane's right hand and introduced himself as Clifford Shaw, then stood quietly, no doubt waiting for Jubal to state his business.

Kane took the note from his pocket. "Win Clayton told me to give you this," he said. "I guess you could call it a short letter of introduction."

Shaw accepted the note, then set his basket of eggs on the ground. "How is Win doing nowadays, anyway?" he asked.

"I think he's getting along very well. He still needs to lose some of that weight and get a little more exercise, though."

"He's always been fat," Shaw said. He unfolded the note, then began to move his lips silently as he read Clayton's hurried handwriting. Then he spoke again: "Well, this reads like Win thinks you're a pretty nice fellow, even says that your pa is a good friend of Harlan Mitchell." He refolded the paper and shoved it into his pocket. "What can I do for you?"

"Well, my pa grew up with Harlan Mitchell back in Kentucky, and he'd like to renew their friendship. He's not able to do much riding nowadays, so he asked me to try to locate the man. I've been trying to find somebody who knows where the Mitchells went after they left Bandera County, but I haven't had much luck. I had a talk with Mr. Clayton this morning, and he seemed to think you were the man I should talk to." He tied the roan's reins to the rail, then turned to face Shaw again. "You see, Pa wants to find Mr. Mitchell pretty bad. He didn't actually say so, but it sounded to me like he might even owe the man a good deal of money. I know they were in business together about the same time I was born."

Shaw stood quietly for some time, running his right hand over the white stubble on his jaw. "What's your pa's name?" he finally asked.

Jubal answered with the only truthful words he had spoken since introducing himself: "Bernard Kane," he said.

"Bernard Kane," Shaw repeated softly. He shook his head a few times, then spoke the name again. "Don't reckon I ever heard Harlan mention anybody by that name."

Jubal leaned against the hitching rail and held his tongue.

"Did Clayton say how come he thought I might know where Harlan went?" Shaw asked after a while.

"No, sir. He just said that it seemed only natural for the two of you to keep in touch, since you both lived in the same section of the county for several years, and appeared to be the best of friends."

Shaw nodded. "We were friends, all right, even hunted cats together every year. He gave me the best pack of lion hounds in this country when he pulled out. Of course, the dogs all died of old age a long time ago."

Jubal nodded and smiled, but remained quiet.

Shaw scratched his jaw and stood staring at the ground for a while. "You say your pa might owe Harlan some money. Do you have any idea how much?"

"I'm sorry, sir, but I don't. I just remember Pa saying that Mr. Mitchell got disgusted and left Kentucky way too soon; said that if he had stuck around till the business caught on, he would have gotten his investment back a hundred times over. Pa sold the company eventually, and he hasn't had to work a day since."

"The hell you say. What kind of business are you talking about?"

"Warehouses. At the time he sold out, Pa owned a string of thirty warehouses within a twenty-mile radius. The whiskey companies were there to lease 'em just as fast as he could build 'em.

"They aged their liquor in the warehouses, stacked barrels almost to the roof. Pa had to furnish a security force and a crew to keep the buildings warm in the wintertime, but other than that, it was all profit. The companies would lease the buildings for five years at a time, 'cause that's how long they aged their whiskey. Pa explained it all to me after I got old enough to understand it."

Jubal could tell by the man's facial expression that he had bought the story. Shaw rubbed a knuckle across his chin. "Did you think to try asking about Harlan around Houston?" he asked.

"No, sir. I don't know why, but it just never occurred to me."

"Well, that's where he went when he left here. He said he was gonna try to get hold of some lowland property, try his hand at growing rice."

Jubal was already untying the roan. "I guess Houston's my next stop, then. I certainly appreciate the information, sir, and I should be able to find the man by asking around."

"You might have to do a right smart of asking, 'cause that's a big town and Harlan pretty much keeps to himself. He's certainly around there, though. He sent me word last year that he was still alive and kicking. The fellow who brought the message said that Harlan lived a few miles south of Houston, and that he was doing right well for himself." .

Jubal threw his leg over the saddle. "I'm on my way to Houston," he said. "You've been a big help to me, and I thank you much." He kicked the roan in the ribs and soon disappeared over the hill.

Two hours later, he turned the roan over to the hunch-backed liveryman, then hurried up the street toward the courthouse. He arrived just as Win Clayton was leaving the building. "Have you already been out to Shaw's place?" the lawyer asked, stepping through the doorway and joining Jubal, who stood leaning against the wall a few feet from the door.

Kane nodded. "I went straight out there after I left your office. I just got back a few minutes ago."

Clayton raised his eyebrows. "And?"

"Mr. Shaw suggested that I try my luck in Houston," Kane said, smiling. "That's where Harlan Mitchell went when he left here."

"Does Shaw think he might still be there?"

"He was there last year, even sent a messenger by to say hello to Shaw. The rider told Shaw that Mitchell was living somewhere south of Houston, growing rice and do-ing well."

"Well, I'll be damned," Clayton said. "I'll bet a dollar that the son of a bitch who killed your pa is hanging around there, too."

Kane nodded. "I intend to find out in the very near future, Mr. Clayton. The reason I came back by here again this afternoon, was to ask you to keep all of this under your hat. News travels fast, and I'd hate for Calvin Mitch-ell to get the word on me before I get a chance to intro-duce myself."

The attorney chuckled. "It won't happen, Jubal Kane. At least, nobody's gonna hear it from me." He tapped Jubal on the chest lightly. "I fully expect you to kill Mitchell within the next week or two, and I can guarantee you that I'll hear about it not too long after." He reached for Kane's hand and gave it a firm grip. "You just be careful, Jubal; that son of a bitch you're hunting is the scum of the earth, and he'll shoot you right between the shoulders if he gets a chance." He shook Jubal's hand and patted Kane on the back, then disappeared around the corner.

A few minutes later, Jubal was sitting in the restaurant with his hat in his lap. The same young girl was his waitress, and she seemed a little friendlier this time around. She smiled prettily, and seemed to be in no hurry to leave after handing him the bill of fare. "Hi," she said softly, fluttering her eyelashes.

"Hello," Jubal said, ignoring the menu he now held. "My name is Jubal Kane, and I promised myself that I'd ask yours the very next time I saw you."

She wiggled her nose. "My name is Jenny Hilton," she said, then pointed to the menu. "Order up."

He held the menu playfully against his chest. "Just one more thing," he said, "then I'll eat. You see, for the time being, I'm traveling around the country a lot on business, and I was wondering if it would be all right for me to write to you here at the restaurant sometime."

She answered quickly. "I think I'd like that, but you probably should write me at my father's place of business. It's called Hilton Feed and Supply, and it's located up the street by the livery stable."

"I've read the sign on the building," he said, handing the menu back without looking at it. "Just tell the cook to send me whatever he considers his best steak."

"You mean whatever Sally considers her best steak. She does her own cooking, Mr. Kane."

"Well, all right," he said. "But I do wish you'd call me Jubal. Just listen to this: 'Jubal and Jenny Kane.' Don't you think that has a nice ring?"

She wiggled her nose again and headed for the kitchen.

He was soon served the best steak he had eaten in months. By the time he finished his meal, the restaurant was crowded and Jenny had no time for idle conversation. He laid a quarter on the table and waved good-bye, then paid for his food and left the building.

He had a drink at the Cypress Saloon, then walked to the hotel just as darkness closed in. When the last hint of daylight disappeared around the edges of the window shade, he was already in bed. He had come into the building as quietly as possible, for another conversation with Barney C. Witt was completely out of the question. Kane felt that he already had as much information as he was likely to get in this town, and that the hotelkeeper could add nothing. Jubal lay on his bed thinking of the beautiful Jenny Hilton for a while, then slept the night away.

9

★

He ate breakfast in the restaurant at sunrise, then headed for the livery stable. The hostler was standing in the wide doorway with a cup of coffee in his hand. "You cutting your visit short?" he asked. "Or are you just gonna ride around a little more this morning?"

"I'll need both of my horses," Kane answered. "I'm leaving town."

The man nodded, but said no more. He dashed his coffee grounds out of his cup and set it on the office door-step, then headed down the hall toward the corral. A few minutes later, he helped Jubal arrange the packsaddle on the black, and insisted that Kane allow him to saddle the roan. "Part of my job," he explained.

Jubal paid the man and gave him an extra quarter, then rode out of the barn. A short distance farther down the street, he tied his animals to the hitching rail in front of a grocery store. His food supplies were getting low, and he also needed some matches and a small container of lard. When he stepped through the doorway he was greeted by a tall, gray-haired woman, who immediately went about gathering and sacking up the things he requested. Finally, when she had it all lying on the counter, she asked, "Will this be everything, sir?"

"I'll have two bags of those," he said, pointing to a stack of oatmeal cookies.

He spent a few minutes loading and balancing his supplies on the black's packsaddle, then rode out of town. Houston was on a straight line due east from Bandera, and well over two hundred miles away.

The settlement of Houston, located just south of Buffalo Bayou, and named in honor of the victorious military commander at San Jacinto, General Sam Houston, had served as the capital of Texas from 1837 to 1839, and was incorporated as a city in 1839. Situated on the flat Gulf Coastal Plain in an area drained by short, sluggish bayous, the area had grown only slightly during the first few decades, but eventually came to be considered the transportation center of southeast Texas.

The first European settlement in the area had been started by a man named John Harris in 1826, and was called Harrisburg. The settlement was destroyed in 1836 by the Mexican general Antonio López de Santa Anna, however, shortly before his defeat by the Texan army at San Jacinto. That same year, two land speculators, the brothers Augustus and John Allen, laid out a new settlement and decided that it should be called Houston, after the famous general.

Jubal Kane rode into Houston ten days after leaving Bandera. The sun was already disappearing for the day when he halted at a livery stable on the edge of town. He turned his animals over to an elderly hostler who introduced himself as Tyson.

Then, with his saddlebags lying across his shoulder, and his rifle and a change of clothing under his arm, Jubal leisurely began to walk up the street. It was past dark by the time he rented a room at the Andrews Hotel, which was the first one he came to. Unlike most of the hotels Kane had stayed in this year, the young male desk clerk insisted that Jubal sign his name on the register. "Hotel policy," he said. When Kane was halfway down the hall toward his room, the clerk called after him: "Gonna be in town long?"

Jubal stopped in his tracks. How many times had he answered that question this year? And why in the hell did it matter how long he was gonna be in town? He turned to face the young man. "Let me tell you how you can figure that out all by yourself," he said sarcastically. "I'm gonna pay you every day, if I intend to sleep here that night. Then, when the first day comes along that I don't pay you, you'll know that I won't be around at nightfall."

The clerk, who appeared to be not yet out of his teens, dropped his eyes and nodded. The expression of hurt on the young man's face did not go unnoticed by Jubal Kane, who suddenly felt terribly ashamed.

He was back at the desk quickly. "I had no right to speak to you that way," he said. "And the fact that I'm hot and tired is a damn feeble excuse. I hope you'll accept my apology, because I truly am sorry."

The boy smiled and nodded.

"The truth is," Kane said, "I really don't know how long I'll be around. Maybe two days, maybe two weeks."

The boy nodded again. "Yes, sir," he said.

Jubal smiled, and patted the youngster's shoulder. Then, promising himself that he would try to be more considerate of other people's feelings from now on, he walked down the hall and turned his key in the lock.

When he stepped through the doorway he knew even before he lit the coal-oil lamp, that he would sleep much cooler than usual. The windows that were already open on two sides of the room created a draft that he had felt the moment he opened the door. Once he had put a match to the wick and replaced the globe on the lamp, he could also see that the windows were covered on the outside with wire netting. He closed and relocked the door, then walked back to the bed. He ran his hand along the mattress and smiled, knowing that soon he would be lying there enjoying the cool breeze. And with the wire netting over the windows, he would have no reason to be concerned about the bloodthirsty mosquitoes that the Houston area was noted for.

He laid his gunbelt on the bed, then doffed his sweaty clothing. He poured the washpan half-full of water, then, taking advantage of the soap, washcloth, and towel provided by the hotel, shaved his face and washed his body as best he could.

Half an hour later, dressed in clean clothing and feeling much better, he walked into the lobby. He nodded to the young clerk, then followed an arrow that pointed the way to the hotel restaurant, which a large sign proclaimed to be "under new management." A tall, skinny waiter met him at the door. "Right this way, sir," he said in a Northern accent, then led the way to a table that Jubal could have very easily found on his own. "We have a special on fried shrimp and oysters tonight," the waiter said, pulling out a chair and motioning for Jubal to seat himself.

Kane took the chair, but was none too happy about it, for he simply did not like being coddled. He could have chosen any one of at least a dozen tables, for they were all vacant, and he was plenty capable of pulling out his own chair. And the fact that the waiter pushed the chair in closer to the table while Jubal was in the act of seating himself, much like Kane had often seen his father do for his mother, just went against the grain.

However, remembering that he had no more than an hour ago decided to be more considerate toward others, Jubal spoke to the waiter cordially. "I'll have the fried oysters," he said.

The young waiter, who had never produced a bill of fare in order for Kane to look over alternatives to the special that the restaurant management seemed to be pushing, nodded and bowed halfway, then headed for the kitchen.

While awaiting the preparation of his meal, Jubal sat looking around the room. There were only two diners in the place besides himself, and he thought he knew at least one of the reasons why the restaurant did not have more customers: Texas men simply did not want long-legged waiters pushing chairs under their asses while they were trying to sit down.

Such treatment no doubt worked well wherever the new management had come from, but most Texans, both male and female, were of a highly independent nature, and too much pampering was likely to send them and their business elsewhere. Jubal decided that the sign in the lobby might just as well be left in place, for he believed that the restaurant would be changing hands again before long, even if the food they served was good.

An hour later, he removed all of his clothing and stretched out on his bed, his Colt lying on a small table at arm's length and his Winchester leaning against the nearby wall. He had just eaten an outstanding meal, and what he needed now was a good night's sleep. He was very tired, for, having climbed into the saddle at daybreak this morning, he had traveled close to forty miles this day.

He had resisted the urge to visit some of the saloons asking questions, for he had decided to see how much he could learn on his own before turning to strangers for information. Besides, if a dead body should turn up somewhere in the vicinity, the fewer people he talked to, the fewer would know that he had been here. At any given time a large segment of the population of Houston was transient, and Jubal doubted that anyone would even remember him if he kept his mouth shut.

He slept soundly till daybreak next morning, then lay on his bed for a while, thinking. He had already decided that everything he did around this town would be done leisurely. He would speak to people only when necessary, and even avoid making eye contact with men he met on the street. He would also be careful to eat his meals at peak times of the day, for when a waiter was very busy, he would be less likely to remember any particular diner. He would do his eating at sunup, noon, and sunset, and he would not eat in the same restaurant twice.

He ate a breakfast of pancakes and ham in a small establishment halfway down the block, then walked to the livery stable for his roan. Half an hour later, he was headed south by southeast. When Jubal had casually asked what lay in that direction, the liveryman had said that marshlands abounded all the way from Houston to the Gulf Coast, and that they were littered with one rice farm after another. "Anywhere people run across enough moisture, they plant rice," he said. "Some of 'em even dug ditches and canals and turned a lot of dry ground into rice paddies, 'cause there's money to be made. Hell of a lot more money than raising cotton or cattle. At least, that's what I've been told."

Jubal shook his head and curled his lip all the time the hostler was talking about rice, then asked enough additional questions to create the impression that he was totally disinterested in rice farms. When he mounted the roan, knowing that the hostler was standing watching in the doorway, he headed toward the center of town. Once out of sight of the livery barn, however, he circled to the south and pointed the animal down the road toward the marshlands.

He began to see rice growing on both sides of the road after only a few miles, but saw no one in or around any of the fields. He rode past one field after another till mid-morning, and was about to turn back toward Houston when he saw a rider coming up the road in his direction. Jubal continued on at a walk, trying to decide whether or not to question the rider when the two met.

They were still thirty yards apart when Jubal knew that he would definitely have something to say to the man, for he suddenly knew that he was about to come face-to-face with Calvin Mitchell. Even from this distance he could easily make out the man's facial features, which had changed little since the day Jubal had seen him in the barn. In fact, Mitchell appeared not to have aged a day during the past seven years.

By the time the distance had closed to ten yards, Kane could even make out the blue eyes and the dirty blond hair. There was not even the slightest room for doubt. He had found his man, and knowing that shooting Mitchell here in the road would be unwise, he racked his brain for a way to handle the situation. Then, as they came alongside each other, Kane raised his arm and spoke with a voice that sounded as if it belonged to someone else. "Hello, there," he said, beaming from ear to ear. "I thought I recognized you. You're Calvin Mitchell, and I remember you from our days in the Huntsville pen together."

Mitchell stared stonily at Kane for a moment, then spoke: "I can't say that I remember you. What's your name?"

The voice—the same voice Jubal had been hearing in his dreams for the past seven years! "My name's Woody Eason," he answered, his smile constant. "Of course, you and I never did have too much to say to each other, probably because I was a few years younger than you, but I sure remember you, even remember when you and your cousin Leroy Lively escaped." He paused for only an instant, then added, "Whatever happened to old Leroy, anyway?"

"I ain't seen him in years," Mitchell said, both his voice and his facial expression softening. "I heard he was up in Indian Territory, then somebody said he was hanging around Waco. Me and him fell out over a woman back in 'seventy-two. It turned out that she weren't worth a shit for nothin', but neither one of us knowed it at the time we was squabblin' over her."

Jubal shook his head. "I know what you mean," he said. "Damn women have broken up more good buddies than anything else I can think of." He sat his saddle thoughtfully for a few moments, then asked, "You headed into Houston, Calvin?"

Mitchell nodded. "Thought I'd ride in and have a drink or two. Fellow can't have much more'n that nowadays: Every saloon in town's gone up at least a nickel a drink, and a bunch of 'em's gone up a dime."

Jubal shook his head. "That's exactly the reason I don't do much of my drinking in saloons," he said. "A man can't tie one on anymore without coughing up an arm and a leg." He turned in the saddle and pointed down the road in the direction from which he had come. "I just came out on the road to exercise my horse a little. My camp's about a quarter mile back there on the creek, and I've got plenty of whiskey." He smiled broadly, then began to turn his horse around. "If you'll follow me, I'll let you break the seal on a quart of Jim Beam."

Mitchell nodded. "I've got to say that I've heard worse suggestions," he said, then laughed aloud. "The price is right, too." He kneed his black gelding, then headed down the road alongside Kane.

It was only when Jubal got back to the creek that he noticed the thick patches of weeds growing along the south bank in either direction. Not only was there no trail alongside the creek, but not a single weed or blade of grass had been pushed out of shape. Mitchell would surely know that no horse had traveled that route recently, Kane was thinking, and the north bank was probably no different. "We can make it to my camp a little quicker by turning off here," he said, glancing at Mitchell in an attempt to read his expression. "I rode down the other side of the creek yesterday and this morning because it's a little easier traveling over there, but my campsite is actually here on the south bank." He turned off the road and Mitchell followed, showing no signs that he might have become suspicious.

Jubal led the way till they were around a sharp curve and about two hundred yards from the road, then stopped, allowing Mitchell to come alongside. With lightning speed, Kane drew his Colt with his right hand and grabbed the bridle of Mitchell's horse with his left. "Raise your hands, Calvin Mitchell," he said harshly, "and don't even bat a damned eye."

Though slow to comply, Mitchell finally raised his arms above his head. "Wha—?"

"Lift that gun out of its holster with your thumb and forefinger," Jubal interrupted, "then toss it in the creek."

Mitchell unholstered the weapon, and a moment later both men heard the splash as it hit the water. "Now," Kane continued, "I want you to dismount very slowly, then start walking toward the creek. I'll tell you when to stop."

The man stepped from the saddle and took a few steps. "Right there!" Jubal said loudly. "That's far enough. Now, turn around and see if you can face me after you hear what I've got to say." The man complied.

"My name is not Woody Eason," Kane began, "and I've never served time in the pen. My name is Jubal Kane, son of the late Bernard Kane. You remember Bernard Kane, don't you Mitchell? Don't you remember reading his name in the newspaper? You probably even laughed when you read it. Of course, it could be that you don't know how to read, and in that case I'll remind you that Bernard and Tess Kane are the names of the couple that you, Leroy Lively, and a sandy-haired squirt with a squeaky voice left lying dead in a puddle of milk.

"You do remember that, don't you, Mitchell? You three sons of bitches gunned them down in their own barn while they were milking their cow. It all took place in Nacogdoches County, seven years ago this month."

Mitchell stood listening with his mouth half open. His complexion had suddenly turned the color of ashes.

"You want me to jog your memory a little more, Mitchell? You remember that squeaky-voiced son of a bitch asking you to let him look in the barn loft? You told him nobody was in that loft, and ordered him to saddle the horses instead. I'm living proof that you were wrong, mister. I had just climbed up there to throw down some hay for the horses. I lay in that loft almost too scared to breathe, while you put two shots in my pa's chest, then ordered Leroy Lively to do the same to my ma. After the three of you rode our horses out of the barn, I peeked through the cracks and watched you ransack our house. Do you remember that, Mitchell?"

Mitchell finally found his tongue. "How can you be sure that it was me in that barn, and who told you my name?"

"I can be sure because I saw you with my own eyes, mister. I watched you shoot my pa down in cold blood, and I committed your face to memory. It was easy enough to find out your name after I figured out how to do it. You see, I just went to the Huntsville penitentiary and good old Warden Jack Brady let me look at your file. Your name was right there under your picture, just as pretty as you please. I know your life history, old buddy; it was all right there in the folder.

"I'm gonna ask you one more question, Mitchell, and you might live a little longer if you answer it. Who was the squeaky-voiced little man in that barn with you and Lively?"

Mitchell spat in the dust, then spoke with a snarl: "Ain't got nothin' to say to you," he said.

Jubal cocked the Colt. "Your choice, Mitchell," he said. "But since you're not gonna talk to me, I've decided that you're not gonna be talking to anybody." He pointed the gun at the man's chest. "Think on this for a few seconds, Mitchell: I'm about to kill you, and there's not a damn thing that you can do about it. You see, at this particular moment you're completely helpless, just like my pa and ma were the day you sons of bitches burst into their barn and gunned them down."

Kane looked Mitchell straight in the eye as he pulled the trigger. He waited for a moment, then fired again. The man had dropped to his knees with the first shot, and the second knocked him sprawling onto his back. Jubal kneed the roan forward a few steps for a closer look. He had only to see the open mouth and the glassy eyes to know that it was all over for Calvin Mitchell.

Kane dismounted and tied the reins of Mitchell's horse to the saddlehorn, then gave the animal a whack across the rump. Three minutes later, he was on his way to Houston at a canter, intending to be in town only long enough to pick up his packhorse. He certainly did not want to be around when Mitchell's body was found, although he felt that, knowing the man's background and reputation, local lawmen would not be overly concerned about apprehending the party responsible for his demise.

He reached the livery stable in less than two hours. After retrieving his packhorse and telling the hostler that he was on his way south to the Gulf Coast, he made a half circle and eventually rode out of the area in a northerly direction. He would know very soon whether or not Leroy Lively was in Waco.

10

★

At midafternoon on the fourth day, Jubal rode into the town of Bryan, which was roughly the halfway point between Houston and Waco. A roadside sign on the outskirts stated that the town had been chartered in 1855, and was located in the same area where Stephen F. Austin's colonists had settled between 1821 and 1831. These things Kane already knew, because Texas history was a required subject in Nacogdoches County schools.

He halted at the livery stable on the south end of town, and turned his horses over to a barrel-chested liveryman. "Are you a blacksmith?" he asked.

The man nodded. "Most of my life," he answered.

Jubal motioned to the packhorse. "I think I heard a rattling shoe on one of his hooves a little while ago, so check him out, if you will." He stood thinking for a moment, then added, "Just look the hooves of both animals over, and correct anything you find wrong. I'll be needing them about sunup in the morning, so if you can get that done this afternoon, I'll appreciate it."

The muscular man nodded again. "That ain't no big job," he said. He waved his arm around to indicate the empty stalls, then chuckled. "I can get on it right now, 'cause you're the only customer I've had since nine o'clock this morning."

Kane shouldered his saddlebags and pulled his rifle from its scabbard, then pointed to the man's office. "I suppose you'll lock up my pack in there, huh?"

"Always," the big man said.

"All right," Jubal said. "What I need right now is a hotel room, a cold beer, and something to eat."

"That ain't no problem, neither," the man said. "You'll find all three of them things under one roof up the street a ways. The Bryan Hotel's on the corner at the end of the block. You can't miss it."

"Thank you," Kane said. "I'll see you about sunup."

Jubal paid seventy-five cents for a room on the top floor of the two-story building, and knew the moment he opened the door that he had gotten more for his money than most hotels had to offer. Not only were the walls and ceiling colorfully papered, but there were two tables, two chairs, a chest of drawers, and a clothes closet that was exceptionally large by hotel standards. Not that he had any use for a closet, because he carried nothing around that required hanging.

He mentally checked out the bed, then raised the room's only window, which offered an excellent view of the street below. He stripped to the waist, then shaved his face and washed his upper body with a washcloth. He had brought no clean clothing to the room, for he intended to wear what he had on till he reached Waco. He rebuttoned his shirt and wiped most of the dust from his hat with his kerchief, then headed for the stairway.

A few moments later, he was seated in the hotel restaurant. "I can warm up some of what we had for dinner," the gray-haired lady standing beside his table was saying. "It's our special of the day: all the black-eyed peas and cornbread you can eat, for fifteen cents."

Jubal nodded. "That sounds exactly like something I need, ma'am," he said. He chuckled softly, then added, "As hungry as I am today, I imagine you might lose money on me, though."

The lady was halfway to the kitchen. She paused for a moment, then spoke over her shoulder: "I don't think so," she said. "Peas are down to thirty cents a bushel, and I can get 'em shelled for another twenty cents. Besides, my oldest son planted twenty acres of 'em this year."

Jubal sat smiling as the lady disappeared. Nope, he was thinking, she wasn't going to lose money on anybody. Twenty acres would not only grow enough peas to feed everybody in this town, but several other towns of comparable size as well.

When he had finished eating, Jubal walked through the bat-wing doors and into the adjacent hotel saloon. A fat, middle-aged bartender, who had his few remaining strands of hair slicked down and combed forward in a vain attempt to hide his balding pate, threw up a hand and spoke loudly as Kane walked into the room. "Come on in and have a seat," he said. "Been sitting here by myself looking at that door for the past hour, and I'd just about decided that nobody was ever gonna walk through it again."

"There's always one more around somewhere," Jubal said, taking a stool directly across the bar from the man. "I'll have a beer."

The bartender, whose complexion was almost as white as chalk, served the beer quickly. He accepted Jubal's nickel, then poked his right hand across the bar for a shake. "My name's Joe Crockett," he said with a smile, "but that ain't good enough for most of the drinkers in this town. They all insist that my first name ought to be Davy." He dropped the coin into a metal box on the shelf behind him, then turned back to face Kane. "Don't make a shit to me, though. I'll answer to any damn thing people want to call me, if it'll keep me from having to work out in that hot sun."

Jubal chuckled, and wiped the foam from his mouth with the heel of his hand. "You're right about it being hot," he said. "Almost hot enough to do in a traveling man."

The bartender nodded. "Traveling man, huh? I knew you weren't from around here the second you walked through that door."

Kane had decided to change his tactics. From now on he would ask after Leroy Lively by name. But the name Jubal was about to change was his own. He must assume that by now Lively knew the surname of the couple who had died in the barn, as did most other Texans who read newspapers. And if Lively heard that a man named Kane was on his trail, he would surely become suspicious, and no doubt more cautious. However, if he heard that an old friend was trying to get in touch with him, he might not be nearly as hard to find. In fact, he might actually begin to make an effort to reacquaint himself with that old friend.

"I've been traveling all summer," Kane said, pushing his mug forward for a refill. "My name's Jubal Brown, and I've been hunting an old family friend. He's a few years older than me, but our families were good friends back in Kentucky."

The bartender drew the beer. "An old family friend, huh? What name would that old family friend be using?"

Jubal shrugged, then smiled. "His name was Leroy Lively back home, and I don't guess he'd have any reason to change it."

"Leroy Lively," the man repeated smugly, and drew a beer for himself. "Leroy Lively," he said again, as he turned back to face Jubal and took a sip from his mug. "Six feet tall, blackheaded, brown-eyed, about thirty years old. Does that sound like the man you're looking for?"

Kane nodded. "Sounds exactly like him," he said.

"Well, you're about a year late. He tried to make a go of a freighting business right here in Bryan, but he finally fell on his ass. He pulled outta here a year ago last spring, and that's the last I saw of him. I did hear that he killed a man in a gunfight up in Waco last year, but I don't know how much truth there is to that." He took another sip, then added, "Could be something to it; I've heard it said that he's pretty fast with a gun."

Jubal sat staring at the bar as the information soaked in, thankful that he had decided to stop overnight in Bryan. "This town looks to be plenty big enough to support a freighthauling business, Joe," he said finally. "Do you have any idea why Lively couldn't make it work?"

"Yep, sure do. He did all right when he first started up, but when word got out that he'd served time in prison, just about every merchant in town made other arrangements, saying they didn't want no crook handling their stuff." He drank the last of his beer, then set the mug on the bar noisily. "And you're right about Bryan being able to support a freighting business. There's one located on each end of town right now, and both of them are doing mighty well."

Jubal slid off his stool. "I'll be leaving now, Joe, but I certainly appreciate the information. You wouldn't happen to know what Lively's doing in Waco, would you?"

Crockett shook his head. "Nope, just heard that he shot somebody up there."

Jubal reached across the bar and shook the man's hand. "It was nice meeting you," he said, then began to chuckle. "I'm sure you noticed that I called you Joe, but I've got a feeling that everybody else is gonna keep calling you Davy."

The bartender nodded. "You can count on that," he said.

Kane was in bed at sunset and went to sleep quickly, as was almost always the case after he had drunk a few beers. Aside from the times when he awoke needing to use the chamber pot, he slept soundly, and the last time he opened his eyes he could see that it was well past daybreak.

He ate a pancake breakfast and drank several cups of coffee in the hotel restaurant. The gray-haired lady who had served him the day before was not on the floor this morning, but as the waiter opened the door leading to the kitchen, Jubal had caught a glimpse of her bent over the stove. For some reason, knowing that she would be the one to prepare his meal had given him a good feeling.

"The roan's hooves were in pretty good shape," the liveryman said, when Kane arrived at the stable to pick up his horses. "At least, they looked good enough that I decided not to mess with 'em. I put new shoes on your packhorse's hind hooves, though." He pointed. "The old ones are hanging right there on that ring if you want to take a look at 'em."

Jubal shook his head and reached for his purse. "How much do I owe you?"

"Got to charge you three dollars for the whole works," the big man said, sounding almost apologetic.

"Oats have gone up again this summer, and the price of horseshoes has shot plumb outta sight."

Jubal paid the liveryman with no complaint, and a few minutes later rode out of the barn and took the road to Waco.

Kane traveled steadily throughout the day, halting only to eat cold food and allow his animals to graze for an hour at midday. He rode past Robertson County cotton fields for most of the afternoon, often waving to the dozens of Negro field hands who were busy tending the area's leading cash crop with hoes. The bolls had not opened yet, but Jubal knew that the snowy fields would be nothing short of beautiful a few weeks from now.

An hour before sunset he selected a campsite alongside the Brazos River, a few miles west of Calvert. As he staked out his animals on their picket ropes, he was trying to make an estimate as to how many thousands of mile-long rows of cotton he had seen this day. He knew that he had seen only a tiny portion of the area, and that most of its acreage was devoted to growing the soft, white product for which there was always a ready market.

He doubted that there were many places on earth better suited for the production of cotton than Robertson County, Texas; and the town of Calvert, less than an hour's ride from where he was now standing, boasted the largest cotton gin in the world. He stood for a moment, trying to imagine the vast sums of money involved in such an operation, then shook his head and began to look around for some kindling with which to start his campfire.

Dead leaves, twigs, and bark were easy to find, and he soon had a blaze going under his coffeepot. He ate tinned fish and soda crackers for his supper, then sat sipping from his tin cup. Just before dark he dashed his coffee grounds toward the river, then dragged his bedroll into a thick cluster of bushes. He stretched out immediately, and after slapping at mosquitoes for what seemed like hours, he finally drifted off to sleep.

The town of Waco, located in a rich agricultural region of the Brazos River Valley, had actually experienced two lives: The large, cold springs on the high riverbank had early on been a favorite gathering place for the Waco Indians, and the first white men to visit the area were remnants of De Soto's band in 1542. The Texas Rangers had established a fort near the Indian village in 1837, and the first white settlers came in 1849. Great plantations soon appeared along the Brazos, and very quickly began to prosper beyond the wildest dreams of the men who had built them. Then came the Civil War, which destroyed the agricultural economy and scattered the population to the four corners of the nation.

Another boom was just around the corner, however: When the Western Movement began after the war, much of it passed through Waco, and more than a few of the travelers settled there. In 1870, America's largest suspension bridge was built across the Brazos, which separated the town east from west. It was across this very bridge and right through the center of town, that the great herds of the famous Chisholm Trail would travel, once again putting Waco on the map. With the trail herds and the Great Western Movement creating an almost endless supply of revenue, prosperity came quickly, and along with it, frontier wildness that had nicknamed the town "Six-shooter Junction."

Jubal Kane rode into Waco on a Saturday afternoon, and immediately after crossing the bridge, pointed the roan south. He could see several saloons along the waterfront, as well as the Palace Hotel on the corner. The hotel was his first stop. "Ain't got but two rooms left," the aging desk clerk said, in answer to Jubal's inquiry about lodging for the night. "If you want one of 'em, you better hurry up and get it. Today's Saturday, you know."

"I know," Kane said. Having already read the sign behind the desk stating that the rooms rented for a dollar a night, he laid the money on the counter and reached for the register, where he signed Jubal Brown's name in large letters. He pocketed the key, then walked back to the hitching rail. He returned a few minutes later, carrying his rifle and a change of clothing, his saddlebags hanging across his shoulder.

He climbed the stairs two at a time, then walked down the hall to his room. When he turned his key in the lock, the door swung open of its own accord, which told him that the entire building was leaning to the north. Seeing that the room was furnished with everything he was likely to need, he laid his Winchester and his clean clothing on the bed, then stepped back into the hall and relocked the door. He headed for the stairway, and was soon leading his horses down the street.

The livery stable was located a block south on the opposite side of the street, about twenty yards from the riverbank. A middle-aged man stood out front shoeing a horse, and he nodded when Jubal approached. "Thank you for stopping by, young fellow. I reckon you can see that I'm tied up right now, but my boy'll take care of your needs."

A skinny kid who appeared to be no older than twelve or fourteen, but was already at least six feet tall, stepped from the office. His voice cracked as he asked, "Can I help you, sir?"

Jubal nodded. "I want to leave my horses with you. As far as I know now, I'll be in town for at least a day or two."

"Yes, sir," the boy said, reaching for the reins. "One thing we know how to do around here is take care of a man's transportation." He pointed to a small room beside the office that sported a large padlock on the door. "And your packsaddle will be right there under lock and key."

Kane smiled. "That sounds fine," he said. He spun on his heel and headed back down the street.

Back in his hotel room, he bathed himself from head to toe with a soapy washcloth, then shaved his face and dressed in clean clothing. He brushed his hat with his dirty shirt, then shoved his rifle and his saddlebags underneath the bed. A few moments later, he was down the stairway and out on the street.

The watering hole with the largest and tallest sign was the Texas Saloon, located a few doors down from the hotel. And judging from the number of saddled horses standing at its four hitching rails, it was also the busiest. A short time later, Jubal pushed his way through the bat-wing doors, then stood with his hands on the back of a chair till his eyes had adjusted to the dim lighting.

He knew immediately that the Texas was one of the largest saloons he had ever seen. There was a cast-iron stove that no doubt stayed in the middle of the room year-round, and enough tables and chairs to accommodate at least a hundred men. The bar was close to forty feet long, with stools on three sides and stations for three bartenders. Closer to the rear wall, a piano rested on a riser at the edge of an elevated stage, and there was a hardwood dance floor that reached all the way to a balustraded staircase. A man needed little imagination to figure out what went on upstairs.

Jubal walked to the far end of the bar and slid onto a stool that afforded him a decent view of the entire room. By leaning his body to one side or the other so he could see around the several large posts that held up the roof, he could very easily see the comings and goings of the drinkers. He was left sitting on the stool feeling unappreciated for what he thought was much too long. "I'll have a beer," he said, when a muscular, red-haired bartender finally appeared.

The man grunted, then delivered the beer quickly. "I'm Red Layton," he said, reaching across the bar for a handshake.

Kane was taken by surprise. He had already gauged the redhead as having a sulky nature, for the man had not only appeared to think he was being put upon when Jubal first stepped up to the bar, but his facial expression suggested that he would rather be anywhere on earth than where he was. Nor was he smiling now. Nonetheless, Kane grasped the hand and gave it a firm grip. "My name's Jubal Brown," he said.

"I knew right away that I hadn't seen you before," Layton said, "and I'm always curious to know what name a fellow answers to. Once I learn a man's name, I don't ever forget it, either." He turned and walked back down the bar.

Kane decided that the redhead's sulky expression was probably permanent, but most likely deceiving. Some people were just not smilers, and it had nothing whatsoever to do with how well they may or may not be enjoying themselves at any given time. Looking at the bartender's blank facial features reminded Jubal of one of his cousins. Cousin Rudolph seldom cracked a smile, but if someone told a joke that was truly funny, he would laugh as long and as loudly as the next man. For the remainder of the day, however, his face could have been made of stone.

Jubal finished his beer fairly quickly, for he had been thirsty. When he pushed his mug across the bar for a refill, the bartender was there immediately. "I wish I could have a few of these with you," he said through lips that appeared to have been cut from granite. He set a full beer in front of Kane, wiping at a wet spot on the bar with a dry cloth. "I'm liable to have something a little bit stronger about an hour from now." He glanced at his watch. "I'll be off duty at six o'clock."

Jubal nodded. "The two of us having a few drinks together sounds like a good idea to me, Red. In fact, I like it so much that I'll do the buying." He motioned toward the kitchen, and the roped-off area in front of it that served as a dining room. "Six o'clock, huh? That gives me just enough time to get my eating done for the day." He drained his mug. "Is that all right?"

Layton's face brightened ever so slightly, offering a faint hint of a smile that never appeared. "I don't like that part about you having supper alone," he said. He refilled the mug and set it beside Jubal's elbow, refusing payment. "I have to eat, too, you know. If you'll just sit where you are till six, we'll visit the dining room together. One of the waiters has already told me that they're gonna be serving chicken and dumplings tonight."

Jubal reached for the mug. "Your idea sounds better than mine," he said, then raised the brew to his lips.

Shortly after six o'clock they selected a table in the dining area and both men ordered chicken and dumplings. "I eat in restaurants often," Jubal said, after the waiter had disappeared, "but I seldom see dumplings on the menu."

"They serve 'em about twice a month here," Layton said. "The waiter told me this morning that they were talking about doing it twice a week."

Jubal nodded. "That would probably please a lot of people. I've always thought that restaurants would do better if they served the same kind of food folks eat at home."

"No doubt about it," Layton said. "People don't come to a restaurant thinking they're gonna eat any better than they do at home. They come because they'd rather pay somebody else to fix it than to go to all that trouble themselves."

The waiter delivered their food to the table, then disappeared again. "Looks just like what Aunt Maggie used to fix," Layton said, eyeing the steaming platter. "Probably tastes about the same, too."

They ate in silence for the most part, but when the meal was over and Jubal had ordered more coffee for both men, he decided to go fishing. "I guess you've been around Waco for a good while, Red. Do you know a fellow named Leroy Lively?"

Layton chuckled, then repeated the name. "Leroy Lively." He leaned closer and spoke more softly: "Is he a friend of yours?"

"Nope," Jubal answered quickly. "A fellow in Bryan just mentioned his name, asked me to say hello if I happened to run into him."

"Well, you sure ain't gonna run into him in Waco. Sheriff Dubar gave him a choice of hitting the road or going to jail." He accepted a cup of coffee from the waiter, then continued. "No, sir, Lively ain't never gonna be back in this town. Dubar told him that if he ever caught him in McClennan County again, he'd send his ass back to the penitentiary, even if he had to make up something to charge him with. You know, once the word gets out that a man's done time in prison, it ain't too hard to find a jury that thinks he oughta go back."

Jubal sipped at his coffee. "You're right about that. And I'd say that if Lively is even halfway smart, he'll keep his butt out of Dubar's territory."

"He ain't smart, but he ain't dumb enough to show up around here again."

"What seems to be Lively's problem?"

Layton blew into his cup, then wet his lips. "His problem is that he's a liar, a deadbeat, and a damned thief. He had every chance in the world to make it around here, but it's just not in his nature to do the right thing. They hired him out at the Hester Ranch and kept him on for a month or two, but finally fired his ass because he wouldn't work. Then, when old man Hester put out the word that he was a slacker, no ranch in the area would touch him with a ten-foot pole.

"He's a fair hand at poker, and I think he occasionally made a few dollars that way, but his biggest score was the swindle he pulled on the widow Seals. Took her for more than a thousand dollars, is the way I heard it. Of course, the loss didn't put her in the poorhouse or nothing, because she was well-off. Still is, for that matter; her husband left her rich.

"Not long after Hester fired him, Lively started playing up to the widow—guess somebody told him that she had plenty of money. Now, Leroy ain't really a bad-looking fellow, and Mrs. Seals is getting on in years. I suppose that when he started telling her all the things a woman likes to hear, she bought it hook, line, and sinker. Anyway, he talked her into giving him a thousand dollars by telling her that the two of them were gonna be equal partners in a big advertising business that he was about to start up.

"Now, she never saw that business materializing, and before long it got to where she didn't see Lively, either. She finally went to Sheriff Dubar and the county prosecutor both, but when they talked with Lively, he gave the old woman the lie. He admitted that she had given him money a few times, but swore that they had never even discussed going into business together. Every dollar that she had ever laid in his hand had been a gift, he claimed, and it was certainly true that Mrs. Seals had no evidence to prove otherwise.

"Now, everybody in Waco believed the widow's story, but she simply didn't have any proof that she'd been swindled. You see, Leroy didn't sign a damn thing, she gave him all the money in cash."

Jubal had listened to the story attentively. "So the sheriff just up and ordered Lively out of the county, huh?"

"Well, not right then. He let it rock on for a coupla months, while Leroy was spending money left and right around town. Then I reckon it just got to eating at Dubar, because he was an old friend of Mrs. Seals and her dead husband both. I was behind the bar myself the day he walked right into this saloon and damn near shoved the barrel of his Colt into Lively's mouth. Took his gun away from him and ordered him outta the county. He never did give that gun back to him, either; Leroy rode out of town with an empty holster."

Jubal signaled the waiter for more coffee. "What kind of fellow is the sheriff, Red? I mean, what's he like?"

"Aw, Dubar's all right, he just wanted that man outta the county. He told Leroy that he'd send him to prison if he came back around here, but he won't do that—he'll send him to the graveyard. You see, Lively not only talked Mrs. Seals out of her money, but he killed a man last year that the sheriff had known for a long time. Leroy claimed it was self-defense, but Dubar didn't buy a word of it.

"The dead man's holster was empty, though, and there was a six-gun lying in the dirt beside his body. And since there had been nobody else on the street to say otherwise, Lively's version of the incident would have been accepted by any jury in Texas. So, the only choice the sheriff and the prosecutor had was to let the matter slide.

"Putting all that stuff together, though, I reckon it finally just built up in Dubar's mind. I'll never forget the way he looked the day he walked in here and brought it all to a head. He had fire in his eyes, and there was no doubt in my mind that he was here to send Leroy packing or kill him."

Jubal drummed his fingers on the table, then chuckled softly. "Word gets around fast when the law runs a man out of town. I wonder where a fellow like Lively would go."

"Ain't no damn telling, but no matter where he went, I'd almost be willing to bet that he ain't using his true name."

"The odds would probably be in your favor, Red," Jubal said, then pushed back his chair. "I'll pay for our supper, then we can move over to the bar or go somewhere else. The choice is yours."

"The drinks are about the same price all over town," Layton said. "But if you like to look at female flesh while you drink, the girls are a lot prettier right here at the Texas."

"I'll meet you at the bar," Jubal said, then headed for the counter.

They sat at the bar for more than an hour, with Red Layton doing most of the talking. After a while, Kane announced that he was going to call it a night. He had asked as many questions as he could without sounding too anxious, and had learned everything of importance that Layton knew about Lively.

Nor was Jubal impressed with the painted dancers. Unlike many men, he could not be entertained by women who would bare half of their flesh on a saloon stage, then walk upstairs with a stranger and bare all of it. Nope, he was thinking as he emptied his mug for the last time this night, he was more attracted to the likes of Jenny Hilton. Jenny Hilton—now there was a woman!

Jubal had thought of the young waitress often lately, and had even dreamed of her once. He pushed himself off the barstool. "I've enjoyed talking with you, Red, but I'm gonna tuck myself in. You take care now, and I'll see you at another time." He walked through the front door and straight to the hotel, for tonight he had something to do. Jenny Hilton had smiled when he promised to write her a letter, and he would fulfill that promise right now.

12

★

He awoke much later than usual next morning, then
seated himself in a chair at the small table. In less than
half an hour, he finished the letter that he had fallen asleep
trying to write the night before. He fervently urged Jenny
Hilton to mail an answer to him at the post office in Nacogdoches, for no matter what happened in Waco, Jubal
intended to visit his grandparents while he was this close.
He would leave this town tomorrow morning and head
directly to the Silas Kane farm, which was only a three-
or four-day ride due east.

He ate breakfast in the hotel restaurant, then headed
for the livery stable. The same skinny youngster that he
had dealt with the day before met him at the door. "Are
you leaving us already?" he asked.

Jubal shook his head. "Not for long," he said. "I'd
appreciate you catching up my roan so I can take a little
ride, though."

"Yes, sir," the boy said, then headed down the hall toward the corral.

A few minutes later, Jubal tightened his cinch and shoved his Winchester in the boot. "Now I need a little information," he said to the young man. "Which way do I go to get to the Hester Ranch?"

The boy pointed northwest. "Just take that wagon road that runs behind the hardware store over there. Mr. Hester owns about everything between here and the Bosque River, but if you're wanting to go to Circle H headquarters, you'll have to make a right turn about six miles out of town. You'll see a sign and an arrow pointing the way, so you can't miss it. The big house is about a quarter mile off the main road."

Jubal thanked the youngster, then headed for the wagon road. Just as he rode out of town, a church bell started to ring loud enough to be heard for miles. The sound brought back memories of his childhood, a time when he had spent each and every Sunday morning sitting between Bernard and Tess Kane in church. His mother had sometimes sung in the choir, but his father, who actually had a better singing voice, could never be talked into sitting on the tall riser behind the preacher. He preferred doing all of his singing from his seat in the pew, his big bass voice reverberating throughout the building.

Jubal's grandparents were also religious folks, and though he himself did not believe everything he had heard from any organized religion, he was nonetheless convinced that something more powerful than anything humans could even dream of had put together the fantastic show that he could see simply by looking in any direction on any given day. No doubt about it, he was thinking, as he forded a small stream and looked out across a large field of colorful bluebonnets; there was something at work that was far too complicated for humans to understand—now, or ever.

Jubal followed the signs, and an hour later rode past what appeared to be a new bunkhouse and on up the shaded road toward the ranch house. Long before he reached the house he could see a figure standing under one of the giant oaks that stood on each side of the yard. As Kane came closer, he decided that he might well be looking at someone who had been around since the turn of the century. "Good morning, young fellow," the man said, pointing to a nearby trough. "Water your horse, then get down and tie up."

Kane complied, then walked to meet the man, his right hand extended. "I'm Jubal Brown," he said, "and I think you've got the prettiest ranch in Texas. Best-looking cattle, too."

The old man grasped the hand and pumped it a few times. "We always manage to get by," he said, in a voice that sounded much younger than Jubal had expected to hear. He took off his hat and wiped sweat from his balding head and bushy eyebrows with his shirtsleeve, then spoke again. "I'm Abel Hester. Is there something I can do for you?"

"I hope so, sir. I've been looking for a man named Leroy Lively for more than a year now, and I understand that he used to work for you."

The old man chuckled. "He was around here for a while. I don't know of him ever doing much work, though."

"Yes, sir, I've been told that he was fired for slacking. But the reason I rode out here this morning is because I was hoping that you or one of your hands might have an idea where he is, or where he might have gone after the sheriff ran him out of Waco."

Hester stared at the ground for a few moments, then began to shake his head. "I sure don't have any idea—don't even know where he came from, for that matter." He was quiet for a while, then asked, "Has he done you some dirt?"

Jubal was slow to answer. He stood thinking for several seconds, by which time he had decided to fully trust the old man. "Yes, sir," he said, "a lot of dirt." He walked to his horse and took the newspaper clipping from his saddlebag, and handed it to Hester. "Read this, then I'll tell you the rest of the story."

The old man held the clipping in his hand for a moment, then called out to the house loudly: "Clarabelle, bring Grandpa his glasses off the kitchen table!"

A young girl of about ten was there quickly, and Hester began to read. "I remember reading about this back in 'sixty-eight when it first hit the papers," he said when he finished reading. "Does it have something to do with Lively?"

Jubal nodded. "Yes, sir," he said. "He's the man who shot my ma to death in the barn that morning. I saw it with my own eyes."

"Well, this newspaper account says there were no witnesses. How come—"

"Sheriff Patterson purposely withheld that information," Jubal interrupted, refolding the clipping and shoving it into his pocket.

The old man pointed to the porch. "Some comfortable chairs up there," he said. "I'd like to hear the story about what really happened in that barn."

Kane followed Hester up the steps and took a seat in a cane-bottom rocking chair. "It happened a little more than a month after my fifteenth birthday," he began. He talked for a quarter hour, with the old man hanging on every word. Jubal was careful not to even mention Calvin

Mitchell's name, but gave a full and accurate description of Leroy Lively.

"There ain't no doubt in my mind that you're hunting the right man," Hester said, after listening to the story. "I never did like that shifty-eyed son of a bitch, but my foreman had already hired him, so I went along with it; gave him as many chances to be a regular hand as any man is entitled to. I'm the one who finally put him on the road. I made the decision without even discussing it with Rooster, which is something I very seldom do." He sat looking toward the bunkhouse for a moment, then got to his feet. "Just keep your seat," he said. "I'll be back directly."

He walked down the dusty path to the bunkhouse and disappeared inside the building. When he returned several minutes later, he was accompanied by another man. He halted at the porch, pointing first to one man then the other. "Jubal Kane," he said, "meet Rooster Colfax." As the two men shook hands, Hester added, "Rooster's been foreman of the Circle H for more than ten years now."

Colfax appeared to be about forty years old, and the fact that he had no hair on his head was obvious, for he was hatless at the moment. Jubal supposed that the man had originally been nicknamed Banty Rooster, because he stood at least a foot shorter than Kane himself. Colfax shook Jubal's hand with a firm grip, then smiled. "The boss tells me that you've got a good reason for wanting to find one of our rejects," he said, in a deep voice that belied his diminutive size.

Jubal nodded, and said nothing.

"I remember reading about that shooting a day or two after it took place," Colfax continued, "but I never did hear much about it after that. You saw Leroy Lively in the barn that morning, huh?"

"I watched him shoot down my ma in cold blood."

The foreman shook his head several times. "Well, I'll be damned," he said. He stood staring toward the distant horizon for a few moments, then added, "I don't know if I can help you or not, Mr. Kane. I do know that Lively's the type of man who'll take the path of least resistance, travel whichever way the wind blows. And I know that he bragged a lot about the lower Rio Grande Valley, especially the town of Brownsville. I remember one night in the bunkhouse when one of the hands got tired of listening to him. He spoke up and asked Lively why in the hell he didn't quit talking about it and get his ass on down to the lower Rio Grande Valley."

"Maybe that's what he finally did," the old man said.

"Maybe so," Colfax agreed.

Jubal nodded. "I'll try to find out when the weather cools off a little. South Texas is just too hot for traveling right now." He took a step toward the roan. "I'll be leaving now. I've enjoyed meeting both of you, and I thank you for the information. I'm gonna have to ask you to keep everything I told you under your hats, though. So far, Lively has no idea that I even exist, and I'd sure like to keep it that way."

Both Hester and his foreman promised to keep their mouths shut.

Kane rode out of the yard at a walking gait, then pushed his animal to a canter. When he reached Waco he made an attempt to locate Sheriff Dave Dubar, but was unsuccessful. There was a padlock on the front door of the sheriff's office, and when Jubal finally found a deputy he learned that Dubar was out of the county on official business, and would not return for several days.

When the deputy asked if he himself could be of assistance, Jubal declined. He doubted that the man knew where Lively had gone, so there was nothing to be gained by discussing it with him. After thinking on the matter for a while longer, Jubal began to doubt that the sheriff would know anything, either. After all, it was highly unlikely that a man who was being run out of town would announce his destination. Especially to a man wearing a lawman's badge.

Kane returned the roan to the livery stable and, having no desire to visit another saloon, bought two magazines and headed for the hotel. Except for the hour he spent in the restaurant at suppertime, he stayed in his room for the rest of the day and night.

He rode out of Waco at midmorning next day, headed due east. He was getting a late start because he had waited for the post office to open so he could post the letter to Jenny Hilton. She would be reading it a few days from now, and he was anxious to read her answer. Of course, it was altogether possible that there would be no answer to read, but for some reason that he could not even explain to himself, he believed she would write to him.

There had been some picture postcards for sale in the hotel lobby, but Jubal had not seen them until after he had already written her the letter. Nonetheless, he had bought three of the cards to be posted at a later date, and now carried them in his saddlebag. The one that he thought Jenny would like most was a picture of Waco's current claim to fame: America's largest suspension bridge, with a good view of the Brazos River which flowed beneath it. If she answered his letter, he would send her the postcard right away.

He rode steadily throughout the day, and an hour before dark, made camp at a spring a few miles south of Mexia, near old Fort Parker. He staked out his animals on good grass, then for the first time in many months, threw up his sleeping tent and spread his bedroll inside. It had been looking like rain even when he left the hotel this morning, and he had seen the sun only a few times all day. He fully expected a cloudburst within the next few hours, and had chosen a spot on hard clay that sloped enough to drain the falling water away from his tent.

He kindled a fire and made a pot of coffee, then ate Bologna sausage, cheese, and stale doughnuts for supper. Just before darkness closed in, he spent a few minutes gathering handfuls of dry leaves, bark, and deadwood, then dropped it all inside the tent beside his bedroll. Rain or no rain, he would have dry kindling in the morning.

He dragged his tarp over everything that he did not want to get soaked, including the pot that was still half full of coffee, then stretched out in the tent, his Winchester on one side of his bedroll and his Colt on the other.

The rain came before he even got to sleep. He was just about to doze off when a sheet of water carried by a strong gust of wind hit the side of the tent forcefully, causing it to vibrate and tremble. One gust after another shook the canvas, and even though Jubal knew that he had pegged it well, he began to wonder if the wind was about to blow the tent to hell and gone and allow the rain to fall into bed with him. Even if that did happen, he was nonetheless glad the downpour had occurred, for the area needed the moisture badly.

Half an hour later, the strong wind subsided, the thunder and lightning moved away, and the rain settled down to the kind of steady drizzle that farmers and ranchers dream about. Jubal lay listening to the music of the raindrops bouncing off the canvas for a while, then dozed off. His last thought before going to sleep was to hope that his grandfather's farm was getting the same treatment.

13

★

When Jubal forded the Angelina River at noon four days later, he was immediately on his grandfather's farm. As he rode up the wagon road toward the house he could very easily see that the harvest would be good this year. The corn was fully matured, and the tassels and shucks had turned a golden brown. The stalks had already been stripped of their leaves, and bundles of the drying fodder lined the road on either side. Farther up the slope he could see one rick of hay after another, their number representing at least two cuttings so far this year.

No doubt about it, Jubal was thinking, as he mentally counted the big ears of corn on one particular stalk, Grandpa had enough corn and hay in the fields to swell his bank account this fall, not to mention the garden truck he always sold during spring and summer.

Though many Texas farmers treated cotton as their main cash crop, the Silas Kane farm had never grown as much as one stalk. While working in the cotton fields as a young man, Silas had promised himself that if and when he had a farm of his own, he would never put a single cottonseed in the ground. He had held to that promise, and had never been sorry.

Anyway, there was always a ready market for corn and hay, and both were easier to produce. And easy to sell. If a man dropped the price a little, the ranchers would buy the corn and hay right in the field and do their own hauling. And even after a cattleman had bought as much feed as he was likely to need, he would buy more and put it in storage if the price was right. Not so with garden truck, of course. Once a man had bought all the vegetables his family could eat, and all his wife could put up in jars, he would buy no more at any price. Silas Kane's foreman, Frank Opal, knew about such things, and was always careful to plant no more truck than the market would bear.

Jubal topped the hill and rode past the group of farm workers' cabins known as Cottage Row, then on to the huge barn. As he tied his horses to a post, he noticed that not a single workhorse was running loose in the corral. Not that he had expected to see any of the draft animals loafing, for even though the crops had been laid by weeks ago, there was always something else that needed doing in the fields.

He stood at the corral for a few moments, admiring a big gray saddler that he had never seen before, then glanced toward the bunkhouse, a long, low building where the single workers lived. Even as Jubal watched, Frank Opal stepped from the doorway and stood in the yard, shading his eyes with his hand. "Well, I'll be damned!" he said loudly, then headed for the barn.

The two men were soon shaking hands. "We were just talking about you last night," Opal said. "I told 'em all that you'd be back before the year was out, and here you are." He began to unbuckle the packsaddle from the black, and pointed toward the house. "Mr. Silas and Miz Estelle are gonna be mighty proud to see you. You go on up and give 'em both a big hug. I'll take care of these horses."

Jubal nodded, and headed for the house. The two-story weatherboard building was no longer green as Jubal remembered it, but had recently been painted white. A wraparound porch had also been added this year, one corner of which almost touched one of the two large live oaks that stood in the front yard.

When Jubal stepped onto the porch, his grandmother was through the doorway quickly. "My land, Jubal!" she squealed, then ran across the porch and into his waiting arms. "We've all been worried sick about you and wondering why you didn't write us a letter or something. I've been looking down that road for you every day for the past year, but it never did any good. On the one day that I don't look, here you come." She kissed his cheek, squeezed his arm, and pointed toward the west wing of the house. "Your grandpa's in his den and don't have the slightest idea that you're on the premises. Go on in there and give him the shock of his life."

Jubal took a step toward the door, then turned. "Have you ever known of anything shocking Grandpa?" he asked.

"Well, no," she answered. She stood quietly for a moment, then motioned him on. "But he'll be plenty glad to see you."

In the den, the elder Kane almost jumped from his chair, and crossed the room quickly. He grabbed his only grandson's right hand with his own, and put his left arm around Jubal's shoulders. "I've been talking about you every day and thinking about you more often than that," he said. "Take a seat there, and tell me all about it. Have you caught up with any of the men you left here hunting?"

Jubal nodded, then seated himself and relived the most important events of the past year.

Silas Kane listened without interrupting. "Did Calvin Mitchell beg when he realized that you finally had him?" he asked, when Jubal had finished the story.

"No, sir. He defied me right to the end."

The old man shuffled some papers on his desk, then spoke again: "You think you know where another one of 'em is. Is that right?"

"Yes, sir. His name is Leroy Lively. The law ran him out of Waco, but I've been told that he likes the lower Rio Grande Valley. Especially Brownsville."

The old man nodded. "It is nice down there. I reckon it would be mighty hot at this time of the year, though."

"I think it's even hotter than it is here," Jubal agreed, "and hundred-degree weather takes its toll on horses in a hurry. I'm gonna wait at least a month before I head south. The middle of September ought to be a pretty good time."

"I guess so," Silas said, getting to his feet. He crossed the room and stood staring through the window for a few moments. "I don't suppose your grandma mentioned it to you," he said, as if speaking to the window pane, "but there's gonna be a lot of changes made around here."

Jubal kept his seat, and said nothing.

The old man stood at the window for a while longer, then returned to his desk and reseated himself. "This is the last year we're gonna be farming on this place, Jubal. Last month I bought the two sections of land joining us on the north, and I've already agreed to take delivery of three hundred head of Herefords right after the first of the year.

"You never have been a farmer at heart, son. You proved that during your teen years by hiring out to the neighboring ranchers instead of helping out here. So, we're gonna stock the place with cattle and change the name to the Circle K Ranch. I say 'we,' because I reckon you already know that it's all gonna be yours one of these days."

Jubal got to his feet. "I've never spent any time thinking about things like that, Grandpa."

"Well, it's time you started. We've got six sections of the best land in northeast Texas, and it'll grow grass just as well as it grows corn and hay. I suppose we'll continue to grow a little hay because we'll need it ourselves, but I intend to plow the stalks under and turn the cornfields back to nature. There won't be no shortage of feed for the cattle, though; after we quit plowing the fields, the prairie grass'll be there in no time.

"I know you don't like to talk about these things, but it's got to be done. Your grandma and I are both getting a little more feeble every day, and it stands to reason that neither of us is gonna be around for many more years. This farm has been good to us, and according to what the banker says, we've got enough money saved up to see us through. So, everything else we do around here is gonna be for your benefit." He put an arm around his grandson's shoulder. "You're all we've got left, son."

Jubal swallowed hard and stood quietly for a while, touched by the old man's words. "What are you gonna do about all the farmhands?" he finally asked.

"I'll keep Frank Opal no matter what, because he's been with me a long time and he can do just about anything. Some of the others might want to quit, or I might just have to let them go, but we'll turn as many of the younger ones into cowboys as we can. And like I said, we'll probably grow some hay, which means we'll have to fence in some hayfields. That's enough work right there to keep half a dozen men busy for weeks.

"I'll hire a man who understands the business of raising cattle, and put him in charge of the others. Everything'll work out just fine, you'll see. Of course, when you
get done with this thing that's taking up all your time
nowadays, you might want to run the ranch yourself. It
would do your grandma and me both a lot of good to see
you do that. Fact is, if you'll look around the place and
point out a homesite, we'll build you a house anywhere
you say. The wife and I are hoping to see some great-
grandchildren before we pass on."

Jubal nodded. "I'll do all of that if I can get the
woman I want, Grandpa, and I'm happy that you decided
to turn to cattle. I believe that your decision to start with
Herefords rather than longhorns was the right one, too.
Most of the ranchers I talk with seem to think that longhorns will soon be a thing of the past. Buyers want better
beef nowadays, they say, and in the long run, the buyers
are gonna get exactly what they want.

"You can see the changes taking place by just riding
about the country. Most of the longhorns I see these days
are in a herd headed for the rails, and they're being replaced on the ranches by the heavier shorthorn breeds,
mainly Herefords." He returned his grandfather's hug,
then changed the subject. "Who does that big gray gelding
in the corral belong to?" he asked.

Silas chuckled. "He belongs to you, I guess, because I
sure can't think of anything I can do with him. I bought
him during a weak moment just because I thought he was
pretty. Turns out that he's a lot more horse than I figured
on, way too high-spirited for an old fellow like me. Put a
saddle on him anytime you want to; if you like him, he's
yours."

"Thank you, sir. Do you know how old he is?"

"I bought him for a four-year-old, and his mouth looks like that's about right."

"You say he's high-spirited. Does that mean he still bucks and pitches?"

The old man shook his head. "Naw, I don't reckon he does that. It just seems that whoever taught him to ride, didn't bother to teach him to walk. He's ready to go hell-bent the instant you throw your leg over the saddle, and he'll leave you lying in his dust if you ain't hanging on mighty tight. I have no doubts about him being the fastest thing that I've ever sat down on, but I just don't ever get in that big a hurry these days."

Jubal smiled. "I don't suppose I do, either," he said, "but I think it would be nice to know that I've got some speed under me if I ever do need it. That roan of mine is a good animal, but I sure wouldn't bet any money on him in a horse race." He turned to leave the room, adding, "I'll saddle up the gray and run him for a while, Grandpa. I'll either teach him to walk or run him to death, 'cause a horse that insists on doing his own thinking ain't worth a shit for anything."

"Amen," the old man said.

Jubal walked through the dining room and into the kitchen, where he stopped and hugged his grandmother again. "Whatever you're cooking sure smells good," he said, then kissed the top of her head.

The lady stood a good foot shorter than her grandson, and, like that of her husband, her hair had long since turned a snowy white. The fact that she had spent her early years toiling in the fields was obvious, for the hot sun and the strong winds had taken their toll. Her complexion was the color of old leather, and deep wrinkles ran along her forehead and around the edges of her mouth. "I've got a beef roast in the oven with fresh vegetables in the same pan," she said, "and I guess it'll turn out about like it usually does. Oughta be plenty of that sopping gravy like you've always been partial to." She pointed toward the dining room. "That covered bowl in there on the table is full of tea cakes, if you need a little something to hold you till suppertime. I reckon that's gonna be at least two hours from now."

He paid a quick visit to the covered bowl, then walked into the yard with one of the flat, sugary tea cakes in each hand. He headed for the barn, where he could already see Frank Opal moving around in an adjoining shed, and covered the distance quickly. "I see that your grandma's already decided to fatten you up," Opal said, pointing to the remaining cake in Jubal's hand.

Jubal nodded, then spoke with a full mouth. "I'll certainly do my part to help her. I guess you could say that I haven't been eating too good lately, and I suppose I really have lost a few pounds."

Opal looked Jubal up and down, nodding all the while. "You have fell off a little; I could tell it before you even dismounted." He chuckled, then added, "If you're like me, though, you'd rather be a few pounds underweight than to be fat."

Jubal nodded. "Yep." He stood quietly for a few moments, then pointed to the corral. "Have you ever ridden that big gray, Frank?"

Opal shook his head, a frown suddenly appearing on his face. "I saddled him up and watched your grandpa ride him once," he said. "That was enough for me."

"Well, Grandpa just gave him to me, so I guess I'll climb on him and see what makes him tick."

Opal reached for a rope. "I'll catch him up while you get your saddle, then I intend to stand around and watch the show. I don't know exactly what makes him tick, but I think you'll pretty soon agree that he ticks aplenty."

A short time later, Opal led the gray to the gate. Then, moving about slowly and speaking to the animal in a soft, soothing tone, Jubal laid the blanket across his back, and added the saddle and cinched it down. He continued to talk to the horse as he led him around the inside of the corral a few times and out through the gate. With Opal holding the horse's head, Jubal mounted and gathered in the reins, then nodded for the foreman to let go of the bridle.

The animal stood in his tracks for several seconds, obviously not knowing exactly what was expected of him. Then, when Jubal reined him toward the road and kneed him on each side, the big gray was off and running, leaving the gate so quickly that if Jubal had not grabbed the saddle horn he might have slid over the horse's rump.

Jubal was taking the fastest ride of his life. He traveled down the hill and out of sight in record time, then began to make an effort to slow the big horse down. Jubal's commands of "whoa," and even the seesawing of the reins, had absolutely no effect, for the animal just seemed to take the bit between his teeth and run faster.

When Jubal was sure the gray had carried him farther than a mile, he took to an open field and began to run the horse in circles, first to the left, then to the right. Each time he laid the rein against the horse's neck, the animal obeyed the command instantly, and turned in the desired direction. Damnedest thing he had ever seen, Jubal quickly decided. The animal seemed to understand every single command except "whoa."

After several minutes of circling, when it became obvious that the horse was beginning to tire, Jubal guided him back onto the road and headed for the barn, which was still more than a mile away. He made no further effort to stop the horse, but the animal nonetheless went up the hill at a much slower pace than he had coming down.

When he reached the corral the horse came to a sliding stop of his own accord. Whether it was because he was tired or because he was home again, neither of the men had any idea. Continuing to sit his saddle, Jubal spoke to Opal: "Catch up a good saddler for yourself, Frank, then tie his bridle to the gray's with a piece of rope about four or five feet long. I think we need to give this big fellow a riding lesson right now while he's tired."

Opal soon sat beside Jubal on a saddled horse, with the bridles of the two animals tied together. "I guess this might work best if you don't say anything at all, Frank," Jubal said. "Make your horse follow every one of my commands, and let's see if any of it soaks into the gray." When he kneed the gray, the animal tried to run, but the horse the gray was tied to would have none of it. When they had walked side by side for several yards, Jubal pulled back on the gray's reins and ordered him to whoa. The gray ignored the command, but was quickly brought to a halt by the short rope holding him to the well-trained saddler.

When they had gone through this particular exercise several times, and the gray had surprised both men by himself initiating one of those stops on command, they kicked the horses to a trot, and in less than an hour were traveling at a canter. When Jubal finally remembered that his grandmother had said supper would be ready in two hours, he pointed the gray up the hill and stopped at the corral.

He dismounted and turned the horse over to Opal, saying, "I'd like to work with him every morning till he fully understands how he's supposed to act, Frank. Any day that you're gonna be too busy with something else, I'd appreciate it if you'd let one of the hands off to help me. Next time I leave home I'd like to be riding him, but I sure as hell don't want to ride something that I can't stop."

14

★

Jubal selected his homesite two weeks later. The site, located on the west side of a long, sloping hill that Silas Kane had long since named Cedar Ridge, was almost a mile from the main house. "I'm not surprised that you chose the west side of that ridge," the old man said, when informed of Jubal's decision. "If I had it all to do over, I'd probably build my house over there, too. Your grandma says it's the prettiest place on the whole farm, and with the river no more than a hundred yards away, you sure won't have to carry your fishing pole very far."

Jubal smiled. "That's one of the first things I considered, Grandpa."

The old man took a seat in the porch swing, and Jubal soon joined him. "Are you gonna dig a well before you start building?" Silas asked.

Jubal nodded. "The well's the very first thing. I may be wrong, but I believe I'll hit good water there in forty feet or less."

"Could be," the old man agreed. He sat for a while, jerking hairs out of his nose with a thumb and forefinger, then announced his latest decision. "I know that you're gonna be riding off again any day now, but that ain't no reason for us not to get your house on up and be done with it. With the crops all laid by, there ain't nothing pressing around here right now, and I had in mind assigning about half of the crew the task of building that house for you while you're gone.

"Now, all I want you to do is tell me how big you want it and whether or not you want two stories. I'll hire Jesse Harper to design the building and oversee the construction, then you can probably just pick out your furnishings and move in anytime after the first of the year. Jesse's mighty good, and I'd say that he'd be done and off the premises long before Christmas." He patted Jubal's knee. "Now, I'd appreciate it if you don't give me no argument about this, son. It's something that I've always intended to do, been planning on it since a day or two after you were born. You just enjoy that house, and consider it a gift from your grandma and me."

Jubal sat staring quietly into the yard, clearly moved by the old man's generosity. Though his throat felt exceptionally tight, he finally managed to speak. "I don't know what to say to all of that, Grandpa. I—"

"Don't say nothing," the old man interrupted. "I mean, nothing except how big you want the house to be. You got a woman in mind? You gonna get married and raise a family?"

"Well, yes, I've got a woman in mind. But, hell, Grandpa, I don't have any idea whether she'd ever consider marrying me or not."

The old man chuckled. "Did you ever consider asking her?"

"Nope, not yet. I've been too busy trying to figure out how to ask her to go for a buggy ride. The biggest problem is that she lives way out in Bandera. I wrote her a letter three weeks ago from Waco, and it's about time she answered it if she's ever going to. I'll ride into Nacogdoches after a while and check at the post office." He got to his feet. "What I'm gonna do first, though, is ride over to Cedar Ridge and drive a stake in the ground so they'll know where I want my well dug." He looked the old man in the eye for a moment, then smiled broadly. "Just tell Mr. Harper that I want the well in my front yard, that I want a two-story house, and that I want it facing downhill toward the river."

Silas nodded, and got to his feet. "You go on and drive that stake," he said. "I'll send word to Jesse Harper that I've got a job for him." Then he disappeared into the house.

Jubal jumped down into the yard and headed for the wagon shed, where only the day before he had noticed a short section of two-by-four. He carried it to the woodpile and sharpened one end with an ax, then headed for the corral. He caught the big gray without having to use a rope, and, holding the animal by its lower lip, led it to the corral gate.

The horse accepted the bit and bridle almost eagerly, then stood in its tracks without flinching as Jubal piled on the saddle and cinched it down. He mounted and kneed the horse to a trot, then suddenly pulled back on the reins and ordered the animal to whoa. The gray slid to a halt immediately. Jubal sat for a while, patting and rubbing the horse's neck and talking to him softly, pleased that the two weeks' training had evidently done the trick. He nodded at his thoughts, then urged the gray on down the road, satisfied that the big horse would be his favorite mount for the next several years.

He dismounted at the homesite and tied the gray to the lower limb of a cedar, then walked around till he found a flat rock with which to drive his stake into the ground. When he had marked the spot for his well, he remounted and sat his saddle between the two large cedars that would eventually be standing in his front yard.

Cedar Ridge was not a tall hill, but rather a mile-long strip of land that gradually sloped upward for several hundred yards on its east side. On the western side, however, the elevation dropped off much more quickly, and it was little more than a hundred yards down the steep slope to the swift Angelina River. Jubal sat for several minutes, staring down the hill and making a mental note of the way he wanted things to look. His barn and corral would be south of where he was now sitting, halfway between the house and the main road, which was about eighty yards away. He would remind his grandfather to pass that information on to Jesse Harper.

After looking his new home over through his mind's eye till he was satisfied, he turned the gray down the south slope to the main road, then headed for town at a canter.

He rode into Nacogdoches an hour later. Waving to a man on the street who he had known for most of his life, he rode on to the post office, which was located in a small building adjacent to Welch's General Store. He tied the gray to the hitching rail, then poked his head through the open doorway. "Would you happen to have any mail for me, Mrs. Dillard?"

The postmistress was also someone that Kane had known since childhood. She motioned for him to come inside. "Your name's Jubal Kane, ain't it?" she asked.

"Yep," he said, stepping into the room and up to the window. "I suppose that you knew my name even before I did."

"I certainly did," she said, then turned to a shelf behind her. "You've got a letter here, all right, and judging by the handwriting, I'd say that you've done run off somewhere and found yourself a girlfriend." She chuckled and waved the letter around a few times, then handed it over.

"Thank you, ma'am," Jubal said, and hurried from the building. Stepping into the saddle quickly, he rode to a parking lot behind the bank. He dismounted and tied the gray to one of the many hitching rails, then seated himself on a broad stump that had once held up a large live oak. Pulling the letter from inside his shirt, he sat admiring the beautiful handwriting for a few moments before tearing open the envelope.

My Dearest Jubal, the letter began. He stopped reading for a moment to absorb the salutation, repeating the three words to himself. *Dearest,* huh? Jenny Hilton had called him her "dearest." Damn, that sounded good! The letter went on to say that the young lady was working six days a week at Sally's Restaurant, and that so far this summer she had had little time for anything else. She had been both surprised and pleased by his letter, she wrote, and was already looking forward to the next one.

The letter was almost two pages long, and on the second page she wrote that she had been thinking of Jubal often, and was hoping to see him again soon. She also wanted to talk with him when she was not busy working, and at someplace other than the restaurant. Just above her signature at the end of the letter, she had written, *Affectionately yours.*

Jubal read the letter twice, then folded it and shoved it into his pocket. He knew that he would see Jenny Hilton in the very near future, and he would definitely find a better place than Sally's Restaurant to conduct a courtship. He untied his mount from the hitching rail, then climbed aboard. When he had ridden around the corner to the front of the bank, he dismounted again.

As he tied the gray to the bank's hitching rail, he began to speak to the animal as if it were human. "Are you about ready to haul me out to Bandera, old buddy?" he asked, patting the horse's thick dappled neck. "Sure you are," he said, answering his own question. "You'd try your damnedest to run all the way out there if I'd let you, wouldn't you?"

Jubal withdrew as much money from his account as he expected to need for the remainder of the year, then, leaving the gray tied in front of the bank, crossed the street to Brewster's Saloon, where owner Toot Brewster did most of his own bartending. "Have you got any good wine, Toot?" Kane asked. "I mean, sure-enough good wine?"

"I certainly do, Jubal," Brewster answered. "I've got two cases of the best stuff San Antonio has to offer, and it sells for thirty cents a quart." He poked his hand across the bar for a shake, adding, "Ten quarts to the case—do you wanna buy both cases, or just one?"

Kane grasped the hand and pumped it a few times. "I'll settle for one bottle," he said. "I don't have any desire to see my grandparents drunk."

Brewster chuckled, then set a bottle of red wine on the counter. "I don't guess they'd want to get drunk, but I reckon they still have a sip occasionally. Old Silas bought a quart of this same stuff about a month ago."

Jubal picked up the wine and read the label, then stood thinking for a few moments. "Just give me two bottles, then," he said finally. "One won't last very long if Grandpa likes it well enough to buy it himself."

Brewster set up another bottle. Jubal laid sixty cents on the counter, picked up the wine, and headed for the door. "It was good to see you again, Toot," he said over his shoulder. "Take care of yourself, and say hello to your brother for me."

A short while later, he rode out of town with a bottle of wine in each of his saddlebags. He put the gray to an easy canter, and the big animal seemed content to hold it. Jubal sat his saddle effortlessly, knowing that he was aboard the smoothest-riding horse he had ever straddled. The gray was not only much faster than the roan, but stronger. He evidently enjoyed nothing more than a good, hard run, and now that he had learned to stop on command, he was a pleasure to ride.

Whoever taught the animal to tolerate a passenger on his back had no doubt been a very busy man, for the riding lessons had obviously ceased shortly thereafter. The more Jubal thought on the matter, the more surprised he was that he could determine the direction of travel with nothing more than the weight of the rein lying against one side of the horse's neck. Maybe it was pure instinct, he was thinking, for he seriously doubted that an experienced horse trainer had spent any time with the gray.

Nor was Jubal himself a horse trainer. Every animal he ever owned had been broke to the saddle long before being acquired by him. In fact, he had never even seen an animal trainer at work. Nor had he ever before seen the bridles of two saddle horses tied together. The idea of tying the gray's head to that of a well-trained saddler had just come to him from out of nowhere, and it had worked. Before working out with another horse, the gray had ignored Jubal's jerking on the reins and his commands to stop, simply because he had not understood them.

Kane rode at a canter for several minutes, then pulled the gray to a walk and began to pat him on the neck. The big fellow was going to be all right now, he decided.

Silas Kane was sitting on the porch in his rocking chair when his grandson rode into the yard. Jubal dismounted and leaned across the porch, handing his grandfather the bottles of wine. "I brought you and Grandma something," he said. "I remember that both of you used to like a glass of red wine of an evening."

"Still do," the old man said, paying close attention to the label. "I bought a bottle just like this not long ago, and it was some of the best I ever tasted. Your grandma thought so, too, and we drank it all before bedtime." He set both bottles on the floor beside his chair, then began to laugh. "I like to hear her giggle like she did when she was young," he said. "She'll do it, too, if I can get more'n one glassful down her."

Jubal nodded, then smiled broadly. "I hope she giggles all night, Grandpa," he said, then turned and led the gray toward the barn. He had many things that he wanted to do before nightfall, for he expected to be on the road to Bandera about sunup in the morning.

15

★

Both Silas Kane and his wife stood at Jubal's stirrup next morning as he was about to ride off the premises. He had been sitting aboard the gray for more than five minutes, and the anxious beast had been stomping its feet in anticipation ever since being mounted.

Jubal tightened up the packhorse's lead rope. "Right now I'm on my way to Bandera," he said, speaking to both grandparents. "To the best of my memory that's about a ten-day ride. I expect to spend a few days around there on personal business, then head for the lower Rio Grande Valley, which'll take another ten days. I'd say it's probably gonna be early October by the time I get to Brownsville, but I will get there, and if Leroy Lively is anywhere in that valley, I intend to find him."

"I'm sure you will, son," Silas Kane said, his lower lip quivering slightly. "Then you come on back home, 'cause you're gonna have an awful lot of good things waiting for you."

"That's right, Jubal," his grandmother agreed. "You hurry up and get all this running-around out of your system, then trot right on back here and learn to live like normal people."

"Yes, ma'am," Jubal said, then kneed the gray toward the road. "Don't look for me till you see me coming, though."

Except for a noonday stop beside a shallow stream, where he ate his dinner and allowed his animals to graze for an hour, he traveled steadily all day. After crossing the Angelina River he had ridden due west through the thick woodlands of Houston County, then turned southwest when he reached San Antonio Road. He would follow the well-known route all the way to San Marcos, a distance of more than two hundred miles.

He halted for the day at a boxed-up spring two miles northeast of Crockett. Named for frontiersman Davy Crockett, who died at the Alamo, the settlement was among the oldest towns in Texas. As Jubal unburdened his animals at the spring, which was located between two large oaks in a well-used campground, he began to wonder if maybe Colonel Crockett had once unsaddled his own mount at the same watering hole.

Jubal supposed that the spring had been bubbling just as it did now for thousands or maybe even millions of years, and that if there was any truth to the legends, it was altogether possible that Crockett had once drunk from the spring, tied his horse to one of the oaks, and pitched his tent on this very same spot.

Jubal staked out his horses forty yards away, then dragged his saddle and his packsaddle up beside a cluster of bushes, among which he had decided to spread his bedroll. The sun was still an hour high when he kindled a fire under his coffeepot. He would do no cooking tonight, for his grandmother had seen to it that he had a half-gallon jar full of ready-cooked lima beans and a pone of corn-bread in his pack.

Unlike most men, having hot food at every meal was something that Kane neither expected nor thought about. Of course, he preferred eating vittles that had recently been exposed to heat, but that was not a priority. He was perfectly content to eat whatever was available when he was hungry, and had long since decided that if something tasted good when it was hot, it would at least be tolerable when cold.

A short while later, he pulled the coffeepot off the fire and filled his cup. He broke off a chunk of the cornbread, then began to eat the beans right from the jar with a large spoon, washing it all down with strong coffee.

He heard the rattling of trace chains and the sound of broad wheels crunching the hard earth long before he saw the wagon. He screwed the lid back on the bean jar and sat sipping his coffee, keeping his eyes on the road in the same direction from which he had come. Finally, a big, canvas-covered wagon topped the hill. Jubal could see the driver pulling on a rope to activate the brake as the heavy vehicle's coasting ability forced the team into a fast trot. The animals were soon walking again, however, for the road leveled off just before it reached the campground.

A man who was well past middle age and a bonneted woman sat on the front seat of the wagon, which, though neither as large nor as heavy, was built along the same lines as the Conestoga. Kane waved as the vehicle passed the spring, and his greeting was acknowledged by both the driver and his passenger. The man drove the team only a short distance farther, then pulled off the road. He stepped down from the wagon and helped the lady to the ground, then began to unharness the horses.

Jubal was sipping his second cup of coffee when the man led the team to the spring to drink. As the animals sucked up water noisily from the runoff, Kane spoke to the man: "I've got more hot coffee there than I'm gonna drink," he said, pointing to the blackened pot. "Fact is, there's enough for you and the lady both, and you're welcome to it."

The man shook his head. "I guess not," he said, "but I appreciate the offer. We've gotta build a fire to boil some potatoes anyway, so we might as well make our own coffee." Then, with his coiled picket ropes hanging on his shoulder, he led his animals toward the grassy meadow.

The lady took some kindling from the bed of the wagon and built a campfire. Then, nodding to Kane as she passed, she filled a water bucket from the spring and returned to her wagon. Both the man and the woman were soon seated on the ground, peeling potatoes. Though Jubal had little interest in their actions, he could scarcely keep from seeing what they were doing, since they were directly in front of him and no more than twenty yards away. He got to his feet and walked to the spring, where he seated himself and began to mentally count the tadpoles on the bottom. Anything to keep the couple from thinking that he was staring at them.

He stayed where he was until dusk, at which time he saw the man extinguish the fire and boost the woman into the back of the wagon, then climb in after her and drop the canvas flap. Undoubtedly they had had a long day, he was thinking, and were eager to rest their weary bones.

Full darkness found Jubal stretched out on his bedroll inside the cluster of leafy bushes, with both his Peacemaker and his Winchester close by his side. He had made good time today, he was thinking, but knew that tomorrow would be a different story. For one thing, he had heard a rattling shoe on one of the gray's hooves as he was leading the animal to graze, and that would certainly have to be taken care of before he continued on his way. He would look the hoof over in the morning and, if necessary, lead the horse to town instead of climbing into the saddle. A place the size of Crockett would surely have a good blacksmith.

He awoke once during the night, and lay on his bed quietly for a while, trying to figure out whether or not he had heard something in his sleep. Finally he crept to the outer edge of the cluster of bushes and stood listening. When several minutes had passed and he had seen or heard nothing, he peed in the top of a short willow and returned to his bedroll. He was quickly asleep.

Jubal was in the meadow at daybreak, looking over his saddler's hooves. The left front shoe was loose, all right, but was probably in no immediate danger of falling off. He watered the animals at the spring, then cinched the saddle down on the gray. All the time he was putting his pack together and buckling the packsaddle on the black, he could see that someone was moving around inside the wagon. The travelers had never shown themselves, however, and even as he mounted and headed for town, the tailgate was still up and the canvas flap down.

As was often the case, the livery stable was also a blacksmith shop, and was the first establishment Jubal came to as he rode into Crockett. A middle-aged man who was both bald and beefy stood in the wide doorway. "Good morning," he said in a deep voice, as Jubal rode around the corner of the corral.

Kane returned the greeting, then dismounted. "The gray's got a loose shoe on the left front," he said. Jubal had only to look around him to see that the big man was swamped. "I can see that you've got plenty of other things to do," he said, "but I'm hoping you can take the time to check him out."

The man flashed a snaggletooth. "I've been backed up on work for weeks," he said. "I can see that you're a traveling man, though, and I'm sure you'd like to be on your way." He accepted the reins and led the gray toward the adjacent room that served as his blacksmith shop. "Don't reckon this'll take very long, anyway." He pointed to the office. "Hot coffee in there on the stove if you want some—cups and sugar on that little table."

"That sounds good," Kane said, "but I was thinking about eating breakfast while you're taking care of the horse. Is there any particular restaurant in town that you'd recommend?"

The big man shook his head and laughed aloud. "I ain't never been one to tell a fellow where he oughta eat," he said. He pointed toward the center of town. "Three eating places on the right-hand side of the street, and I reckon they're all about the same, especially for breakfast. Ain't many ways to mess up a pancake or an egg, you know."

Kane chuckled along with the blacksmith. "Thank you," he said. "I'll see you in about an hour." He walked up the street past two saloons that were not yet open, then stopped at the first restaurant he came to. When he stepped inside the door, a young waiter who appeared to be still in his teens followed him to a table. Jubal seated himself and waved away the bill of fare the youngster offered him. "Just bring me a good breakfast," he said. "Whatever everybody else is eating."

"We've got pancakes, sausage, and eggs for twenty-five cents, sir."

Jubal nodded. "That sounds exactly right," he said.

The restaurant was not crowded at the moment, but judging from the untidy appearance of most of the tabletops throughout the room, the establishment must have been filled to capacity early on. Just by watching the activity around him Jubal could tell that the waiters were not expecting more customers in the immediate future, but were concentrating on cleaning up after the ones who had already come and gone. After all, the sun was more than an hour high; long past the time when most Texans had eaten their morning meal and begun their workday.

Kane's meal was hot when it arrived, and had been prepared well. He forked a bite of scrambled eggs into his mouth immediately, appreciative of the fact that the cook had not fried them to a crisp. Then he poured a river of syrup over the pancakes and sausage, and finished off the platter of food in short order. When he was done eating, he waved the waiter down and ordered another cup of coffee, which he sipped very slowly. He must allow the blacksmith enough time to take care of his horse, he was thinking. Besides, the restaurant had the best coffee he had tasted all year.

Finally, he laid a nickel beside his empty platter and walked to the counter to pay for his meal. "That was the best breakfast I've had since I don't know when," he said to the lady who accepted his money. "You folks must have about all the business in town."

She smiled, and dropped the quarter in a metal box. "Lord, no," she said, "we don't even come close." She chuckled softly, adding, "I'd say that at least one of the other restaurants in town does a dollar's worth of business every time we take in a dime. They've got a new brick building and fancy, cushioned chairs, you know."

Jubal shook his head. "No, ma'am," he said, "I didn't know. But I do know that I'll stop right here if I ever come through this town again." He turned and headed for the door.

"You do that," the lady called after him as he stepped through the doorway. He had walked for only a short distance when he came upon the couple who had spent the night beside him at the campground. Their wagon was parked directly in front of the bank. Seeing the couple standing at the rear of the wagon, with a half-circle of men gathered around, Kane crossed the street and joined the crowd.

The tailgate of the wagon had been lowered to form a table and was being held in a level position by a small chain on either end. What was probably most of the couple's portable possessions were spread out in the rear of the wagon and along the tailgate for the inspection of the crowd. The travelers had obviously run out of money, and were willing to part with some of their belongings in order to remedy the situation.

Even from where he was standing, Jubal thought he saw a hand-cranked Elias Howe sewing machine, the exact same kind his mother had used to make his clothing when he was a youngster. To this day the machine stood in his grandma's sewing room, and Jubal had noticed and commented on it only last week. He took a few steps forward to make sure his eyes had not deceived him. The machine was an Elias Howe, all right, identical to the one Tess Kane had been so proud to own.

While the man was busy arranging the goods that made up the display, the woman stood a few feet from the wagon staring at the ground, her bonnet hiding most of her face. "The wife and I have run into some bad luck, fellows!" the man said loudly. "I lost my money pouch a week ago, and it had every dollar we had in the world in it.

"We even crawled around on our knees looking for it for several hours, but finally decided that it was long gone." He pointed to the odds and ends scattered along the tailgate. "We ain't got no choice but to trade some of these things for money, 'cause we've got to get on to San Antonio no matter what. We've been out of grain for the horses for four days, and to tell you the truth, we ain't even had no breakfast ourselves." He laid his hand on the sewing machine. "Now, I reckon this Elias Howe here would be worth more than anything else we've got, and there ain't no doubt in my mind that some of you men have got womenfolks who could put it to good use."

"What's the bottom dollar you'll take for it?" a man asked loudly. "Now, if you get the price down low enough, I just might—"

"The sewing machine is not for sale!" Kane interrupted. Then he stepped forward and spoke to the woman. "Was it your idea to sell the machine, ma'am?"

She raised her eyes for the first time. "Got to give up something," she said. "We've got to eat, and so do the horses. They can't keep pulling this heavy wagon on what little grass they get."

Jubal bit his lower lip. "Do you know how to use the machine?" he asked.

She offered a feeble smile. "Been using it for years. Sewed my own things and clothed three children with it; made about everything my husband wore, too."

Jubal nodded, then addressed the man. "How much money do you think you need, mister?"

"Well . . . I was hoping to get about ten dollars. We need grain, groceries, a can of axle grease—"

"Put your belongings back in the wagon," Jubal interrupted, laying a double eagle in the man's hand.

The man stood quietly for a few moments, turning the coin from side to side. "Twenty dollars?" he asked. "I don't reckon we need no twenty dollars."

Jubal shook his head emphatically. "Any man who has just lost every penny he had, needs twenty dollars, sir."

He pointed across the street. "Take your wife to the restaurant and buy her a good breakfast, then pick up the other things you need for the trip to San Antonio." He spun on his heel and headed for the livery stable.

"What's your name?" the man called after him. "Where do you want me to send the money once I get in shape to repay the loan?"

Kane stopped and turned sideways. "The name is Jubal Kane," he said. "And the money was not a loan."

Then he began to walk toward the livery once again. After Jubal was out of earshot, one man in the crowd asked of another, "Did you ever in your entire lifetime see a whiter deed than that, Bruno?"

"If I did, I sure can't remember it," Bruno answered. "It could be that the young man's got a lot of money and just wanted to show off, but I don't think so. He struck me as a fellow who came from good stock. At least, I'm gonna chalk it up in my own mind that way, 'cause it makes me feel a little better about the human race."

Both of Jubal's horses were standing in front of the smithy when he arrived. He raised the gray's left front hoof and saw that a new shoe had been nailed on. "I put four new ones on him," the big man said, as he stepped from his office. "He was about to lose that left front, and neither one of the hind pair was gonna hang on much longer."

Jubal released the horses's hoof. "That's fine," he said. "Did you happen to check out the packhorse?"

"I looked him over good," the blacksmith said, closing the distance between them. "Didn't see anything that needed doing, though." He was quiet for a few moments, then added, "I guess you know that the price of horseshoes is way up, so I'm gonna have to charge you a dollar-thirty for shoeing the gray. A dollar for the shoes, and thirty cents for my labor."

Kane nodded and handed over the money. "No complaint here," he said. He mounted the gray and yanked on the packhorse's lead rope. "Good day to you, and I appreciate you dropping whatever you were doing in order to do me a favor."

The big man chuckled loudly as Kane rode away. "Did myself a favor, too," he said. "About everything else I do is on credit, but I figured you'd pay cash."

When Jubal reached the center of town he saw that the couple's wagon was parked in front of the general store, and both the man and his wife were busy placing sacks of groceries inside the tailgate. "I'm gonna pick up some grain at the feed store," the man said to Jubal, "then stop somewhere outside of town and feed these horses. We'll cook and eat our own breakfast while they eat theirs. We can fix three or four meals on the road for the price of one in a restaurant, you know."

"I know," Kane agreed. He tightened the lead rope. "You folks take care of yourselves, and I hope you have better luck from now on."

"Just a minute," the man said. "I mean, I think my wife wants to ask you something." He turned to the woman. "Go ahead, Lucy."

The lady pushed her bonnet away from her eyes. "I just told my husband that I'd like to make you a shirt or a sweater or something. Would that be all right with you?"

Jubal offered what was probably his broadest smile of the year. "Yes, ma'am," he said. "If you make a shirt for me I'll treasure it for the rest of my life."

She nodded. "Where do you want me to send it to?"

"The Silas Kane farm, in Nacogdoches, Texas. Do you think I should write down the size?"

She shook her head. "I've made things for tall, muscular men before," she said. "It'll fit."

Kane nodded, and smiled again. As he rode around the wagon and headed out of town, the man called after him: "One of these days when you get a package in the mail from somebody named Lucy Dunlap, you'll know what's in it!"

16

★

The gray was a fast walker, and covered the twenty miles between Crockett and the Trinity River by midafternoon. Jubal watered his animals and refilled his canteens, then re-mounted and forded. The river was no more than a foot deep where it crossed the road, and there was a good campground on the west bank. Kane supposed that the Dunlaps would spend the night there, for if they stayed on the move throughout the day, they should reach the Trinity about an hour before sunset. As for himself, he had enough daylight left to travel several more miles before spreading his bedroll.

He rode another ten miles before deciding to call it a day. The sun was low and shining directly in his eyes, when he came to a roadside sign reading WATER, with an arrow pointing to a deep-rutted wagon road that turned off to the north. He followed the road till it played out at a large spring about two hundred yards away. He dismounted and stood for a few moments, staring into the clear water, watching the strong vein shoot particles of sand up from the bottom.

He could easily see that he was not the only one to use the campground this summer. Piles of ashes were scattered over a fifty-yard radius, and the fact that the majority of the fires had been extinguished with water from the spring was evident.

Kane tied his horses and relieved them of their burdens, then gathered up several half-burned pieces of wood left over from other campers' cooking fires. He kindled a blaze easily, for the wood was very dry. When the fire was burning to his satisfaction, he washed the soot from his hands in the spring's runoff, then led his animals closer to the treeline, where the grass appeared to be greener. He put each of them on a long picket rope, then returned to his fire.

He made a full pot of coffee, for what he did not drink this evening, he would reheat in the morning. He cut off a sizable chunk of cheese and heated several slices of smoked ham in his iron skillet, then opened a can of peaches. After supper, he spread his bedroll a few yards from the spring and stretched out. He dozed off quickly, and slept the night away.

Jubal rode into San Marcos two hours before sunset, four days later. With the livery stable being on the west side of town, he rode right down Main Street. He had been here before, and had long since decided that it was one of the prettiest towns in Texas. Seat of Hayes County, and often called "the Gateway to the Hill Country," the town was once the site of two Spanish missions, relocated from east Texas because of French and Indian difficulties, and had been laid out for Anglo-American settlers in 1851.

The surrounding area was cattle country at its best, with an abundance of water, shade, and perennial grasses of many kinds. Large springs within the town itself gave rise to the clear, cold San Marcos River, known throughout Texas as one of the state's most productive fishing streams.

As he rode down the street, Jubal nodded a greeting to several men who were standing around the hitching rails, or leaning against the posts that held up the roof over the boardwalk. He rode past two saloons that he would most likely visit before the night was over. The building on the corner just before he reached the stable would be the first one he visited, however, for the sign above the front door read: MOMMA COOPER'S RESTAURANT.

He continued on to the livery stable, where he was greeted by a young man who was just beginning to sprout a little patch of white fuzz on his upper lip. "Can I help you, sir?" the youngster asked in a squeaky voice.

Jubal dismounted. "I believe you can," he said. "Can you feed, water, and put my horses up for the night?"

"Yes, sir," the young hostler answered, "that's what we're here for." He took the reins of both horses and tied them to a post inside the building, then unbuckled the packsaddle from the packhorse. "I'll put this in the storeroom beside my cot."

"That'll be fine," Kane said, pulling his Winchester from his saddle scabbard. "I usually hit the road about sunup. Are you gonna be open that early?"

The boy chuckled. "Be open long 'fore that," he said. He pointed to a small room off in the corner. "I sleep right there. Anytime you want something and I ain't up, all you gotta do is call out or knock on the wall."

Jubal nodded. "I'll remember that," he said. He threw his saddlebags across one shoulder and a change of clothing across the other, then headed for the San Marcos Hotel, which was directly across the street from the restaurant. "Upstairs or downstairs?" the muscular young desk clerk asked, when Kane requested a room.

"I suppose it's a little cooler upstairs, if you've got one with a window," Kane said.

"The upstairs room on the northeast corner's got two windows," the young man said. "If you raise 'em both, you'll get a little draft going." He ran his finger down what Jubal supposed was a price list lying on the desktop. "That's a seventy-cent room, but there sure ain't no chinches in it. You in the mood to pay that much?"

Kane laid the money on the counter, and the clerk handed him a key.

Once inside the room he raised the windows, and as he had expected, felt the cool draft immediately. He stripped off his clothing and washed himself all over with a soapy washcloth, then shaved his face and changed into clean jeans and a blue flannel shirt. He brushed most of the dust off his hat with his hand, then locked his door and headed for the stairs.

Momma Cooper's Restaurant was considerably larger than most, and, at the moment, was doing a land-office business. The tables were arranged in separate sections with wide aisles in between, and another rarity was the fact that a pretty young hostess greeted each diner at the door. "Good evening, sir," she said flirtatiously, as Jubal entered the establishment. "Welcome to Momma Cooper's. Will you be dining alone?"

Kane nodded. "I guess so," he said, chuckling, "unless I can talk you into eating with me."

She giggled softly, and motioned across the room. "Follow me," she said. He was soon seated at a table along the east wall, near the rear of the building. When his waitress arrived, he decided immediately that she was a dead ringer for the hostess. "Is that your sister at the front door?" he asked.

The girl smiled broadly. "My older sister," she said. "My mother says she's about ten minutes older."

"You're identical twins?"

She nodded and smiled again. "Yes." Then she turned to the business at hand. "Let me know when you decide what you want to eat," she said, handing him the bill of fare. Then she was gone to another table.

He studied the full-page menu for a while, then caught the girl's eye again. "Have you got these stuffed pork chops tonight?" he asked, when she was back at his table.

"Yes, sir," she answered. "The stuffed-pork-chop platter is our biggest seller. I'd say that's what half the people in here are eating right now."

He handed back the menu. "I suppose half the people know what's best," he said. "I'll join them."

She giggled, exactly like her twin, then headed for the kitchen.

The meal was very good, and he sat at the table sipping coffee and watching people long after he was done eating. Though several young women were in the restaurant dining with their men, none was half as pretty as the twins, who were surely among the most beautiful females Jubal had ever seen.

From where he was sitting, both girls were in his view most of the time, and he could not help wondering what it would be like to carry one of the curvaceous, dark-haired beauties to the hotel room he had just rented. Even as the thought crossed his mind he discarded it, for he knew that either of the girls could have her pick of the men in this town. Nor did he believe that it would do him any good to exercise his powers of persuasion, for no doubt both of the twins had heard it all. That decided, he slid a dime under his plate, then walked to the counter and paid for his food. A moment later, he was back on the street.

The Horseshoe Saloon was his next stop, a few doors down and on the same side of the street as Momma Cooper's. Less than half the size of the restaurant, the saloon had a twenty-foot bar against the west wall, behind which stood a lone bartender who appeared to be too young for the job. The bar was lined with a brass rail and leather-bound stools, and the remainder of the room was devoted to tables and chairs.

The cast-iron stove that stood in the middle of most saloons year-round was noticeably absent in the Horseshoe, but the two joints of stovepipe hanging from the ceiling suggested that the stove was not far away, and would be reconnected at the first sign of cold weather.

There were only two drinkers in the saloon at the moment, both of them seated at the far end of the bar. Kane took a stool closer to the front door and spoke to the tall, blond-haired bartender, who appeared to be no more than eighteen years old. "Is the beer cold?" he asked.

The young man turned and drew a mugful of the foamy brew. "Cold as I can make it," he said, sliding the mug across the bar to Jubal's elbow. "The icehouse is just up the street."

Kane dropped a nickel on the bar and took a sip. "Plenty cold," he said, wiping his mouth with the heel of his hand.

The bartender nodded, then moved to the far end of the bar to check on the drinkers seated there. The two dark-haired men appeared to be in their early twenties, and bore a strong resemblance to each other. Both ordered straight whiskey.

The bartender had just served them and moved away when the bat-wing doors opened noisily. A tall, stoop-shouldered man stepped inside the building and headed toward the far end of the bar. As the man walked by, Jubal saw that a deputy sheriff's badge was pinned to his vest.

Halting beside the whiskey drinkers, the lawman pointed to the smallest of the two. "You're under arrest, Kearney Jessup!" he said loudly. "I'm arrestin' ya fer beatin' up old man Atticus, an' ya know good an' well 'at ya done it." The deputy was considerably larger than the man he had called Kearney Jessup, and though he had never drawn his gun, his attempt to intimidate the smaller man was obvious. He moved closer and spoke even louder: "Gitcha ass off'n 'at stool an' come along, dammit. I ain't got all day!"

Though Kearney Jessup did not move a muscle, the man beside him was on his feet instantly, slapping his right leg noisily. "You ain't takin' my brother no damn whur!" he said, as he leveled his Colt between the deputy's eyes. "Jist ease 'at gun outta th' holster'n lay it on th' bar, there."

The red-faced deputy quickly complied.

"Now," the man with the gun continued. "Move over there in th' center of th' room an' set down at a table. You damn well better stay there for a while, too."

When the deputy was seated, the speaker picked up the lawman's gun from the bar and shoved it behind his own waistband, then the brothers headed for the front door, each of them nodding a greeting as he passed Jubal's stool. A moment later, they were gone.

The deputy was on his feet quickly, but he did not rush to the front door. He stood in his tracks for a few moments, then began to lash out at the young bartender. "Why in th' hell didn't ya do sump'n? Ya got a damn shotgun behind 'at bar, don'tcha?"

Then, not waiting for an answer, he pointed to Kane. "An' you! Ya set right there an' watched 'im disarm a officer o' th' law, and ya didn't eeb'n lift a damn fanger. Ya got a Colt Peacemaker hangin' on ya hip, too."

Jubal nodded curtly. "You had one hanging on your hip, too, Deputy." He took another sip of his beer, then added, "The biggest reason I didn't lift a finger, though, was because it wasn't my gun he was taking."

"Humph!" the deputy said, then walked to the front of the building. He stood looking out over the doors for a moment, then turned halfway around and spoke to the bartender. "Th' sheriff'll be roundin' their asses up purty quick, an' I'll damn shore tell 'im about you not helpin' me out when I needed you." Then he pointed to Kane, speaking much louder now. "I'll be tellin' th' high sheriff o' this county about yore insolent mouth, too!" He shouldered his way through the bat-wings, leaving them flapping back and forth behind him.

Jubal upended his beer mug, then spoke to the bartender: "Is the deputy always that nice?"

The young man chuckled. "Yep. Just about always. I doubt that he knew exactly what he was up against just now, though. That was the Jessup brothers, Kearney and Moe. Moe was the one holding the gun, and I have no doubt that he would have used it if the deputy had given him any shit. Most folks around here call him Shooter, and I believe there's a good reason for that."

Jubal slid off the stool. "I'm gonna call it a night," he said. "I've already seen the show."

The sun was still two hours high when Jubal rode into Bandera two days later. Nobody paid any attention to him as he traveled through the center of town, for it was a Saturday afternoon, and the street was more congested than it had been at any time during his earlier visit. Men hurried along the boardwalks in either direction, and a few had women and children with them.

Several men on horseback were moving up and down the street, which was cluttered on both sides with wagons parked at any old angle the driver chose. It appeared that the busiest place in town was the Cypress Saloon, for each of its three hitching rails held as many saddled horses as it could accommodate. Jubal smiled as he rode past, knowing that he himself would most likely be among the establishment's patrons before the night was over.

The hunchbacked hostler was waiting in the doorway of the livery stable, for he had seen Jubal coming. "Good to see you again, young fellow," he said, as Kane drew up and dismounted. "I see you've been trading horses."

Jubal handed him the reins of both animals, then shook his head. "I haven't actually done any trading," he said. "I just turned the roan loose in my grandpa's corral after he gave me the gray."

"Sounds like a good deal to me," the hostler said, then began to unbuckle the packsaddle from the black. "I see you've still got the same packhorse, though."

Jubal nodded. "The black's about as good as they come," he said, beginning to strip his saddle from the gray. "If he's got any bad habits, I can't remember what they are."

Kane placed his saddle on a wooden rack, then stood by watching as the man led the animals down the hall and put them in separate stables. Then he dipped one bucket, then another, into a metal grain bin. "If you had come along yesterday, I wouldn't have had these oats," he said. "The young fellow I do business with in San Antonio brought me out thirty bushels about three hours ago." He pointed southeast with his thumb. "If you rode in from that direction, you probably met him on the road."

Kane nodded. "I suppose that was him I met right after I crossed Pipe Creek. He appeared to be about the same age as me, and he was sure driving an empty freight wagon."

"That was Joe, all right."

While the hostler was busy taking care of the horses, Jubal leaned his rifle against the wall and took a seat on the office steps. He rummaged through one of his packs till he found clean socks and clothing, then opened the office door and lifted the packsaddle inside. He was still sitting on the step when the hostler returned.

"I took the liberty of putting my packsaddle inside your office," he said. "I remembered that you kept it in there the last time I was here."

The hostler nodded. "I always keep a man's valuables locked up in there," he said. "One thing I don't like, though, is to be held responsible for somebody's gun. I always recommend that a fellow take his rifle with him." He glanced at Jubal's Winchester leaning against the wall. "I can see that you intend to look out for your own."

Jubal nodded. He sat quietly for a while, then pointed through the doorway. "Is that buggy out there for rent?" he asked.

"Absolutely," the hostler said, then chuckled loudly. "I'm in a position to offer you a mighty good deal on it if you'll rent it for the rest of the year."

Kane smiled. "I had a little shorter contract in mind," he said. "More like five or six hours."

"Dollar a day for the buggy and a horse to pull it. Don't make no difference whether you use 'em one hour or all day long, the price is the same. If you're thinking about using it tomorrow, though, you'd better get here early. It's the only one I've got nowadays, and it's usually gone by ten o'clock on Sunday morning."

Jubal fished a dollar out of his pocket and laid it in the man's hand. "Will this make sure that it's here tomorrow if I happen to need it?"

The hostler shoved the money into his pocket. "This'll make sure it's setting right out there waiting for you in the morning," he said. "Only difference is, it'll have a horse between the shafts."

Jubal laid his saddlebags and his clean clothing across his shoulder, then picked up his rifle. "I'll see you tomorrow," he said, then headed for the street.

A short while later, he stepped inside the hotel and knocked on Barney C. Witt's door, which opened immediately. "I wondered what the heck happened to you," the smiling man said loudly, stepping forward and lifting his arms as if he intended to hug his guest.

Kane moved backward out of the man's reach. "I'm still traveling around the country," he said, "and I thought I'd stop by and spend a few nights with you. Can I have the same room I had before?"

Witt handed him a key and pointed to the first room inside the front door. "By all means," he said. "We gonna have us a little sip, like we did the last time you stayed here?"

Jubal accepted the key, then turned toward the room. "I don't know, Barney," he said. "Let's just wait and see how things work out."

Kane entered the room and closed the door with his foot. He laid his things on the bed, then raised the window. He stripped to the waist, and as he dug his razor and his shaving soap out of his saddlebag, he heard a knock, then the door opened. Witt stood there holding a kettle, a towel, and a washcloth. "Brought this hot water to you 'cause I thought you might be wanting to shave." He laughed loudly. "If you steam them whiskers good enough, they'll damn near fall off of their own accord. Of course, the trail dust comes off a little easier with hot water, too." He set the kettle on the table, dropped the washcloth and the towel on the bed, then disappeared through the doorway.

There had already been a washpan full of water on the table. Jubal carried it to the front door and dashed half of it on the ground, then returned to the room and finished filling the pan with water from the kettle. He steamed his beard with a hot towel for a few minutes, then got a much better shave than he had ever gotten using cold water from a spring, creek, or river.

That done, he bathed himself from head to toe with the washcloth, then slipped on the clean jeans and a blue flannel shirt. He ran a comb through his hair a few times, then sprinkled his hat with water and wiped it dry. A few moments later, he was out on the street.

He stood in front of the hotel for a while, then crossed the street to Sally's Restaurant. Even before he touched the door he decided that he had arrived during the establishment's busiest hour of the week. Every hitching rail in the vicinity was filled to capacity with wagon teams, buggy horses, and at least a dozen saddle horses. Nonetheless, he turned the knob and stepped inside, taking his place in a line of about twenty people. He felt especially good tonight, and the fact that he had to stand in line bothered him not in the least. Sally's food was something special, and besides, one look at Jenny Hilton would make the wait worthwhile.

That look at Jenny Hilton did not come until more than fifteen minutes later, after he had been shown to a table along the east wall. She was stationed on the west side of the building, and would not be his waitress for this meal. Instead, the tall Mexican waiter handed him a menu, then stood by, awaiting his order.

"I'll have the roast beef and mashed potatoes," Kane said. He handed back the menu with one hand while he laid a quarter in the young man's hand with the other. "Will you tell Jenny Hilton that Jubal Kane is in the building?" he asked.

The waiter nodded. "First chance I get, sir," he said.

At least ten minutes passed before the waiter and the waitress were in the kitchen at the same time, then the recognition that Jubal had hoped for was quick in coming. Jenny Hilton was beside his table quickly, and placed her hand on top of his own. "I can't talk now," she said, "they'll raise Cain with me. I'll be off at eight o'clock; wait for me outside if you want to." Then she was gone.

He sat staring after her, forgetting for the moment that he had ordered a meal. "Here's your food, sir," he heard the waiter say, then turned to see the young man standing at his elbow with a steaming tray. "Sorry you had to wait so long," the youngster added, "but we haven't been this busy since I don't know when."

"Did I have to wait a long time?" Jubal asked, picking up his knife and fork. "I didn't even notice."

He dug into the scrumptious meal and scarcely came up for air until all of it was gone. Seeing that Jubal had wolfed down his food in a hurry, the waiter was soon back at his table. "We've got coconut cake if you want something sweet, sir," he said.

"Good," Kane said. "Bring me two slices." He handed over his empty coffee cup. "I suppose you should bring me something to wash it down with, too."

A quick glance at his watch told Jubal that he had another hour to kill before Jenny would be off work, and since there was no longer a line of people waiting to be served, he was in no hurry to vacate his table. He drank still another cup of coffee, and after buying a San Antonio newspaper from a stack on the counter, paid for his supper and left the building.

He did not even consider going to the saloon for a beer, for the last thing he wanted at the moment was the smell of alcohol on his breath. He crossed the street to his hotel room and turned his key in the lock. As he opened the door, he heard Witt's voice behind him. "I trimmed the wick and finished filling up your lamp with coal oil," the hotelkeeper said, "then put some matches on the table next to it. I just happened to remember that you like to read a little before you go to sleep."

"Thank you, Barney," Kane said, then struck one of his own matches on the sole of his boot. Inside the room he touched the match to the wick and replaced the globe, then set the lamp on a smaller table closer to his bed. When he turned to close the door, he saw that Witt was still standing in the doorway of his own quarters with what appeared to be a glass of whiskey in his hand. Jubal waved good-night to him, then pushed the door to.

Lying on his bed fully clothed and with his boots on, he scanned one page of the paper after another, making a mental note of the articles that he would read later. On page three there was a large picture of Sheriff Randy Bacon, along with a half-page political ad soliciting votes in his bid for reelection. The ad praised his accomplishments as the county's top law official in the highest terms imaginable, extolling the unequaled number of undesirables that he had hanged, sent to prison, or chased out of the county. The election would be held on the second Tuesday of next month, and Jubal expected Bacon to win by a large margin. Bacon was a very popular man, not only in his own county, but throughout the state of Texas.

Jubal crossed the street again at ten minutes to eight, and stood leaning against a post in front of the restaurant. He could see no one on the street at the moment, and decided that most of the diners who had crowded Sally's earlier had probably gone home. Those who had not gone home were most likely sitting on a barstool in one of the saloons.

Carrying a small umbrella, Jenny Hilton stepped from the restaurant right on time. She crossed the boardwalk quickly and found his hand with her own. "I'm so glad to see you again, Jubal," she said, squeezing as hard as she could. "Thank you for coming."

"I'm happy to see you again, too," he said.

Jubal had known pretty girls in the past, a few of them intimately, but never before had he held hands with a creature as lovely as Jenny Hilton. And though he was racking his brain for something clever to say at the moment, what came out of his mouth was, "I see you've got your umbrella, are you expecting rain?"

"No," she said quickly. "I just bring the parasol to the restaurant with me every day, then carry it home at night." She squeezed his hand again. "I haven't gotten wet a single time since I acquired that habit."

Jubal continued to hold her hand, feeling more foolish by the moment. He had thought of Jenny Hilton every waking hour since their first meeting, and now that she was responding favorably to his overtures, he was suddenly tongue-tied, and his mind seemed to have gone on strike. "I didn't expect what I said to sound quite that silly," he said with a chuckle.

She ignored the remark, and tugged on his hand. "Let's move over against the wall," she said. "I'd like to get out of the light shining through that window."

When they reached the shadows, Jenny loosened her grip on his hand and spoke softly: "The day I got your letter from Waco, I made up my mind that I was going to do this the next time I saw you." She stood on her tiptoes and put both arms around his neck, then pulled herself up and kissed him full on the mouth. "There," she said, returning her weight to her own two feet. "I've done it."

Jubal had found his tongue. "You sure have, little girl," he said, sliding one arm around her waist and the other around her shoulders. "You certainly have." He pulled her to him and held her tightly, kissing her hard on the mouth. "I've been hoping I would eventually get to do this, Jenny, even dreamed about it a few times."

"Me, too, Jubal," she said, returning his kiss hungrily. "I've dreamed about it, too."

They continued to embrace each other, dropping their arms to their sides only when a man walked by on the boardwalk. He turned his head in an attempt to get a better look, then walked on without speaking.

Jenny squeezed Jubal's arm with both hands. "This is not a good place for us to be," she said. "Do you want to walk me home?"

"Of course. Where do you live?"

She pointed. "In the white house behind my dad's store," she said. "Only two and a half blocks from here."

He nodded, then took her hand in his own. "I was hoping it would be a lot farther than that," he said, then led off.

When they had turned the corner at the feed store, she stopped. "Do you wear that gun on your hip all the time?" she asked.

"It's been there pretty regular for the past few years, but there's a reason for it, Jenny. I'll explain it all to you when I get a chance."

"You mean you don't have a chance right now?"

"No, that's not what I mean. What I mean is that it's a long story, and this is not the time to go into it." He was quiet for a moment, then added, "I've already rented a buggy for tomorrow. If you'll go riding with me, we can discuss the matter of the gun then."

She squeezed his arm again. "Sure, I'll go on a buggy ride with you. I'll even supply the blanket and the picnic basket."

"Ten o'clock all right?"

"Nine o'clock would be better. It takes about two hours to get to Pipe Creek, and that's where all the pretty picnicking places are."

He kissed her nose. "Nine o'clock, then."

They had walked only a few steps before she stopped again. "The gun on your hip doesn't bother me, Jubal, and neither would it bother my dad; he carries one himself part of the time. But I'm afraid my mom would hit the ceiling, so I'd appreciate it if you'd keep it out of her sight." When Jubal said nothing, the girl added, "At least, for a while."

He hugged her to him. "I don't guess she'll see me tonight; I'll hide the gun out somewhere tomorrow, though."

They were soon standing in front of her home. Jenny stood on her toes and kissed him once again, then ran up the steps and disappeared inside.

Jubal stood in his tracks for a few moments, then began to stroll back toward the hotel, his mind occupied with thoughts of the beautiful girl he had just been holding in his arms. He had held and kissed pretty girls before, but the feeling he had experienced tonight was totally new to him. Just the touch of her fingers made his skin tingle, and when her tongue touched his lips something inside him that he had not known existed seemed to suddenly come alive.

As he headed for his room he felt that all was right with the world, and the knowledge that he would be holding Jenny Hilton in his arms again in just a matter of hours gave him a good feeling. He eased himself inside the front door as quietly as he could, for he was not in the mood for a conversation with a drunk hotelkeeper.

18

★

He shaved and washed his body again at sunup, then walked across the street for breakfast. The pancakes and sausage that he was served by the Mexican waiter disappeared quickly, then Kane sat sipping coffee and wondering what Jenny was going to have in her picnic basket. Whatever it was, he would most likely be hungry again by then, for he doubted that they would eat until sometime in the early afternoon.

When he arrived at the livery stable at eight-thirty, the buggy was parked at the hitching rail, between the shafts a black mare with two white stockings. The fact that the stable's front door was closed and the hostler nowhere in sight mattered little, since Kane had already paid for a day's use of the vehicle. He watered the mare from a nearby trough, then unbuckled his gunbelt and shoved it under the seat of the buggy, spreading a dirty shirt that he had brought from the hotel over it. He could get to the weapon quickly if he needed to, but Jenny's mother would certainly never know it was there.

At a quarter to nine, he stepped into the buggy and guided the mare toward the Hilton residence, which was less than five blocks away. He drove into the yard, and had not even finished tying the mare when Jenny suddenly appeared at his side. "Both of my parents are anxious to meet you, Jubal," she said. Then, speaking much more softly, she added, "My dad's name is John. A lot of people around town call him Wink, because he has an uncontrollable blink in his right eye, but he hates the nickname, and he'll like you better if he never hears you use it."

Jubal shook his head. "I wouldn't think of it," he said.

"My ma has a nickname, too, but she loves hers. She'll want you to call her Tiny, although she's not quite as little as she used to be."

Jubal smiled. "Anything to please," he said, then followed her up the steps.

The middle-aged couple met them as they stepped onto the porch. Jenny made the introductions then excused herself, explaining that she still had to finish putting her picnic basket together. Mrs. Hilton squeezed Jubal's arm, then joined her daughter in the house.

John Hilton pumped Kane's hand several times, then pointed to some chairs. "Let's sit down over there and get acquainted," he said. He was a big man, about the same height as Jubal and of a similar build. He had a full shock of brown hair, and appeared to be about forty years old.

"Jenny says you're from Nacogdoches," he said, when both men had seated themselves.

"Yes, sir," Jubal said. "I spent a lot of my growing years on my grandpa's farm, a few miles west of town."

Hilton nodded. He sat quietly for a while before asking his next question: "Do you intend to spend the rest of your working years farming?"

Kane shook his head. "No, sir, this year was our last crop. Grandpa's getting on in years, and he recently informed me that he wanted to do something different with the rest of his life. He's already bought a herd of Herefords, and he's right now in the process of turning the farm into a cattle ranch."

Hilton nodded. "Probably the smart thing to do," he said. "I'll tell you one thing, there's some good money to be made with Herefords."

"I hope so," Jubal said. "As far as I know now, that's what I'll be doing for the rest of my life."

Jenny's mother was back on the porch now. She was a short woman who had no doubt gained more than a few pounds since her younger days. She had dark hair and eyes, and appeared to be about the same age as her husband. She pulled up a chair and sat down, then spoke to Jubal: "Did you ride all the way from Nacogdoches just to see our Jenny, Mr. Kane?"

"Yes, ma'am," Jubal answered. "That's exactly what I did."

"Oh," she said excitedly, "that's so sweet." She turned to her husband. "Isn't that sweet, John?"

Hilton emitted an audible sigh, then sat staring up the road. "Yes, Tiny," he said finally. "I reckon it's sweet."

When Jenny reappeared, she was wearing a blue bonnet on her head, held in place by ribbons tied under her chin. Jubal was quickly on his feet, and relieved her of both the blanket and the picnic basket.

The Hiltons followed the young couple down the steps, then stood beside the buggy. As Jubal helped Jenny into the vehicle, Mrs. Hilton pointed to the bundle under the seat, then spoke a word of caution to her daughter: "Be careful not to step on that shirt, honey. There's probably a gun under it."

Jubal said nothing as he untied the mare and climbed to the seat. He backed the animal up a few steps, then turned the buggy sharply and headed for the main road. The Hiltons stood in the yard, watching till the vehicle was out of sight.

"What do you think of my folks?" Jenny asked, once they were on the road east of town.

Jubal reached for her hand. "I thought they were very nice," he answered, then chuckled softly. "Of course, I'm sure you know that I'd claim to like them whether I do or not."

She wiggled her nose at him. "I suppose so," she said. "They both liked you, though; I could tell by the way they talked and acted." She squeezed his hand, and smiled broadly. "While we were in the kitchen, Ma told me that you were the handsomest animal that had ever stood on our front porch."

Jubal laughed. "Your mother said that?"

"Yes." She lifted his hand and pressed it against her cheek. "And I think she was right."

He pulled her to him, and said nothing more on the subject. Since he was on a good road at the moment, he slapped the mare's rump with the reins, sending the buggy toward their destination at a new pace. He had traveled this way more than once, and knew that the stretch of road between Pipe Creek and Bandera was one of the smoothest in the entire state. Even now it appeared to have been scraped recently, and the drainage ditches on either side were deep and unclogged. He pointed up ahead. "Who takes care of this road, Jenny? Is there a county road crew?"

"I don't think so," she answered. "I remember my dad working on it a few years ago, and he's never been on the county payroll. Some of the boys I went to school with helped out in the summertime, too, but I never heard any of them say they got paid for it."

Jubal nodded. "I guess they get as many volunteers as they need," he said. "They do a mighty fine job, too."

They rode in silence till they reached the creek, then Jenny pointed to a road that ran along the bank in a southerly direction. "The prettiest places on the creek are down that way," she said. "Lots of tall pecans and willows, and the bank is almost free of undergrowth."

Jubal guided the mare onto the grassy, seldom-used road. "You sound as if you've done this before," he said.

She wiggled her nose. "Of course I've done it before. You don't think you're the only man to ever ask me on a buggy ride, do you?"

"No, ma'am," he said, chuckling. "Not by a long shot."

When they had traveled about three hundred yards, she motioned to a thick grove of willows. "If you'll pull up in those trees, we'll be out of sight of anybody traveling on the road, and the ground is pretty level down close to the water." She was quiet till he had made the turn, then with a touch of sarcasm, she added, "Considering the fact that I've picnicked on this creek with about every man in the county, I must have used this same spot a thousand times."

When Kane didn't speak or smile, she elbowed him in the ribs. "Don't take everything I say seriously, Jubal. The truth is, I've only been here once before, and that was two summers ago when I was still in school."

He touched her lips with his own, then stepped down and tied the mare to a willow limb. When he walked back to the buggy, Jenny offered him one of her hands, gathered her ankle-length skirt together with the other, and jumped to the ground as well as any man.

Jubal untied her bonnet and laid it in the buggy, then pulled her to him and kissed her passionately several times. When he finally released her, he reached under the seat for the blanket. "Show me where you want me to spread this, then we'll be in business."

She pointed to a level spot between two large pecans, then led the way. Jubal spread the blanket on the high bank, then picked up a fist-sized rock and dropped it into the water ten feet below. The action had been to test the depth of the creek, and he very quickly decided that it was considerably deeper than five or six feet.

When he returned from the buggy with the picnic basket, he also laid his gunbelt on the corner of the blanket, pulling the same dirty shirt over it.

Jenny motioned to the bundle, then spoke softly: "Like I told you before, the fact that you keep the gun around doesn't bother me at all. If anything, it makes me feel . . . protected."

Kane nodded, and squeezed her hand. "That's the whole idea for having it," he said.

Without another word, Jenny spread a cloth napkin on the blanket, then laid out the contents of the picnic basket: fried chicken, baked ham, biscuits, two slices of pound cake, and a quart jar of lemonade that they would pass back and forth between them. "Twist the lid off the jar for me," she said, "then eat up."

They talked little during the meal, after which Jenny carried the basket back to the buggy. Reseating herself on the blanket, she smoothed out her skirt and patted her thighs. "Lay your head in my lap and tell me why you always carry a gun on your hip. You promised to tell me the whole story, remember?"

He pecked her on the cheek, then stretched out on the blanket, his head on her thigh. "It all started the year I was fifteen," he began, then told her of the cold-blooded murders in the barn, the promise he had made to his dead parents, and the measures he had taken so far to fulfill that promise. He concluded by saying, "I promised Ma and Pa both that I would let nothing stop me from dealing with their killers."

Jenny had listened to the narration intently, wiping her eyes occasionally. "Oh . . . Jubal," she said haltingly. "I know it must have hurt something awful to have your parents murdered right before your eyes." She dabbed at her eyes again, then asked, "Did you say you've already dealt with one of the killers?"

He took his time about answering. "Yes," he said finally. "And I'm on my way to south Texas right now to look for one of his partners."

She said nothing during the next few minutes, but continued to hold his head in her lap, running her fingers through his hair. "What are you going to do after you've dealt with those other two men?" she asked finally.

"I intend to go home to the ranch and raise Hereford cattle," he said. "The carpenters are in the process of building a home for me right now, and I expect to raise a family there if I can find a wife."

She slapped him on the forehead playfully. "If you can find a wife!" she said, her tone of voice suggesting that she believed he could marry most any woman he wanted to. "If you can find a wife!" she repeated.

"I haven't seen many young girls running loose in Nacogdoches County," he said. "And the way I travel around the country, I don't meet a whole lot of women of any age." He lay quietly for a moment, then added, "Besides, I've got a particular type of woman in mind that I'd like to carry off to my den.

"You see, I like small women with big bosoms, and I prefer that they have dark hair and eyes." He was thoughtful for a few seconds. "I'm a little bit picky about names, too," he added. "I like the name of Jenny a whole lot. Jenny Kane just seems to have the right sound."

Neither of them spoke again for a long while, then she asked, "Was that a marriage proposal, Jubal?"

He reached for her hand. "Yes, it was," he said. "Would you consider becoming my wife?"

"I've considered it already," she said quickly. "The answer is yes."

He continued to lie in her lap quietly, and began to stroke the calf of her leg.

A moment later, she asked, "When?"

He rose to a sitting position and pulled her to him, pressing her face against his chest. "Early next spring, I hope. I'll even let you pick out the furnishings for your new home."

"You . . . you think you'll find those men you're hunting before then?"

"I believe I will," he said. "If not, we'll just have to postpone the wedding. Hunting down the man who pumped two bullets into Ma's chest is something that I have to do no matter what."

She touched his lips with a forefinger. "I understand," she said. "Then you're going to settle down to ranching?"

"Absolutely. As soon as the manhunting's done, I intend to take charge of the day-to-day operation of the ranch. Calling the shots myself will not only keep me on top of things, it'll save the cost of a foreman's wages— money we can put to good use somewhere else."

He pulled her to him again, then gently pushed her down on the blanket. He smothered her face with kisses and searched the inside of her mouth with his tongue, then began to explore her curvaceous body with his hands. She allowed him to continue for only a short while, then wiggled out from under him and got to her feet. "I . . . I'd like to go home now," she said.

He was on his feet quickly, holding both of her hands.

"I'm so sorry," she was saying. "I just knew that the situation was about to get out of hand, and I was afraid I couldn't say no." Tears rolled down her cheeks as she snuggled against his chest. "I want us to be husband and wife when it happens, Jubal."

He squeezed her tightly. "We will be, Jenny," he said. "I can wait; it's not gonna be forever."

He put his gunbelt back in the buggy and laid the shirt over it, then rolled up the blanket. A few minutes later, they were back on the main road. He held the mare to a walking gait, for he wanted to spend as much time as possible with the girl he was going to marry. Besides, they had plenty of important things to talk about; for instance, how many children were they going to have? As many as they could feed, clothe, and educate, was the number Jenny suggested.

"You might think it's a silly thing to do, since I'm over eighteen years old," she said, as they neared her home, "but I wish you would ask my pa for my hand."

He looked at her out of the corner of his eye. "I don't know how to do that," he said. "What am I supposed to say?"

"It doesn't matter how you say it," she said, playfully tapping his knee with a tiny fist. "Just ask him. I think it'll make him like you more."

Jubal did the asking while the two men were sitting on the porch having a glass of homemade wine, with both of the women out of earshot. For the past several minutes he had been racking his brain for just the right words to use. The hell with it, he decided finally, then said, "Is it all right if I marry your daughter, Mr. Hilton?"

Hilton set his empty glass on the table noisily, a hint of a smile at one corner of his mouth. "I reckon Jenny's the one you ought to be asking," he said. "She turned nineteen years old a month ago, and it sure as hell ain't up to me to be saying who she can marry."

"I've already asked her, sir, and she said yes. She just thought it would be nice if I cleared it with you."

Hilton shook Jubal's hand, squeezing it firmly. "Well, I reckon by God you've cleared it," he said. "You want another glass of wine?"

Jubal handed over his glass. "I believe so," he said. "It goes down mighty easy."

"I put this particular batch up nearly three years ago," Hilton said, stepping inside the front door. "I guess it did turn out pretty good."

Jubal and Jenny were sitting in the porch swing an hour later, with the girl's parents nowhere to be seen. "How do you think your grandfather will feel about your bringing a wife to the ranch?" she asked.

Kane laughed aloud. "Grandpa asked me no more than a month ago, when was I gonna settle down and start raising him some great-grandchildren. Since he knows that I can't produce the kids by myself, I expect him to hug your neck and buy you something pretty."

When the Hiltons reappeared an hour before sunset, Jenny filled them in on the wedding plans. Everything had been decided on except the exact date, she said, and that would be worked out shortly after the first of next year. Jubal had many things to do in the meantime, she explained, such as turning a hay farm into a cattle ranch, and seeing that his new home was finished.

Tiny spoke to Kane: "You intend to build your own home?" she asked.

He nodded.

"It might be done already." Jenny said loudly and proudly. "Jubal said the carpenters started on it about two weeks ago."

Kane had moved to the edge of the porch, just above the steps. "The sun'll be down by the time I get the mare and the buggy back to the stable," he said, "so I've got to be going." He hugged Jenny's mother, then extended his right hand to her father. "I'll be leaving town early in the morning, sir, and I won't be back till I come after your daughter next spring. I'll bring a covered wagon big enough to haul the things she can't bear to part with, and we'll be married right here in her own church." He released Hilton's hand, then walked down the steps.

Jenny followed him to the yard and stood by while he untied the mare. As he pulled his future wife to him and gave her a long, passionate kiss, her parents stood on the porch applauding. He squeezed her hand one last time, then climbed into the buggy. After backing the mare up a few steps, he waved good-bye to them all and headed for the road. He was quickly out of sight.

19

★

Kane stepped into the saddle at sunup and left the town of Bandera at a trot, expecting to be in San Antonio by nightfall. Although the town was a few miles out of his way, he must pass through it or travel cross-country, for all good roads in the area led through San Antonio. Though most died there, some connected with routes heading north, south, or east. Good roads leading west were practically nonexistent, however, for the majority of the population of Texas lived north and east of Bexar County.

After a good night's sleep in San Antonio, he would take the Corpus Christi road and stay with it for at least three days. When he reached Live Oak County, he would turn south and head for Brownsville. He had traveled the road before, and knew that it was good.

Making only a short stop at noon, he stayed in the saddle for the remainder of the day, and rode into San

Antonio no more than half an hour before dark. He smiled as he rode past the Menger Hotel, knowing that he would most likely never sleep there again. He had better things to do with his money than pay four or five dollars for a bed that he could rent elsewhere for fifty cents.

Remembering that it was a long walk from Roscoe Nemecek's place back to town, Jubal chose a different livery stable, a few doors down from Trader Paul's. A black-haired hostler of indeterminate age introduced himself only as Charley, then began to unburden the packhorse, saying, "I guess you'll be staying in town overnight."

Kane nodded. "You guessed right," he said. "Just feed my horses now, and again in the morning. I guess I'll be back here pretty early—what time of day do you usually get up?"

"Don't matter whether I'm up or not, just knock on the door whenever you get ready for your animals. I won't ever be in bed after daylight, though."

Jubal nodded. "I'll see you in the morning," he said. With his saddlebags across his shoulder and his rifle under his arm, he headed back up the street to the Blackstone Hotel, a two-story building that had obviously been around for many years, and was badly in need of a coat of paint. He stepped inside and inquired about a room. "Got three left," the aging desk clerk informed him, "all of 'em upstairs. Considering the way the nights have been cooling off here lately, though, I'd say that a man could get a good night's sleep in any of 'em."

Kane paid the man for a room, and locked his saddlebags and his rifle inside. He was soon back out on the street looking for a restaurant, for his noonday meal had been meager. He settled on a shabby hole in the wall across the street and a few doors down from the hotel.

The large bowl of beef stew he was served tasted as good as he had ever eaten, and he ordered a second helping. The coffee was also good, and he had three cups. Because the lady at the counter charged him only twenty cents for his supper, he stopped off on his way to the front door and left a dime on the table for the waiter. Then he was on the street again.

A sign above the door of a large building across the street stated that the establishment was the Beehive Saloon, and judging from the number of saddled horses tied at every nearby hitching rail, the place was aptly named. Without a second thought, Jubal pushed open the batwing doors and stepped inside. He moved against the wall and stood till his eyes adjusted to the dim lighting, then walked on to the far side of the bar. "I'll have a glass of beer," he said to the waiting bartender, then laid a coin on the bar.

Mainly because he had been sitting in the saddle all day, Jubal ignored the many vacant seats. Standing between two barstools with his elbows on the bar, he leaned forward and began to sip at his beer. "There you are, you son of a bitch!" a loud voice called from somewhere behind him. Kane turned his head to see a dark-haired man of about thirty pointing to him from twenty feet away. "There you are!" the man repeated. "I knew damn well I'd run into you again if I kep' lookin' long enough, an' by God, there you are!"

Kane set his mug down slowly, and backed away from the bar. "I don't have the slightest idea what you're talking about," he said, "but I don't like people pointing—"

"Pointin' ain't all I'm gonna do!" the man interrupted. "I'm gonna put your ass in the graveyard." He motioned to Jubal's Peacemaker. "See how quick you c'n git that Colt off'n your hip. Do it now!" he shouted, "or I'll shoot you down right where you're standin'!"

Kane took him at his word. Making a draw that would be talked about for years to come, he put a bullet in the speaker's mouth before the man even realized that he had moved his hand. The man died instantly, and crumpled to the floor with his right hand still on his gun, which was about halfway out of its holster.

Kane stood in his tracks with his six-gun ready for action. At the same instant he fired, he had recocked the weapon with his thumb in case he needed a follow-up shot. Of course, he could see now that none was necessary. After a few moments, he holstered the Colt and spoke to the bartender: "Do you know who that fellow is?" he asked, pointing.

The barkeep nodded. "I know who he was," he corrected. "He went by the name of Allred—Sparky Allred. He's been in here every day for the past two or three weeks, and if it's really true that you didn't know him, it sounded to me like he mistook you for somebody else."

"Well, it's damn sure true!" Kane said defensively. "I've never seen that man before in my life." He pushed the half-full beer mug across the bar. "I'm not in the mood for that anymore, either."

Several men stood around the corpse now, talking among themselves in low tones. Jubal watched and listened for a few moments, then spoke to the bartender again: "Would you mind telling me what your name is?"

"The name is Buddy. That's all anybody ever calls me."

Jubal nodded. "All right, Buddy. You saw it all and you heard it all. When it comes out of your mouth, I expect it to be straight." When the bartender said nothing nor otherwise did anything to indicate that he had even heard, Kane shrugged, and laid an eagle on the bar. "I'm leaving this money to pay for Allred's burial," he said. "Any man who does the job can claim it." He stepped around the cluster of men standing over the body, then walked through the front door.

He walked to the Blackstone at a fast clip, then climbed the stairs to his room two at a time. He did not light the lamp, but locked the door and felt his way across the room in the dark. He raised the window, then pulled up a chair and sat watching the street below. He could not see the entire length of the boardwalk, for it had a roof over it in places, but there was a forty-foot stretch where there was neither roof nor awning, and anyone walking there would be in plain view.

Kane knew that his shooting of Allred had been cut-and-dried self-defense, but he nonetheless had an uneasy feeling about it. Hadn't the bartender clammed up when Jubal told him that he should tell the truth about what he had seen and heard? Yes—and there was no telling what that crowd of gawkers might say.

Jubal kept asking himself the same questions over and over: Who was the man called Sparky Allred, and who had he mistaken Jubal Kane for? Had he been wronged by a man who resembled Kane so much that he truly had been fooled? Or was he merely a would-be gunman seeking a reputation? Kane seriously doubted that he had been an experienced gunfighter. Somebody would have killed him a long time ago, Jubal believed, for his draw had been much too slow to take any man with know-how.

Continuing his vigil from the window, he decided that some of his questions might soon be answered, for even now he could see three riders headed up the street toward the hotel, and they all had the look of lawmen. Might be the town marshal, he decided, coming to hear Jubal Kane's side of the story.

Kane sat in the dark room waiting for what seemed like an hour, then there was a loud knock at the door. "Be with you in a minute," he said, then struck a match on the sole of his boot and lit the lamp. "Who's there?" he inquired.

"Marshal Stevens," a deep voice answered.

When Jubal opened the door, three men stepped quickly into the room. The marshal pointed to the others. "These men are my deputies," he said, "Clark and Pittman."

"I would invite you in," Kane said, "but I see that's not necessary. What can I do for you?"

"I'd like to talk to you in my office," Stevens said. "Want to get to the bottom of what happened down at the Beehive."

Jubal spun on his heel and walked to the window, intending to reseat himself in the chair. "I can tell you anything you need to know right here, Marshal," he said, then turned to see that Stevens and both of his deputies had Colt revolvers in their hands, all of them pointed at his head.

"Just unbuckle that gunbelt and let's go," the marshal commanded. "I'm charging you with the murder of Sparky Allred."

"Murder?" Kane asked loudly. "You're charging me with murder? Hell, that man challenged me to a gunfight, Marshal; said he'd shoot me down right where I stood if I didn't draw. I didn't even know him, never saw him before in my life!"

"Well, I guess that'll all come out in the trial," Stevens said. "Right now, I'm asking you to drop that gunbelt and come along quietly." He waved the barrel of his Colt back and forth. "The truth of the matter is, you ain't got much choice."

Jubal stared at the lawman for several seconds, then slowly unbuckled his gunbelt and handed it to one of the deputies. He pointed underneath the bed. "My saddlebags and my rifle are down there," he said. "Do you mind if I carry them with me?"

"The deputy'll take care of that," the marshal said, then motioned for one of his men to look under the bed.

A short time later, the four men were walking down the middle of the street. The deputy named Clark led the three horses, while Stevens and Pittman prodded Jubal along with drawn guns. In an obvious attempt to draw attention to the proceedings, the lawmen continued to carry on a loud conversation between themselves. Several men already stood on either side of the street, watching and listening.

The walk was not a long one, and the building Jubal was herded into was hardly an office, but a large, adobe shell built around an iron cage. "Got another one here for you, Pedro," the marshal said to a middle-aged man who was obviously the jailer. "This one's a shooter, too."

The jailer, a medium-sized man of Mexican descent, accepted Jubal's guns and his saddlebags from the lawmen and placed them behind his desk. Then he took pad and pencil from the desktop and spoke to Jubal: "Your name, please?"

When he had written down the name, he returned the pad to his desk, then ran his hands over Kane's body in search of a weapon. "Straight ahead," he said then, motioning to the nearest of several individual cages.

Jubal obeyed the order without a word. He took a seat on the cell's only bunk as he heard the heavy door close with a loud, metallic clang, then watched as the jailer turned the oversized key in the lock. "Better get some sleep if you can," the man said. "They say the first night's always the hardest."

After the marshal and his deputies had said their good-byes and vacated the premises, the jailer seated himself at his desk, turned down the wick and pulled the lamp closer to his elbow, then resumed his reading of a dime novel that he had no doubt been enjoying before he was interrupted.

"Are you gonna sit there burning that lamp all night?" Kane asked.

The jailer turned his head only slightly, answering, "The lamp burns all night every night, but I won't be sitting here that long. My relief comes to work at ten."

Kane was sitting in the same position when the second jailer arrived. About the same size and age as the first jailer, he was also of Mexican descent. After listening to their conversation for a while, Jubal decided that both of them spoke better English than did most Texans, himself included.

Sometime before midnight, he leaned back on the bunk and went to sleep; his anxiety had finally been overruled by fatigue, for he had ridden more than forty miles this day. He awoke once during the night to use the slop jar, then dozed off again quickly. The next time he opened his eyes, he could see daylight coming from someplace farther down the hall, where several other cages exactly like his own were situated.

There was no daylight to be seen in the other direction, however, and the fact that the front of the building was windowless was hardly an oversight. With no windows for prying eyes to peek through, whatever went on in the city jail could very easily remain a secret between the marshal and his hand-picked underlings.

Jubal had just glanced at his watch to see that it was eight o'clock, when the deputy named Pittman came through the front door and set a tray of food on the desk. Then he drew his Colt and spoke to the jailer: "I'll stand back and keep watch on the prisoner while you feed him," he said. "Guess you better put him a bucket of water in there, too. Looks like today's gonna be another hot one."

Kane was soon sitting on the bunk with the tray across his knees. He had only to remove the cloth napkin covering the food to know that it had been catered by a restaurant, for he doubted that true jailhouse food would ever have such an appetizing appearance. The generous portions of ham, scrambled eggs, buttered biscuits, a pile of jelly, and a large breakfast roll, made a meal good enough for any man, and the oversized cup full of strong coffee was still warm. Jubal ate it all, then slid the empty tray under the cell door and out into the hall.

"The marshal mentioned a trial last night," he said to the jailer, when the man came to pick up the tray. "Do you have any idea when they might hold court on me?"

The man shook his head. "Ain't no telling," he said. "Might be a few weeks, might be a few months. I know that the city court and the county court both are backlogged with cases."

"Well, hell," Kane said. "A fellow can get out on bail, can't he?"

The jailer shook his head again. "Ain't no bail on murder," he said, then picked up the tray and disappeared.

Sitting on the bunk and staring at the adobe wall surrounding the cages, Jubal was doing some strong thinking: What the hell had he gotten himself into? Why had he not just eaten supper and gone to his hotel room, instead of traipsing off to the Beehive Saloon to sit and mouth the rim of a damn beer mug till all hours of the night? If he had gotten a good night's sleep, he would have been several miles down the trail to south Texas by now. And although he knew that the thing with Allred had been pure and simple happenstance, he also knew that it would not have occurred if he had been asleep in the bed he had rented.

He continued to give himself a hard time for most of the morning. He had just wound his watch and noticed that the time was twenty minutes to eleven, when the jailer came through the front door and walked down the hall rattling a ring of keys. "Up and at 'em, Kane," he said, pushing a key into the lock. "Looks like you've got friends in high places." He pulled the door open, adding, "If I were you, I'd be getting my ass out of this town in a hurry."

"You're turning me loose?"

The jailer nodded. "That's my orders," he said.

"What happened? Did the marshal drop the charges?"

"Don't ask so many questions, dammit. I don't know what the hell they did or didn't do. All I know is that the word came down that Sheriff Bacon wants you back on the ground. Now, in this town, what Randy Bacon wants, Randy Bacon gets."

With a feeling of jubilance, and a deep appreciation for the sheriff's actions, Jubal darted from the cell. He paused at the front desk only long enough to accept his guns and his saddlebags from the jailer, then stepped out on the street. He covered the distance to the livery stable almost at a run, and a few minutes later, rode out of San Antonio at a lively canter.

20

Only after he could no longer see the city of San Antonio did Jubal change his pace. Then, except for a few minutes spent watering his animals during the afternoon, he continued at a fast walk till he was out of Bexar County. He let out a sigh of relief as he crossed the Atascosa County line, for he knew that he was now safely out of Marshal Stevens's grasp.

He would be forever grateful to Sheriff Bacon for interceding on his behalf, but he doubted that he would ever visit Bexar County again. Nor would he ever be seen in San Antonio again, not unless he knew beforehand that a different man occupied the marshal's office.

He had made up his mind in the jail cell last night that, if he ever got his feet on the ground again, he would give the whole area a wide berth. The knowledge that it was entirely possible for a man to hang for something he knew absolutely nothing about, had been brought home to him by the marshal's steadfast refusal to listen to the facts. No, sir, he was thinking as he reached the Atascosa River, that crazy bastard would not get another crack at him.

Kane already knew that there were campers at the river, for he had seen their smoke from several hundred yards away. He watered his animals on the east side, then forded the shallow stream. When he climbed out on the west bank he found that a covered wagon was parked almost in the road. An oversized team of gray mules stood in the shade of a nearby oak, each of them concentrating on a pile of cured hay.

A couple who appeared to be well past middle age sat on a log beside the gray coals of their cooking fire, and a white-haired man who looked to be at least twenty years older than either of them, sat on the ground on the opposite side. Although darkness would not be along for more than two hours yet, it was obvious that their traveling was over for this day. And though it had been raining off and on all afternoon, they apparently had had no problem preparing their supper, for each of them had a bowl in one hand and a soup spoon in the other. Jubal nodded as he passed.

"Don't go ridin' right on by, young fellow!" the old man called, then held up his bowl. "We've got enough venison stew here to feed an army, and we'd feel honored if you'd share it with us."

Kane was hungry. He pulled up and sat staring between the gray's ears for a moment. Then, with a wide grin spreading from one corner of his mouth to the other, he turned to face the old man. "Well, if it's gonna make you feel all that good, I certainly wouldn't want to be the one to deny you the opportunity." He chuckled loudly. "Are you sure you've got enough?"

"Got plenty," the lady said, pointing to the blackened pot that had already been pulled off the fire. "I must've put at least five pounds of meat in that thing."

Kane dismounted, and tied both of his horses to the same bush. "It smells mighty good from here," he said, "and I can't think of many things that I enjoy eating more." He walked on to the fire, then added, "Besides, it'll save me the trouble of trying to cook my own supper with wet wood."

"We already had deadwood in the wagon," the younger of the two men said, "so we didn't have no problem getting a fire started. It's been sprinkling a little every once in a while, but it ain't never rained hard enough to put it out." He took a bowl and a large spoon from a wooden box, and handed them to Jubal, adding, "Just help yourself to that pot. It's like the wife said, we've got plenty."

After dishing up a bowl of stew, Kane accepted a tin cup from the lady and poured it full of coffee. Then he seated himself cross-legged on the ground and began to eat.

The younger of the men, having already finished his own meal, was on his feet now. He walked to the tree where the mules were tied, then returned. "They're just about done with that hay," he said to no one in particular. "I'll stake 'em out on that good grass out yonder in a few minutes." He extended his right hand to Kane, who was still seated on the ground. "I'm Hansel York," he said. When the handshaking was done, he jerked his head toward the lady, then the older man. "That's my wife, Adelle, and that gentleman over there is her pa. We've been calling him Grandpa for so long that I sometimes forget what his real name is."

Kane nodded to both the lady and the old man, then introduced himself. That done, he stepped to the pot and refilled his bowl. As he sat down and recrossed his legs, he made eye contact with the lady. "This stew is mighty good, ma'am," he said. "The hot pepper you added really agrees with my taste buds."

The lady nodded and smiled graciously, but her husband was the one who did the talking. "We appreciate the compliment," he said. "Eating good on the road ain't very hard to do when you ain't going no farther than we are, though. You can take along about anything you want to.

"We ain't been traveling but two days, and I reckon our trip'll be over by sunset tomorrow. We live down in Bee County, just a short walk from Beeville, and we're on our way to San Antonio to spend the winter with our son and our grandkids. One grandson up there more'n a year old that we ain't never even seen, and Grandpa ain't never laid eyes on none of his three great-grandchildren."

Jubal had finished eating, and was in the process of refilling his coffee cup. "It sounds like you're going to enjoy your visit," he said, "and I know the kids will."

The rain began to fall again at that moment. Nobody moved for cover, however, for there was not a cloud in the sky. "Can you beat that?" Hansel asked. "Pouring down rain with the sun still shining just as pretty as you please."

"The devil's beatin' his wife again!" the old man said loudly.

"Oh, Pa," the lady said. "You don't really believe that."

"Of course I believe it!" her father answered indignantly. "I've heard people a whole lot smarter'n any of us, say it. To the best of my recollection, Preacher Eagleton said it not long 'fore he died. I know for a fact that Brother Emmons believed it, and you know what a smart man he was. Last year he lived, they even made him a deacon in the church." He was quiet for a moment, then added, "Yes, sir, anytime it rains and shines at the same time, the devil's beatin' his wife."

A few seconds later the rain stopped. "There!" the old man said, pointing a finger at his daughter then motioning toward the sky. "You see? He quit hittin' her, and it quit rainin'. He don't never whup her for more'n a little while at a time, 'cause a woman can't stand many licks from somebody as strong as the devil."

When nobody argued with him, the old man dragged himself over to the log and leaned against it, a look of satisfaction on his face.

Jubal got to his feet. "Now that you folks have fed me so well, I'm beginning to think you had the right idea when you decided to camp here." He pointed to the meadow. "Looks like there's plenty of grass on the north side of the road, so I'll picket my horses on it and sleep out there with them. I'll pitch my tent just in case it decides to drizzle some more during the night."

"It ain't gonna rain tonight," the old man said, as Jubal headed for his horses. As Kane led the animals across the road, the old man called after him: "We're gonna be havin' deer steaks right here at this fire about daylight. You be shore to come by and fill up 'fore you hit the road."

"Yes, sir," Jubal said, then continued on across the meadow. He dropped off his saddle and his packsaddle after about forty yards; then, with his coiled picket ropes hanging on his shoulder, led his horses closer to the river before staking them out.

The grassy spot he chose for the tent was almost level, with just enough slope to drain away the water if it should come. The old man had said it would not rain tonight, but Jubal was taking no chances. He had seen storms blow up in a matter of minutes, and an hour later the creeks would be out of their banks. "Only fools and newcomers try to predict Texas weather," Jubal had heard Silas Kane say on many occasions, and he believed that his grandfather knew what he was talking about.

He set up his tent and put his bedroll, packsaddle, and rifle inside, then walked behind a cluster of bushes to relieve himself. A few moments later he spread his felt saddle blanket on the wet grass beside the tent, and sat there till after sunset, thinking about how lucky he had been in having Sheriff Bacon come to his rescue. Finally, just before darkness closed in, he crawled inside the tent and slept the night away.

No rain fell during the night, and Jubal struck the tent at daybreak. He stepped behind the bushes once again, then walked down to the river to wash his face and hands. Seeing that York was just now beginning to kindle his breakfast fire, Jubal led his horses to water, then began to ready them for the road. When he led them across the road a short while later, the lady had already taken over the cooking chores.

He tied his animals to the same bush as the day before, then walked to the fire.

"Good morning," the lady said. "Did you sleep well?"

"Yes, ma'am," he answered. "I was mighty tired, and I guess I went out like somebody had hit me with a hammer."

She poured a cupful of coffee and handed it across the fire. "Reckon this'll wake you up."

Jubal nodded his thanks, accepted the coffee, and took a seat on the far end of the log, well away from the fire. The lady merely raised the volume of her voice, however, and continued to talk: "Pa and Hansel are both off in the woods doing their morning things," she said. "I reckon they oughta be back anytime, though."

Kane nodded again, and sipped at his coffee.

"I'll have some meat for you in a jiffy," she said. "Don't want to get it too done, 'cause the longer you leave it in the skillet, the tougher it gets. That was a tough old doe Hansel shot, anyway, and the onliest reason the meat worked so good in that stew, was 'cause I boiled it for more'n two hours straight."

Jubal dashed his coffee grounds toward the road, then offered the lady a big smile. "Don't worry about me, ma'am," he said. "I'm easy to please, and I've got good teeth. I believe I can chew about anything you can cut with a knife."

A few moments later she brought him a tin plate containing a warmed-over biscuit and a venison steak still sizzling in its own juices. "It may not be quite as bad as I made it sound," she said, puncturing the thick slab of meat with a fork. "See? That fork goes into it just as easy as you please."

"Yes, ma'am," Jubal said. "It's gonna be just fine." He set the plate on the end of the log to cool, and refilled his coffee cup. Then, after slicing the venison into bite-size chunks with his pocketknife, he began to enjoy a tasty breakfast. The lady had refilled his plate and Jubal had emptied it again, before Hansel York and his father-in-law lumbered noisily out of the woods.

"There's a whiskey still right out yonder in them woods!" York said loudly, pointing over his shoulder. "Me and Grandpa ran across a little trail and followed it for a ways just to see where it went. It led straight to that still."

"Don't look like they do none of their cookin' in the daytime," Grandpa said. "Reckon they know the smoke would give 'em away. They've put up a whole lot of tin around the cooker to keep folks from seein' the fire at night, so I reckon they wait till after everybody else is asleep 'fore they get down to business."

Hansel spoke again: "Two vats full of corn and stuff that's already beginning to smell like whiskey, and a big pile of empty jugs to pour it in once they get done running it off." He pointed into the woods and smiled at Jubal. "You want to go look at it, Mr. Kane?"

Jubal was on his feet, shaking his head. "You couldn't hire me to go messing around that still," he said.

"Oh, it's all right," Hansel said. "Ain't nobody over there. We looked all around, and we didn't see a soul."

"Maybe so," Kane said, "but I think it's highly possible that a soul saw you." He dropped his plate and cup into the wooden box that the lady indicated, then continued: "It just seems to me that when a man goes to the expense of putting up a still, buying the corn, the sugar, and everything else that it takes to make a run of whiskey, he's mighty likely to keep an eye on his investment. I'd almost be willing to bet that his camp is no more than three hundred yards from his still."

Hansel York and his father-in-law exchanged glances. "Never thought about it that way," Grandpa said. Hansel shrugged, and reached for a plate.

Jubal thanked the people for their hospitality, then motioned toward the road. "It's time I got moving," he said. "I think my horses are even ready to go."

"We'll be in San Antonio for the rest of the year," Hansel said, "but if you happen to be down Beeville way next spring, look us up. Far as I know, we're the only Yorks in the whole area, so we'd be easy to find."

Jubal nodded and waved good-bye. A short time later, he mounted the gray and led the black up the hill. Once he was out of sight of the Yorks, he pulled to the side of

the road and dismounted. He walked back to the packhorse and took his slicker out of his pack, then tied it
behind his saddle so he could get at it quickly. Judging
from the looks of the sky, the devil would probably beat
his wife again today.

21

★

Kane stayed in the saddle all day, fording both the Frio and the Nueces Rivers during the afternoon. An hour before sunset, he spread his bedroll on the south bank of the Nueces, and picketed his animals a few yards away. Though the fall season was here and much of the grass had cured on the stem, it still held its nutrients, and the horses would eat it when they could find nothing green.

Nonetheless, he had decided to ride through Beeville in the morning and buy a sack of oats. His animals were working hard, and graining them was the only way to keep them in good condition now that the green grass was gone. A nosebag filled with oats twice a day would do the trick, and starting tomorrow, the black would carry a sack of grain on his back every day. With those thoughts, Jubal ate a cold supper, then slept the night away.

*   *   *

Located on Poesta Creek, the settlement had first been named Maryville, in honor of Mary Hefferman, the only survivor of a family massacred by Indians in 1853. The town became the seat of Bee County in 1860, and was renamed Beeville-on-the-Poesta. However, with most of its residents being somewhat lazy of speech, the name was very soon shortened to a single word.

Jubal reached Beeville at ten o'clock in the morning. Coming in from the north, he was just about to ride down the town's main street, when he was almost run over by three men on horseback. Two of them paid no attention whatsoever to him, but the third—a dark-complected man who sat uncommonly tall in the saddle—nodded a greeting as he swerved to miss Kane's packhorse. Riding at a full gallop and continuing to whip their horses, they left the road at the edge of town and headed out across the countryside. Jubal had no problem deciding that they were running from something, for men simply did not push their horses in such a manner except in emergencies. He sat his saddle, watching till they disappeared in the northeast.

A few moments later, a crowd of men came running up the street, one of them sporting a deputy sheriff's badge. "You let 'em get away!" the lawman said loudly, pointing at Jubal with a forefinger. "They just robbed the bank, and you sat right there and watched 'em get away. You never even tried to stop 'em!"

When Jubal said nothing, the deputy, a tall, skinny man with a snaggletooth, spoke again: "Whatcha got to say about that?"

Kane was slow to answer. "I don't know that I need to say anything," he said finally, "but I guess maybe I will. First, I had no way of knowing that they had robbed the bank, and second, I'm not a lawman, and it wasn't my job to stop them." He turned the gray's head toward the

livery stable at the opposite end of the street. "Besides,"
he added, kneeing the animal on, "I didn't have any
money in that bank."

He went down the street at a trot, and did not look
back until he reached the livery. When he dismounted, he
saw that the deputy was hurrying toward the stable, leading ten men—half of them mounted, the others afoot. Jubal moved to the side of the open doorway, then stood
holding his horses.

The panting deputy and his followers arrived a moment later. "We need some horses, Henry," the lawman
said to the hostler. "Get every one of these men mounted
just as quick as you can." The liveryman quickly moved
to comply with the order. The men who needed horses
followed him down the hall to the corral, while the five
who were mounted sat their saddles beside a hitching rail
several yards away.

Then the deputy spoke to Jubal, and pointed to his
mount. "I'll be needing that gray, too," he said. "He looks
like he could cover some country in a hurry."

Kane dropped the horse's reins to the ground.
"Nope," he said, shaking his head emphatically.

"The hell you say!" the lawman bellowed. "I'm
George Fendly, and I'm a Bee County deputy sheriff. The
law says that I can requisition anything I need, any old
time I want to!"

Jubal shook his head again. "You're not gonna requisition the gray, Deputy."

Looking as if he could not believe his ears, the lawman
stared at Kane disdainfully, his eyes eventually coming to
rest on the Colt at Jubal's hip. A large vein popped out
on his scrawny neck. "Refusing to cooperate with a lawful
requisition is a serious offense," he said, "and I intend to
see that the sheriff hears about it. You just make sure you
don't go off nowhere; I'll deal with you when I get back

from this manhunt." He turned and trotted down the hall after the others.

Jubal leaned his back against the wall, his eyes on the mounted men at the rail. Each of them was holding his prancing animal on a tight rein, obviously awaiting orders to move out. They were not only busy talking among themselves, but were too far away to have heard his exchange with the deputy. With his arms crossed against his chest, he stood waiting till he heard the sounds indicating that the posse members in the stable were finally mounting, then he moved a little farther down the side of the building.

A moment later, they came through the doorway at a trot. Joined by the riders waiting at the rail, the deputy led his ten-man posse through town at a hard run. At the north end of the street, they headed cross-country in a northeasterly direction, just as the robbers had done.

Jubal continued to watch. The deputy was still whipping his mount when the posse went out of sight, which reminded Kane that, except for his own steadfast refusal, the animal that was about to be run into the ground would have been his gray.

The hostler was standing in the doorway now. Jubal led his horses up, and nodded a greeting. "I don't know how many chases that deputy's been involved in," he said, "but I sure don't think that's the way to go about it." He pointed the way the posse had gone. "At that rate, they'll all be afoot after a few miles."

"Hell, I know it," the hostler said. He was a short, thick-chested man, with a flat nose, square chin, and a firm mouth. He appeared to be in his late thirties. "George Fendly ain't too bright," he said, "but I've got to put up with his shit in order to get his business. Sometimes, what I get from the county is about all that keeps me going during the slow months." He shook his head several times, then added, "Hope he remembers to stop and let 'em blow once in a while. I've got nearly two hundred dollars tied up in them six horses, and I can't afford the loss."

Jubal took his empty grain bags from his pack, then stated his business. "I'll wait while you feed my horses, then I'll be needing some grain to carry along." He handed over the bags. "Put forty pounds of oats in each one of these so they'll balance out on the packhorse."

The liveryman accepted the reins. "Ain't sure I'm gonna have eighty pounds of oats after I feed these horses, but I'll sure sell you what I've got. Be a penny a pound, however much it is." He looked at Jubal with raised eyebrows in an effort to confirm that the price was agreeable. After receiving a curt nod, he led the horses down the hall toward the stables.

Kane took a seat on an upended crate while he waited. A short time later, the hostler was back with a gunnysack, which he placed on the scales just outside the office door. "Ain't got but sixty-eight pounds of oats," he said. He crooked his finger at Jubal, adding, "I'd appreciate it if you'd come and take a look; I always like for a man to see exactly what he's being charged for."

Kane walked the few steps and read the scale. "That's fine," he said, then returned to his seat.

The hostler laid one of the empty bags on the scale and began to put oats into it with a scoop. "All I gotta do is put thirty-two pounds in this bag," he said, almost as if talking to himself, "then the other one'll have to be right."

Jubal smiled, and said nothing. Though he disagreed with the man's figuring, he thought it was close enough, and doubted that the packhorse would ever notice the difference.

When the hostler disappeared down the hall to attach the grain bags to the black's packsaddle, Jubal walked to the general store a short distance away. A tall man who appeared to be at least seventy years old, got to his feet as Kane entered, and spoke with a surprisingly strong voice. "Come right in and look around, young fellow. If we ain't got it, we can get it."

"I need a stick of cured meat for the road. Have you got smoked sausage?"

The old man chuckled. "Not only have I got it, I've got the best there is. The Germans mix it and cure it up in San Antonio, and there ain't none better." He led the way to the back of the room, where the meat was displayed under a showcase. "The little sticks are a quarter," he said, pointing, "and the big ones are forty-five cents."

Jubal motioned to a small one, because he believed that he would be tired of sausage by the time he ate it. The man sacked it up, then asked, "Anything else?"

"Yes, sir. I'll have a small jar of mustard and a bag of those cookies up there on the counter."

When the old man had sacked up the merchandise, Jubal paid him and left the building. When he reached the livery stable, the hostler was standing in the doorway holding his animals. "I fed and watered 'em good," he said. "The gray's acting nervous as hell, like he's ready to hit the road." He pointed to the grain on the packhorse's back. "Counting them oats there, the charge comes to ninety-eight cents."

After adding his new purchases to his pack, Jubal paid the hostler. Then, having neither asked the man's name nor mentioned his own, he mounted the gray and rode out of town. Brownsville was more than two hundred miles to the south.

22

★

The southernmost town in Texas, Brownsville began when General Zachary Taylor had established Fort Brown. Although its purpose had been only to confirm the Rio Grande as the national boundary after the Republic of Texas became a state, the establishment of the fort was the very incident that had touched off the war between the United States and Mexico. By the time the fighting was over, however, the river had been unquestionably accepted as the boundary between the two countries.

Located in a fertile valley with a near-tropical climate, Brownsville prospered wildly during the next few decades. People from all over America and beyond flocked to the area, many of them with the means to establish ranches or plant large citrus groves.

Jubal rode into Brownsville on a Friday afternoon during the second week of October. As he passed through the center of town he could see that the war was truly over, for clusters of whites and Mexicans mixed readily, standing around hitching rails or leaning against buildings talking with each other.

As in most Texas towns, the livery stable was easy to find. Standing at the edge of town with ample room for traffic to pass on either side, the huge barn and corral were wider than the street itself. The large sign above the hayloft, sporting letters two feet tall, was enough to guide a traveler to the establishment from almost anyplace in town. Jubal soon dismounted in the open doorway.

A muscular young man not yet out of his teens, stepped from the office. "Can I help you sir?" he asked.

Kane nodded. "Have you got room for a couple more horses?"

"Yes, sir," the boy answered quickly. "Got room for a dozen more. This is the biggest livery stable in the lower Rio Grande Valley."

Jubal took a change of clothing out of his pack, then laid his saddlebags across his shoulder and unsheathed his rifle. He pointed to a separate room in the corner. "Will you be locking my packsaddle in there?"

"Yes, sir. Will that be all right?"

Kane nodded. "That'll be fine," he said, then walked up the street.

As usual, he entered the lobby of the hotel closest to the livery stable. "Come right in, sir!" the middle-aged desk clerk said loudly, sounding much like some of the hawkers Jubal had heard at medicine shows. "Welcome to the Bundy Hotel, where a single dollar buys you the best room in south Texas!"

Kane laid his clothing and his saddlebags on the counter, and leaned his rifle against the wall. "How much for a room about half that good?" he asked.

The man sat eyeing him for a moment, grinning sheepishly. "A second-story room is seventy cents," he said finally.

Kane laid the money on the counter, then pointed to the register. "Do I have to sign that thing?"

The clerk shook his head. "Not unless you want to," he said. "Some men sign it; some men don't."

Jubal shoved the key into his vest pocket, then picked up his belongings and climbed the stairs. When he unlocked the room, which was no more than six feet from the top of the stairway, he saw immediately that it contained everything he was likely to need. A washpan and a pitcher of water were set on a middle-sized table, along with a folded towel and washcloth, and a mirror that was larger than a man's head, hung on the wall.

He crossed the room and raised the window, then sat down on the bed and pulled off his boots. That done, he stripped off his clothing and washed his body with the washcloth. He stropped his razor and shaved his face, then dressed in clean jeans and the tan shirt his grandmother had made for him the year he turned eighteen. The fit now was just as good as it had been then.

He combed his hair and brushed the dust from his hat, then headed for the stairway. He would get something to eat first, then begin to make the rounds of the watering holes. He had learned early on that the best sources of information were usually the bartenders. He had also learned that the best and often the only time to talk with them, was during the afternoon, before the evening rush.

When he stepped from the hotel and onto the boardwalk, he could already see two restaurants. He quickly decided on the nearest one, which was directly across the street, but he was in no hurry to get there. He stood leaning against the wall in the shade of the awning for a while, paying close attention to the vehicles and the saddle horses on the street, as well as the foot traffic moving up and down the sidewalk.

Of late, he had been looking over every man he met a little closer than usual, for Rooster Colfax had said that Lively bragged about the lower Rio Grande Valley all the time, and specifically, Brownsville. If he was in this town, it was entirely possible that Kane might come face-to-face with him at any moment. Jubal had even added a sixth shell to the cylinder of his Colt back in the hotel room. A fellow just never knew when he might need some extra firepower.

He finally crossed the street and entered the small restaurant, not bothering to read the name above the door. Once he had seated himself at a table, a homely Mexican waitress was there with a menu. "When you've decided what you want to eat," she said in perfect English, "just let me know." Then she was gone.

He glanced at the bill of fare for only a moment, then raised his hand. The girl was there quickly. He gave her a toothy smile, then said, "I'll have the pork chops and applesauce, pretty lady."

She blushed instantly, and wrote down his order. "You know I'm not pretty," she said.

"Sure you are," he insisted. "Prettiest girl in this town."

She smiled and took the menu from his hand, then cut a wide swath toward the kitchen with her extra-wide hips.

The meal Kane was served was one of the very best he had ever eaten. The pork chops were delicious, the biscuits and the coffee were hot, and there had even been a dish of butter on the table. Then, without asking if he wanted it, the girl returned with a large slice of chocolate cake, and refilled his coffee cup. He accepted it all with a smile, knowing that his compliments had earned him special treatment.

When he had finished his last cup of coffee, he laid a dime under his plate, then paid his way out of the building. He moseyed up and down the street for an hour, then pushed his way through the bat-wing doors of a saloon called Big Don's. Even from the doorway he could see that business was slow, with only a handful of drinkers scattered around the room.

He held his position just inside the door for a few moments. He could see that a tall man who appeared to weigh at least three hundred pounds was standing behind the bar polishing glasses. It was only after Kane closed the distance, that he saw the second man. Of equal size and bearing a strong likeness to the first, he sat on a stool behind the bar doing nothing, though he did have an apron around his waist.

The men were brothers, Kane decided quickly; most likely twins. And one of them, no doubt, was Big Don.

The man on the stool had been reading a newspaper, but put it aside and got to his feet as Jubal approached. "Howdy," he said, a fleeting smile crossing his lips. "What'll you have?"

Kane pulled out a stool. "A beer."

"Yes, sir," the big man said. He drew a mugful of brew and set it at Jubal's elbow, then wiped at a wet spot with a dry cloth. He scooped up Kane's coin and dropped it into a metal box, then returned to his seat. "Just sing out if you need something else," he said, then began to read the newspaper again.

Jubal sat on the stool quietly for the next half hour, and was now sipping his third beer. He had counted six drinkers in the room, and decided that all were loners, for no two of them sat together or carried on a conversation. Five of the men sat at the same number of tables, and the sixth sat on the far side of the bar with the brim of his hat pulled low over his eyes, and his shoulder leaning against a post. He had been in that position ever since Kane entered the building.

"He does that every afternoon," the bartender said, when he noticed Jubal eyeing the sleeping man. "He'll come out of it after a while, then be wide-awake till closing time." He turned a page, then went on with his reading. A short while later, he thumped the paper loudly, and called out to his brother at the opposite end of the bar. "You remember Leroy Lively, don't you, Don?"

Suddenly Kane was all ears.

Don answered with a question of his own: "How could I forget him, John?" he asked. "Took me one whole month to get him to pay a lousy two-dollar bar bill."

John thumped the paper again. "Well, it says here that he killed a gunfighter over in Mission two weeks ago. Shot him right between the eyes in what the constable said was an even draw." He laid the paper down, and got to his feet.

"Maybe Lively is as fast as he claims to be."

Don stood shaking his head. "I never heard Leroy himself say anything about being fast, but I've been told by a few other men that he's mighty quick of hand. I reckon that's one of the reasons people around here always let him get away with so much."

"Maybe so," John said. He pointed to the paper again. "That article says that he owns a saloon over in Roma, and I can't help but wonder how in the hell he managed to get it. You and I both know that he didn't have a pot to piss in four or five months ago."

Don chuckled. "Maybe he met another rich woman," he said. "I think that's his specialty. One fellow told me that he heard Lively bragging about his ability to talk women out of big bundles of money.

"The way I heard it, he fills 'em full of shit till they get to thinking the sun rises and sets on him, then the next thing they know, he's cleaned them out lock, stock, and barrel. With Lively being such a handsome man, I don't

guess it's too hard for him to pull off something like that."
He was quiet for a moment, then added, "Now, I ain't
the one calling him handsome, I was just quoting one of
my waitresses. Handsome and exciting, is the way she described him."

John laughed. "Well, the exciting son of a bitch has
obviously come up with some money from somewhere,
'cause that paper says he's a saloon owner out in Roma
nowadays."

Kane upended his glass, then slid off the stool. "The
beer was good and cold," he said, speaking to both men,
"and I enjoyed it. Three glasses is about my limit, though,
so I'll be on my way." He headed for the front door and
never looked back.

He bought a newspaper at a drugstore, then walked
to his hotel room. Knowing that he would not leave the
room again until after daybreak in the morning, he
stripped off all of his clothing and sat down on the bed.
He began to scan the paper, and very quickly found the
article that the big man had mentioned.

The gunfight had taken place on Main Street in the
town of Mission, on the thirtieth day of September. According to the article, the argument had started in the
Greenbrier Saloon, when a local gunman named Hartsfield had objected to the attention Leroy Lively was paying
to a particular saloon girl. Hartsfield accused Lively of
trying to recruit the dancer for his own saloon in Roma,
and challenged him to a gunfight in the street.

It turned out to be a challenge that had cost Hartsfield
his life, for according to the witnesses, he had been nothing close to a match for the quick-handed Lively. The local
constable, a man named Duvall, stated that he himself had
been inside the saloon when the argument started, and had
heard every word spoken. He had tried to prevent the
bloodshed by talking with both parties, he said, but had

been unable to calm Hartsfield down. Finally, along with several other men, he had stood on the boardwalk in front of the saloon and watched the fight play out in the middle of the street. Only one shot had been fired. Hartsfield had not even cleared his holster when Lively shot him between the eyes. The constable, along with half a dozen others, had proclaimed Lively's action to be self-defense.

Jubal dropped the paper on his chest and lay thinking. The fact that Lively was purported to be fast with a six-gun mattered not at all to him, for he did not intend to give the man a chance to draw the weapon. He was not hunting Leroy Lively merely to test his gunfighting skills, but to kill him. The lady in the barn was completely defenseless when her senseless execution had occurred seven years ago, and her killer would eventually go out in the same manner. Lively would be as helpless as a newborn babe when Tess Kane's son called his number.

Jubal wondered for a moment if the dancer who had been the object of the dispute had left town with Lively, then quickly decided that most likely she had. If not, she had probably headed for Roma shortly thereafter.

The dust motes that only a few minutes ago had been dancing in a shaft of sunlight from the window, were gone now, and twilight had arrived. Jubal pulled the bedside table closer and lit the lamp, for he intended to use the newspaper to read himself to sleep.

He doubled his pillow to prop up his head, then began to scan the paper again. An article on Palmito Hill Battlefield caught his attention right away. He already knew the story from studying Texas history, but enjoyed reading about it again anyway.

The last engagement of the Civil War had been fought at Palmito Ranch. The Confederates, commanded by Colonel John S. Ford—not having heard of General Lee's surrender at Appomattox a month earlier—routed and captured a force of Union soldiers in a running encounter on the twelfth and thirteenth of May, 1865. After the battle, when the Confederates learned from their prisoners that the South had capitulated, the victors quickly became the captives of their former prisoners.

By the time Kane finished reading the full story, his eyelids were heavy. He dropped the newspaper to the floor, then blew out the lamp. He must get a good night's sleep, for the town of Roma was more than a hundred miles to the west.

23

Kane left the livery stable an hour after sunrise next morning, his packhorse carrying eighty pounds of oats on its back. A few more pounds were added to the animal's burden at a nearby grocery store, where Jubal replenished his own food supplies. His final stop was at the same small restaurant where he had eaten breakfast almost two hours ago.

The morning crowd had eaten and gone, and the waiter had already begun to stack chairs on top of the tables. After listening to Kane's request, the lady behind the counter referred him to the cook, who was sitting on a stool nearby, smoking a cigarette. "I was wondering if you have some leftover biscuits that you'd sell," Jubal said.

The fat cook got to his feet and crooked his finger, an invitation for Kane to join him in the kitchen. Once there, the man said, "I always cook more than we need, but I'd rather have too many than not enough." He pointed to a full pan of brown biscuits, now cold. "You can have the whole dozen for a dime."

The biscuits were exceptionally large. "Can I get half of them for a nickel?" Jubal asked.

The cook nodded, then emptied the pan into a paper bag. "You can get all of them for a nickel," he said.

Jubal added the sack of biscuits to his pack. Though he might never eat all of them himself, he knew that his animals would. Horses loved biscuits, and at the price of a nickel a dozen, they were damn sure cheaper than oats.

He rode northwest when he left Brownsville, for the road ran parallel to the Rio Grande. He would travel in the same direction all morning, then the course of both the river and the road would turn due west. Two days from now, he expected to be in Mission, which was roughly the halfway point between Brownsville and Roma.

He would most likely spend a night in Mission, for it was very possible that he might see or hear something that would work to his advantage. He believed that he would hear Leroy Lively's name mentioned without asking a single question, for he knew that people tended to talk about gunfights long after they happened, embellishing the facts with each telling. He smiled at his thoughts; he would not be surprised if next year he heard that six or eight shots had been fired during the Lively-Hartsfield shootout, and that both men had been hit several times. For that reason, he had torn out the newspaper article for future reference.

He halted at a spring an hour after noon, having traveled about fifteen miles. Though it was obvious that the spring was a regular stopover for travelers, no one else was near it at the moment. It was here that both the river and the road turned due west, and, according to his map, would continue in that direction for the next forty miles.

He lightened the packhorse's burden by unloading the grain bags, but did not remove the packsaddle. Nor did he strip the saddle from the gray. He led both animals a little closer to the river, where there were still a few bunches of green grass, and staked them out on their picket ropes.

He raked up handfuls of leaves and dead mesquite twigs easily enough, and soon had a fire going. He dipped his coffeepot into the spring, set it on the fire, and dumped in a handful of grounds. He opened the bag of cookies he had bought at the store that morning, then sat waiting for hot coffee to wash them down with.

He stayed at the spring longer than he had expected to, reluctant to drag his horses away from the only decent graze they had found lately. He led them back to the spring after an hour, however, and reloaded the grain on the packhorse. He had just climbed aboard the gray, when a wagon drawn by a team of black mares rounded the curve from the direction of Brownsville.

The driver halted the team in the shade of the tall mesquites, only a few feet from where Kane sat his saddle. With the wagon having no cover, its load was obvious: two plows, several sacks of grain, and twice as many bales of hay. A boy who appeared to be about ten years old sat on the seat, and Jubal gauged the man holding the reins to be at least seventy. Most likely grandfather and grandson, he was thinking.

The youngster got to his feet and jumped to the ground in one fluid motion. Not so with the old man, who, while holding on to the top board of the wagon with one hand and the seat with the other, stepped to the wheel, then to the hub, then to the ground. He smiled at Jubal, then chuckled, saying, "That damn wagon gets a little higher off the ground every year, son."

Kane nodded. "I remember hearing my grandpa say the same thing," he said. "He finally solved his problem by building himself a little set of steps, with metal hooks on one end. He hauls it everywhere he goes, and when he wants to get down, he just hangs the hooks on the top board of the wagon and drops the other end to the ground." He chuckled, then added, "Nowadays, it looks like he gets off the wagon just as easy as he walks down the doorsteps at home."

The old man stood looking from the wagon to the ground for a moment, as if gauging the distance. "Hell, I could do that," he said, laughing. "Reckon I just never was smart enough to think of it." He mentally measured it again. "Actually, I wouldn't ever have to worry about the steps being too long or too short when I went from one place to another, 'cause it's always gonna be the same distance from the top of the wagon to the ground."

Jubal smiled and chuckled again. "Yes, sir," he said. "That, you can count on." He tightened his packhorse's lead rope, then motioned to the spring. "I don't know that I've ever tasted better water than that," he said. "I guess you already know how good it is, though."

"Yep," the old man said. "Best I ever drank." Seeing that Kane was about to leave, he waved good-bye. "Good luck to you, young fellow, and thank you for telling me about them steps."

Jubal nodded to both the old man and the youngster, then kicked the gray to a trot. A few moments later, he was out of sight.

He traveled for another ten miles or so, then halted at another spring an hour before sunset. He put the nosebags on his horses, then took a seat on the edge of a boulder while he waited for them to eat. He gave them their final drink of water for the day, then led them several hundred yards off the road, where he put them on their picket ropes. Seating himself on the ground beside his pack, he ate a cold supper of German sausage and biscuits, washing it down with water from his canteen.

He stretched out on his bedroll as darkness closed in, but sleep was slow in coming. He lay for a long time trying to imagine how his new home was going to look. That it would be both sturdy and easy on the eyes he had no doubt, for Jesse Harper had the reputation of being a master builder. Jubal was eager to see the finished product, of course, but even more eager for Jenny Hilton to see it. What would she say when she first saw Cedar Ridge? Would her eyes light up when she stood on the porch of her new home and looked down the slope to the Angelina River for the first time? Of course they would, for the view was breathtaking.

And the time when he would have the beautiful Jenny all to himself was not as far off as it used to be. In just a few months she would be sleeping in his bed, and she would be naked. And he would draw her to him and make love. Just thinking of it gave him a warm feeling. How many times could a man do it in one night? He had no idea. Though he had bedded women on several occasions, he had never done it more than once on the same day. Could a man do it five times in one night? Ten times? He certainly intended to find out once he had Jenny Hilton in his bed. He finally went to sleep, and sometime during the night, dreamed that he did it twenty times.

The town of Mission had been established in 1824 by oblate fathers who planted an orange grove, the first of many experiments leading to the citrus culture of the lower Rio Grande Valley Though the area soon became known throughout America and beyond for its subtropical climate, its population remained relatively low due to a shortage of women. Most of the ladies who came to visit refused to linger, and very quickly spread the word that Mission, Texas, was "a thousand miles from nowhere."

Jubal rode into Mission an hour before sunset. With the livery stable being at the east end of town, it was the first building he came to. He sat his saddle, looking around for a while, then halloed the stable, for the door was closed and he had seen no one moving about.

"Sí!" a man answered in a loud voice. A moment later, an aging Mexican walked across the corral, bending at the waist to step between two of the poles. Now able to get a better look at his customer, he switched to English: "Yes, sir," he said. "Can I do something for you?"

Kane had already dismounted. "You got room to put up my horses?" he asked.

"Yes, sir," the man answered quickly. "I just closed that front door 'cause I didn't expect any more business today." He hurried to the door and swung it wide, then took the horses' reins from Jubal's hand. "Ain't got no oats, but I got plenty of shelled corn. Got a whole wagonload in about dinnertime yesterday."

Jubal nodded. "Corn's good stuff," he said. "They both love it." He followed the hostler inside the barn. "Do you know which hotel has the best rooms and rates?" he asked.

"I reckon I do," the man said, appearing to choke back laughter. "That would have to be the Adobe House, 'cause it's the only hotel in town. I never have heard anybody bragging about its rooms or its rates, but I'd say that it probably beats sleeping on the ground." He pointed west. "You can't miss it, it's the only house on that street built out of adobe bricks. Seems like there's a sign in the yard, too."

Kane shouldered his saddlebags, and unsheathed his Winchester. "Thank you," he said. "I'll see you sometime in the morning." Then he was gone up the street.

24

★

Kane dropped off his rifle and his saddlebags in a rented room at the Adobe House, then seated himself on a bar-stool at the Greenbrier Saloon a few minutes after dark. Jubal was the only customer in the building at the moment, and the bartender, a tall, balding, middle-aged man with a copper-colored mustache, was a talker. "I reckon I know about everybody living in these parts," he said, as he delivered the beer Kane ordered, "so I guess maybe you're just passing through."

"You guessed right," Kane said, then lifted the glass to his lips.

When Jubal said no more, the bartender continued: "We had a killing here in this town a coupla weeks back."

"Really?"

"Had a gunfight out there in the middle of the street during broad daylight. The main argument started right here at the bar, though."

"Oh, that," Kane said. "I read about that in the paper over in Brownsville."

"In Brownsville? You read about it all the way over in Brownsville?" He was quiet for a moment, then leaned across the bar, speaking more softly. "Did they say anything about me, Theodore Lucas?"

Jubal pulled the newspaper article from his vest pocket, and handed it to the bartender. "Here," he said. "You can read what they wrote for yourself."

Lucas moved closer to the lamp, and stared at the print for so long that Jubal began to wonder if he even could read. Finally the man bounced a fist off the bar. "This ain't right, dammit!" he said loudly. "This shit ain't nowhere close to right!"

Kane took another sip of his brew. "What's the problem with it?"

The bartender refolded the article and handed it back. "Well, for one thing, it says that Duvall tried to talk 'em into settling their differences without gunplay." He bounced a fist off the bar. "That's a lie, mister. The constable never said a damn word to either one of 'em.

"It was me, Theodore Lucas, who tried to talk some sense into 'em, but did the newspaper say that? Hell, no! Did they even mention my name? Hell, no, it was all 'Constable Duvall did this,' and 'Constable Duvall did that.' The truth is, the constable didn't do a damn thing. He was even too scared to go outside and watch the fight."

Jubal pushed his glass across the bar for a refill. "Is it true that Hartsfield challenged Lively over a woman?"

Lucas laughed aloud. "Challenged him?" He shook his head emphatically. "Joe Hartsfield never challenged anybody in his life—hell, he wasn't no gunfighter. Now, it's true that he did argue some when Lively started messing around with a little yellow-headed girl that Joe was sweet on.

"Lively started that fight himself, mister. He began to egg Joe on when Joe balked at letting the girl go to work in Lively's saloon over in Roma, and Lively ended up inviting him into the street. Like I said before, Joe wasn't no gunfighter, but I guess he was ashamed to back down. After all, he had been challenged right in front of his girlfriend."

"I read that just one shot was fired," Jubal said. "Is that true?"

"Hell, no!" Lucas said loudly. "Joe got off a shot, too. He got his gun out of the holster pretty quick, but he'd already been hit by then. He almost shot himself in the foot as he went down."

The bartender excused himself and walked to the front of the bar to greet two customers who had just entered the building. One of them, a tall, middle-aged man who Jubal decided had the look of a rancher, bought a bottle of whiskey. Then, carrying the bottle and two glasses, he joined his partner, who had already selected a table against the west wall.

Lucas returned and refilled Kane's glass, then jerked his head toward the newly arrived drinkers. "Both of them fellows are money men," he said.

Jubal nodded, and sat sipping his brew. "That Leroy Lively must be a mighty good marksman," he said after a while. "I mean, shooting from the hip and hitting a man between the eyes from forty feet away wouldn't be an easy task, especially when that man was moving around trying to get his own gun into action."

Lucas exploded again. "That's some more of that newspaper's bullshit!" he said, almost shouting. He lowered his voice a little, adding, "Ain't nobody been shot between the eyes. Joe Hartsfield was hit in the chest. High in the chest. Probably blowed the top half of his heart off."

Jubal sat staring across the room at nothing in particular. "Probably," he said. He slid off the stool and pushed his right hand across the bar. "I'm calling it a night, Mr. Lucas. I've had a long day, and I don't expect tomorrow to be any different. Good luck to you."

They shook hands, and Jubal headed for the door.

"Stop in again if you happen to be back this way," Lucas called after him.

He was back in his room at the Adobe House a short time later. And though dozens of cockroaches scurried for cover the moment he lit the lamp, he still believed the room was worth the forty cents that he had paid. He had slept in plenty of places that were worse, and besides, cockroaches did not eat people. He walked to the bed and pulled back the covers, then doffed his clothing and blew out the lamp.

He lay in the darkness with his hands folded across his chest for a long time. In his mind he could still hear the bartender cursing. He believed that Lucas was more upset by the fact that his name had not been mentioned in the newspaper, than by anything else. Nonetheless, Kane would take the man's description of the shootout as gospel, for he knew that newspapers were usually more concerned with headlines than facts. Lucas had been on the scene, so it stood to reason that his account would be more accurate.

Lucas had said that Joe Hartsfield had not been a good gunman. Had Lively known that fact before he challenged Hartsfield? Possibly, Kane was thinking. If not, maybe he was so fast and so confident that he never even stopped to consider an opponent's abilities. Had he convinced himself that he was unbeatable with a six-gun? Maybe. Confidence was a necessity for a gunfighter, but overconfidence was a disease that almost always turned out to be terminal.

The old saying that practice makes perfect, did not pertain to gunfighters, for none ever reached perfect status. A man might practice till he was convinced that he could outdraw his own shadow, but there would always be a man down the road with a quicker hand. And a better eye.

With those thoughts, Kane turned onto his side and went to asleep.

He was on the street at daybreak next morning, and was surprised to find a restaurant open. He ate a breakfast of pancakes, ham, and eggs, then headed for the livery stable. He rode out of Mission half an hour later, expecting to make it to Fort Ringgold long before nightfall. There was a settlement close to the fort called Rio Grande City, but Jubal did not intend to visit either the town or the fort. He was hungry for a pot of ham and lima beans, and knew that he could travel the thirty miles and still have time to cook them on his campfire before dark.

The road ran west-by-northwest now, and Kane held his horses to a fast walk all morning. Though he was traveling parallel to the river, thickets two or three miles wide sometimes separated the road from the water. He was paying close attention to the groves of mesquite that could be seen in any direction, and once even left the road for a closer inspection of a particular tree in order to verify that it was indeed a mesquite.

Mesquite trees simply did not grow this tall, he was thinking, as he sat his saddle looking upward. At least sixty, and maybe even seventy feet. He shook his head. Nope, mesquites did not grow this tall or this straight. Nonetheless, here they were. Thousands of them.

He watered his horses at a spring sometime around noon. Knowing that he would make an early camp this afternoon and feed each of the animals a hefty portion of grain, he did not put them on their picket ropes. He ate a few bites of German sausage and climbed back into the saddle.

A mile out of Rio Grande City, the road veered to the south, and very soon Jubal could see the river from his saddle. He rode to the water's edge, then up the riverbank for several hundred yards. He chose a campsite that was shielded from the road by a thicket of leafy bushes and undergrowth, then unburdened his animals and led them to water. He tied them to a limb and put on their nose-bags, then began to gather up fuel for his campfire.

After raking aside several handfuls of ashes left over from other campers' fires, he kindled his own between two smooth rocks that someone had placed side by side for that purpose. A few minutes later, he set his pot of ham and beans on the rocks above the flame. He would wait till the beans were almost done before putting his coffee on.

His bedroll was still rolled up tight, and he had no intention of spreading it anywhere near the fire. He knew that he was in potentially dangerous country, for thieves and cutthroats of every description roamed both sides of the Rio Grande. With the Mexican border only a short distance away, crime of every nature was rampant. Horse thieves abounded all over south Texas, for just across the river, where a Texas brand meant nothing whatsoever, there was always a buyer waiting with ready cash. South Texas law officials, and even the United States Army, advised travelers to be ever aware of their surroundings, and to keep their horses on short ropes. Jubal would not only keep his animals on short ropes, he would spread his bedroll almost under their feet.

He laid another dead mesquite limb on the fire, then walked into the thicket. A cottontail jumped out of a brushpile and hopped a few yards, then stopped and sat twitching its nose. Kane watched the animal for a moment, then smiled. "Not tonight," he said to himself. "I've got a pot of beans and smoked ham on the fire." He walked on, and the lucky rabbit hopped off in the opposite direction.

Jubal walked around in the thicket till he decided exactly where he would tie his horses for the night, and smoothed out a place about ten feet away for his bedroll. Then he returned to the campsite and added a few handfuls of grain to the nosebags. There would be no grazing tonight, for the only grass available could easily be seen from the opposite side of the river. The horses would be fine, however, for he had fed them well. Shortly after dark he would water them again, then lead them one at a time to their hiding place.

The sun was still half an hour high when he began to eat his beans and sip his coffee. Lima beans and ham had been his favorite food for as long as he could remember, and for a traveling man who had the time, there were few things that were easier to fix. A metal boiler was the only equipment needed, and he doubted that the finest restaurant in the land could prepare the same meal any better than he could over an open campfire. Along with hard biscuits and cheese, he ate every bean in the pot, then drank the soup.

Just before dark he washed his pot in the river, then carried his saddle, his packsaddle, and his bedroll into the thicket. He watered his horses and, when it was dark enough that he could not be seen from the south bank of the river, led them into the thicket and tied them to a bush a few feet from his bedroll.

He stretched out for the night a few moments later, but did not go to sleep right away. The mosquitoes had already found him. He supposed that his being so close to his animals added to the problem, but there was no help for it—he must guard his horses. He could easily imagine what kind of price a thief might ask for the gray, for even in Mexico such an animal would not come cheap.

He lay slapping at the mosquitoes and listening to the horses stomp their feet for a long time, then suddenly he was asleep. He slept well, and the only sounds he heard during the night were those made by his animals.

25

★

The town of Roma was founded in 1765 as part of the Jose de Escandon colony, around a mission that had been established a few years earlier. Located on the north bank of the Rio Grande, the town quickly became an important shipping point, and prospered accordingly.

Jubal Kane rode into Roma a few minutes past noon, and very quickly decided to leave only his packhorse at the livery stable. He would need the gray for transportation, for the layout of the town made a horse necessary. Although it was narrow, it was long, with one commercial establishment after another built on lots as close to the river as their proprietors dared.

Even while sitting in the road beside the livery stable, which was located on the east side, Jubal could see that it would be possible for a man to walk several miles without ever leaving town. He sat studying the layout a while longer, then guided the gray off of the road and to the front door of the stable. The liveryman, who had waved a greeting when he first saw Jubal in the road, threw his hand up again. "Get down and rest yourself, young fellow," he said, chuckling. "Maybe if we talk a little, we can talk up some business." He was a fat man, and his midriff shook like a bowl of jelly when he laughed.

Jubal dismounted. "It won't take much talking on my part," he said, handing over the packhorse's lead rope. "I want to leave the black with you, but I think I'll keep the gray with me for now. I don't believe I'm in the mood to walk all over this town."

The hostler pointed up the street. "It's scattered out for half a mile in that direction. Nobody builds nothing to the north; they all want to be by the river. A damn flood don't teach 'em nothing when it washes 'em away; they just build right back." He pointed north. "I bought fifty acres on that side of town, thinking I might make a little money off of it, but I probably couldn't sell it right now for what I paid for it ten years ago." He laughed again. "Would you like to buy it?"

Jubal chuckled, and shook his head. "I'll buy a feed of oats for the black, and another one later on for the gray."

"You got a deal," the man said, beginning to unbuckle the packsaddle. "You want anything out of your pack before I lock it up?"

Jubal nodded, then dug a change of clean clothing and a pair of socks out of the pack. "I think this is all," he said. "Lock it up." He re-mounted the gray, then pointed up the street. "Any particular hotel or restaurant that you'd recommend?"

The big man nodded. "The Dubarry is the best place for everything," he said. "Hotel, restaurant, and saloon, all in the same building. Two blocks up the street on the right-hand corner."

Jubal nodded, and pointed the gray up the street. Paying most of his attention to the establishments on the right-hand side of the street, he deliberately rode on by the Dubarry, for he intended to look the entire town over before renting a hotel room. By the time he had ridden to what was obviously the west end of town, he had begun to wonder why he had not seen more people. He had traveled well over half a mile, but had met only one wagon and two men on horseback.

As he rode back down the opposite side of the street, he was thinking that maybe he had come into town at the wrong time of day. Maybe the town did not come alive until after sundown.

By the time he was halfway down the street, the puzzle had solved itself. Within a matter of minutes, people began to move about on the boardwalks, more than a few of them women. Suddenly Kane understood. The siesta. He had arrived during siesta, the midday period when most Mexicans did little or nothing. And although he was not in Mexico, the population of the area was largely of Mexican descent. He supposed that the first Texans to arrive had readily taken to the idea of a noonday nap, and had simply continued the Mexican tradition. That had to be the answer, he decided after a while, for the boardwalks on both sides of the street were getting more crowded by the minute.

He continued riding east, and soon found himself back at the livery stable. The big barn door was now closed, and Jubal supposed that the hostler might be taking his own siesta.

Kane had ridden the length of the street in both directions. Now he decided to circle the town. He rode north for a short distance, then turned west across the liveryman's fifty acres. The man had stated the situation correctly: There was not a building of any kind north of the main street; just alleyways piled with junk and garbage.

As he rode across the property that the hostler had pointed out as his own, Kane could easily see why the man had expected to sell it at a profit. The elevation was a good ten feet above that of the town, and probably more than twenty feet above the river. If and when the town was wiped out by a flood, the liveryman's acreage would still be sitting high and dry. That fact alone should have been enough to make some of the merchants consider the land, Jubal was thinking, but obviously it had not happened.

Trying to predict the future values of real estate would be a chancy operation at best, Kane was thinking, and a feast-or-famine occupation for those who did it for a living. Jubal himself wanted no part of the real-estate business, for he had long since given up on trying to guess what people might or might not do. He jumped the gray across a narrow ditch that someone had filled with rocks to slow further erosion, then continued to ride west.

By the time he reached the west side of town for the second time, it seemed that every dog in the area was barking at him, and a few people were beginning to poke their heads through windows or doorways. He crossed the street and rode down to the river.

As he turned back east and rode along the north bank of the Rio Grande, he decided immediately that he had found the place where the poor people lived. The area had both the look and the smell of poverty, and the dilapidated shanties closer to the water were all crudely built and badly in need of repair.

Junk of every description, including several rusty wagons that Father Time had reclaimed, was strewn along the riverbank and in some of the yards. But although most of the people he saw were shabbily dressed, they did not appear to be underfed. In fact, even from his saddle Kane could see one person who was going to eat well tonight: a Mexican boy of about twelve was headed toward one of the huts, carrying a long string of catfish, several of which appeared to weigh as much as three pounds.

Half an hour later, he tied the gray at the Dubarry Hotel's hitching rail. He had looked at the town from the middle and both sides, and decided that he had seen as much as he needed to. He had mentally counted the saloons, restaurants, and hotels that he had ridden past. Some of the names he remembered, some he did not. No doubt he had passed the saloon owned by his quarry. The fact that he had seen nothing to indicate that, meant little, for speculators almost always hung on to the original name when they bought an established business.

Jubal stepped into the hotel lobby, and for the first time in his life at a hotel counter, was greeted by a woman. "Good afternoon," she said warmly. "May I help you?" Though silver-haired and well past middle age, she was nonetheless attractive.

"Yes, ma'am," Jubal answered, reaching for his poke. "I'll be needing a room for at least one night. I'll probably know more by tomorrow about how long I'll be in town."

She nodded. "The room will be a dollar a night, but I'll give you a coupon good for a twenty-percent discount on each meal you eat in the restaurant."

Kane laid a dollar on the counter and smiled. "I'll accept the coupon," he said. "I'm as hungry as a she-bear right now."

She took the money and handed him the coupon, then pushed the register across the counter. "Just sign your name, please."

Kane wrote Jubal Dunlap's name in the book, then pushed it back.

The lady glanced at the signature, then handed him a key. "Thank you for stopping at the Dubarry, Mr. Dunlap. We're home-owned and-operated, and we'll do whatever it takes to make your stay a pleasant one. Now, if you need something—I mean, anything at all—I'm the one you should talk to about it."

Kane shoved the key in his pocket and climbed the stairs two at a time. He unlocked the room, then immediately raised both windows, for the air was stale. He sat on the bed for a few moments, thinking. "Anything at all," the desk lady had said. Hadn't she been telling him in so many words that if he wanted a woman in his bed all he had to do was speak up? He believed that to be the case, but he was not interested. He would wait for Jenny Hilton.

He shaved, bathed, and changed his clothing, then headed downstairs to eat, locking his rifle and his saddlebags in the room as usual. He was greeted just inside the restaurant doorway by a young Mexican girl who, if she had caught him in one of his weaker moments, might have been able to make him forget about saving himself for Jenny Hilton.

She had what might have been the most beautiful face he had ever seen, and the loose-fitting blouse she wore did little to conceal her round, upturned bosom. Her long eyelashes fluttered above dancing dark eyes as she spoke softly: "Good afternoon, sir." Then, without waiting for him to speak, she led the way to a table.

When he had seated himself, she laid down the bill of fare. "The stuffed bell peppers are good."

Jubal ignored the menu. "I believe you," he said. "Bring me some."

She smiled flirtatiously, then headed for the kitchen.

He did not see the girl anymore after she brought his food. Although he had no intention of trying to get to know her, she was a real pleasure to look at. Even as he ate his meal he would raise his head now and then, hoping to get another glimpse of her. After finally deciding that he had probably been her last customer of the day, and that she was now long gone, he concentrated on finishing off the well-prepared meal.

He left a dime on the table, then presented his coupon at the counter. The lady discounted the price of his food, then handed the coupon back. "Hang on to this," she said. "You can use it in here just like money, if you get the hotel clerk to update it every morning."

"Thank you, ma'am," he said, then headed for the doorway.

He mounted the gray at the hitching rail, then headed for the livery stable. He doubted that he would need the animal anymore this day, for he had seen the town of Roma in its entirety. Besides, watering holes were the only places a man could expect to find such information as he was seeking, and he had already noticed two saloons between the hotel and the stable.

He turned his saddler over to the liveryman, then walked leisurely back up the street. When he came to the Hobnob Saloon, he stood looking over the tops of the batwing doors for a few moments, then shouldered his way in.

The establishment was larger than most, with a bar along the west wall that ran half the length of the building. Even from the front door Kane could see a piano resting on a riser at the end of a small stage. A long-necked banjo lay on top of the instrument, and there was a small dance floor nearby. A staircase led to an upper floor, where a man could no doubt find female company for a price.

The Hobnob obviously did not sell food, for Kane could see no kitchen or dining area. Except for the dozen or so stools that lined the bar, the entire room was devoted to tables and chairs, with narrow aisles separating them. The fact that the saloon had been set up to attract drinkers rather than diners, did not surprise Kane at all. He recalled a prosperous saloon owner telling him once that he could make twice as much money selling whiskey as he could selling food. "Besides," the man had added, "food spoils; whiskey don't."

As his eyes became adjusted to the dim lighting, Jubal could see that a few drinkers were scattered around the room, and a waitress was moving about on the floor. The man serving the drinks stood at least as tall as Jubal himself, and appeared to be about thirty pounds heavier. Two men who were seated side by side at the bar were laughing loudly at the moment.

Kane stepped to the bar and seated himself a few stools away. He nodded to the bartender. "A beer," he said.

The beer was served quickly, then the man pushed his right hand across the bar. "I'm Dan Wiser," he said. "I don't recall seeing you around before."

"Dunlap," Kane said, gripping the hand firmly. "Jubal Dunlap."

Wiser reached behind him for a towel to wipe up the few drops of beer he had spilled. "Like I say, I don't recall seeing you before," he said. "If I had, I reckon I'd remember it, 'cause you're a whole lot better looking than most of the rogues who pass through this godforsaken place."

Jubal took a sip of his beer, then spoke to the man again. "Have you been living here for a good while?" he asked.

"Little over three years. I came here from Houston in the summer of 'seventy-two. Married a local girl and got two kids already, so I reckon I'm here to stay."

"Sounds like it," Kane agreed. He stared into his beer for a moment, then said, "You're right about this being my first time in Roma. I thought I was in a ghost town when I first got here today. Rode from one end of town to the other, and saw only three people."

"Did you get here around noon?"

Kane nodded.

Wiser chuckled. "People in this town don't do anything during the noon hour," he said. "The siesta is an old Mexican tradition, and it's a habit that's mighty easy to get into. Hell, I liked the idea right off when I got here, and before long I was taking a nap at noon like everybody else." He pointed to the front door. "I've locked this place up plenty of times, and stretched out right here on the bar."

Several customers came and went during the next hour, and Jubal was now on his third beer. The bartender had just mixed a trayful of drinks ordered by the waitress, then he returned to his stool across the bar from Kane.

"I saw so many saloons today that I lost count," Jubal said. "How many are there in this town?"

"I never counted them," Wiser said. "Must be at least twenty. I reckon I've worked in about half of them at one time or another. Been here at the Hobnob for a little over a year, though."

Kane took a swallow of his beer. "Who owns this place, Dan?" he asked.

"Oh, it's changed hands pretty often since I came to town," Wiser answered, "and it's had two different owners since I've been working here. I reckon the fellow who owns it now is the least likable of the bunch, though. He don't come in here but once a week, but when he does, he walks through the front door bitching and complaining about everything in sight.

"Seems like he's always trying to see how loud he can talk; orders all the women around like they were dogs. I just try to stay out of his way and let what he says go in one ear and out the other. When I want to talk about something, I take it up with Bob Penton. He's Lively's business manager."

Knowing that he had finally found his man, Kane bristled, but held his anger inside. "You say the owner's name is Lively?" he asked.

Wiser nodded. "Leroy Lively," he answered. "He bought the saloon back in May, I think it was."

Jubal finished off his beer in short order, then slid off his stool, extending his right hand across the bar. "I've enjoyed talking with you, Dan," he said. "You take care now, and don't let Leroy Lively get to you."

"I won't," Wiser said, pumping Kane's hand. "Like I said, I don't pay him no damn mind." He released the hand. "I guess when you get right down to it, I am dreading tomorrow a little bit, though. Tomorrow's Wednesday, and Wednesday afternoon is always when Lively comes in here raising hell."

Kane headed for the front door. He had not expected it to be so easy. For the most part he had been given the answers without having to ask the questions, and he had not only learned where his man would be, but exactly when he would be there. He pushed the bat-wings aside with his elbows, then stepped out onto the boardwalk.

He made a quick glance toward the livery stable, then decided just as quickly that it was too late for what he had in mind. The county courthouse would already be closed for the day. It had suddenly occurred to him that maybe he should have a talk with the county sheriff. Was it possible that Starr County's top lawman might be as sensitive to Kane's quest as Sheriff Bacon had been? Yes, Jubal was thinking, and he would probably not be hard to find.

First, Kane would have to find out the sheriff's name, a question that could no doubt be answered by anybody in town. Even as the thought crossed his mind, he noticed two old men sitting on a bench in front of a hardware store, talking. He was there quickly. "Pardon me, sir," he said, addressing the man closest to him. "I'm new in town, and think I might have some business with the sheriff of this county. Can you tell me his name, and where I might find him?"

"Reckon I can," the old-timer answered. "His name is John Legget, and he don't never make no secret about where he can be found. He's at the courthouse in the day-time, and he goes home at night. Of course, with you not even knowing his name, I don't reckon you tried his house, huh?"

"No, sir."

The man pointed west. "Well, you just go right on up this street, the same way I saw you riding earlier today. Once you pass the courthouse, you'll be out of town. You go about another quarter mile, and Sheriff Legget lives there on the right-hand side of the road. It's a log house, but it's been painted white."

Jubal cocked an eye toward the sun. "It won't be dark for at least two hours yet," he said. "Do you think he might be at home right now?"

The man nodded. "Don't see why not," he said. "Reckon he's usually there by this time of day."

"Thank you," Jubal said, then headed for the livery stable almost at a trot.

When told that Kane was in a hurry, the hostler roped the gray and cinched down the saddle in what might have been record time. "If it happens to be late when you get done with this horse," he was saying, "I'd appreciate it if you don't wake me up." He pointed to the corner where the corral joined the barn. "Just drop the little end of them poles to the ground, then turn him loose in the corral. Leave your saddle and bridle under that shed there. I'll get 'em in the morning."

26

★

Kane took the reins and mounted, then headed up the street at a fast trot. The old men on the bench waved as he passed. He resisted the urge to push his mount to a canter, for although he doubted that many towns had rules against it, most citizens frowned on the idea of running horses in congested areas. He continued at a trot till he passed the courthouse, then kicked the gray to a faster pace.

A short time later, he rounded a curve and saw the white house about two hundred yards across the treeless plain. A barn and corral were located behind and slightly west of it, along with several smaller buildings. When he turned into the lawman's private drive, Kane was not surprised to find that it was in much better shape than the main road. One of the advantages of being sheriff of the county, he was thinking.

While still some distance from the house, he noticed that someone was sitting on the porch. Hoping it was Legget himself, he kneed the gray to a trot. By the time Kane reached the hitching rail at the edge of the yard, the man had gotten to his feet. He now stood at the end of the porch, leaning against a post. "Howdy," he said in a deep voice, then stood quietly, obviously waiting for Kane to state his business.

Observing Western protocol that a man did not dismount until he was invited to, Kane spoke from his saddle: "My name is Jubal Kane, Sheriff, and I was hoping I could talk with you for a few minutes."

John Legget was short, though solidly built. With a dark complexion and a shock of graying hair, he appeared to be a few years past the age of forty. He nodded, and pointed to a cane-bottom chair beside his own. "Of course you can talk with me," he said. "Just tie up, then come on up here and have a seat."

Jubal met the lawman at the top of the steps, his right hand extended. Once the handshaking was done, he accepted the chair he had been offered. Then he unfolded the newspaper clipping describing the murders of his parents, handing it to the lawman. "I'd like for you to read this first," he said. "Then I'll tell you why I'm in this town."

Legget squinted a few times, first moving the print closer to his eyes, then farther away. Finally, he held the article at arm's length and began to read. When he had finished, he refolded it and handed it back. "Seems like I either heard or read something about that back when it happened," he said, then leaned back in his chair.

Sensing that it was time, Jubal began his story: "Bernard and Tess Kane were my parents, Sheriff Legget. I was fifteen years old at the time they died, and I witnessed the murders."

The lawman was a good listener, and interrupted Jubal only a few times during the lengthy narration. He seemed particularly impressed by the fact that Sheriff Randy Bacon had interceded on Jubal's behalf. "I don't mind telling you that Randy Bacon stands about ten feet tall in my eyes," he said. "He's a man who don't shoot no shit, and he don't tolerate none. If Bacon thinks you're on the right track, I reckon by God you must be.

"I don't know the warden at the state pen personally, but I've been told that he's an upright fellow, too." He paused for a moment, then added, "Sounds like you've had two good men helping you out already, but I sure don't know of anything I can do. We're almost at the end of the world, down here."

Jubal spoke quickly: "The man who murdered my ma is right here in this town, Sheriff."

The lawman was on his feet. "Here?" he asked loudly. "Here in Roma?"

Kane nodded. "He's here. I already knew what he looked like, then I learned his name at the state prison, when Warden Brady let me look at pictures of past and present convicts."

"There . . . there ain't no way you could be mistaken, huh?"

Jubal shook his head. "No way," he said. "I remember his face just as clearly as I remember my name. It's taken a long time and a lot of hard work, but I've trailed him to Roma. He's here, all right."

"Well, I'll be damned!" Legget said, getting to his feet. He stepped to the edge of the porch and stood staring at the main road for a few seconds, then turned around and spoke loudly: "Are you gonna tell me that damn woman-killer's name?" he asked.

Jubal got to his feet. "His name is Leroy Lively," he said.

"Leroy Lively," the sheriff repeated. "Leroy Lively," he said again. "I knew that shifty-eyed son of a bitch was no good the first time I ever laid eyes on him. His reputation for talking rich widows out of their money got here long before he did, but there ain't a thing in the world the law can do about it. All them women are old enough to do whatever the hell they take a notion to.

"I'm not so sure about the young ones who work down there in his saloon, though. Some of them girls don't even look to be out of their early teens yet, but there ain't a damn thing I can do about that, either. They all claim to be eighteen years old, and where in the hell am I gonna find any proof that they ain't?"

Jubal had not spoken while the lawman was talking. Nor did he speak now. The sheriff coughed a few times, then continued. "After listening to your story, I have no doubt that you've found your man, Mr. Kane. What's next?"

Jubal was slow to answer. "Before my ma's body even got cold, I made her a promise that I'd bring her killer to account," he said finally. He looked the lawman squarely in the eye. "I intend to keep that promise, Sheriff."

Legget nodded. "Of course you do," he said. "What I haven't exactly figured out yet, is why you came down here to tell me about it."

Kane stood thoughtful for a moment, then said, "I just wanted you to hear the true story, Sheriff, and I'm hoping you'll lay off me after I deal with Lively."

Legget spoke quickly and loudly. "Lay off you? You bet I'll lay off you! I don't give a rat's ass what you do to Leroy Lively. You'll be doing me and everybody else a favor if you rid this town of that son of a bitch. Don't worry about hiring somebody to put him in the ground, either. If he ain't got enough money in his pocket to pay for a funeral, we'll drop his sorry ass in a hole up on Pissant Hill."

Jubal made a move toward the steps. "Do you think the town marshal will leave me alone, too?" he asked.

"Hell, yes, he will. The town marshal ain't gonna do a damn thing to you, son; you just leave him to me. Besides, he don't like Leroy Lively much better'n you do."

Kane stepped into the yard, and untied the gray. "Thank you, Sheriff," he said. "It was a pleasure meeting you." He threw a leg over the saddle. "I'll try to take care of my business tomorrow afternoon, then get on out of your town." He pointed his saddler toward the main road, then kicked the animal in the ribs. He was quickly out of sight.

He returned to the livery stable just as the hostler was closing the front door. "Looks like I got back just in time," he said, then dismounted and loosened the cinch. "You've got the gray for the night, this time."

When darkness closed in twenty minutes later, Kane was back in his hotel room. He locked the door and lit the lamp, then drew the shade on the window. And though he had no intention of leaving the hotel again this night, he did not undress right away. Instead, he stood in the middle of the room, practicing his fast draw for almost an hour.

His actions were little more than a blur, as he jerked the big Peacemaker out of its holster and brought it up to an imaginary target. Finally he unloaded the weapon and laid the shells on his pillow. For the next half hour, he stood beside the bed quick-drawing and dry-firing, with each click of the hammer falling on an empty chamber representing a round fired.

The quickness was still there; an awe-inspiring degree of quickness. Jubal had become so proficient with a six-gun during his late teens, that he feared no man alive.

Now, at age twenty-two, he was just as confident, and his hand was even quicker.

Finally, he reloaded the Colt, adding a sixth shell to its cylinder, then laid his gunbelt on the bedside table. He undressed and blew out the lamp, then lay on the bed, staring into the darkness, his mind on his quarry. He had long intended to dispatch Leroy Lively in much the same manner as he had Calvin Mitchell, by first disarming him and rendering him helpless, just as Tess Kane had been; then, after allowing him to ponder his predicament for a few moments, executing him.

The circumstances with Lively were not the same as they had been with Mitchell, however, so the situation must be handled differently. Jubal had decided to meet the man face-to-face in his own saloon and shoot him dead. Before the showdown came, however, he intended to make sure every single one of Lively's customers knew that Lively was a conscienceless woman-killer. And he had already figured out exactly how he was going to do it. He fluffed up his pillow, turned on his side, and was quickly asleep.

The next time he opened his eyes he saw sunlight shining around the edges of the window shade and, after looking at his watch, knew that he had slept a full hour longer than usual. He threw his legs over the side of the bed and sat yawning and stretching for a while, thankful for a long night of such restful sleep.

He dressed and washed the sleep from his eyes, then headed downstairs to the restaurant. The same beautiful little Mexican girl met him at the door. Once she had led him to a table and taken his order, just as had been the case the day before, he never saw her again. His breakfast was delivered by a skinny, long-legged waiter.

He wasted no time looking around for the girl this morning, however. She no doubt had been told how beautiful she was all of her life, and was probably spoiled rotten because of it. When he finished his breakfast he left a dime on the table for the ugly waiter, then walked to the counter. He paid full price for his meal because he had failed to have his discount coupon updated, then stepped out onto the boardwalk.

He walked east for two blocks, noting as he passed the Hobnob that it was not yet open, and crossed the street just before he reached the livery stable. Then he strolled back up the opposite side, coming to a halt when he reached the second corner. He leaned his shoulders against the wall of a drugstore and stood looking toward the Bank of Texas, located on the corner across the intersection.

Even as Jubal watched, a one-horse buggy rounded the corner, with a black, blaze-faced mare between the shafts. The vehicle pulled up to the bank's hitching rail, and a tall man jumped to the ground and tied the animal. He then retrieved a small satchel from the seat and disappeared inside the building.

Kane bristled, then stood seething, for he had instantly recognized the man as Leroy Lively. And except for the fact that he was now expensively dressed, the man's appearance had changed little since the day of the murders. Nor had Kane's presence on the opposite corner of the street aroused his curiosity, for he had merely given Jubal a quick glance, then gone on about his business.

Kane walked to the hotel at a fast clip, then trotted up the stairs to his room without even touching the handrail. A few minutes later, he was back on the street with his Winchester under his arm and his saddlebags across his shoulder. He was at the livery stable in less than five minutes, and spoke to the fat hostler. "I know it seems like I'm always in a hurry," he said. "But I need my horses as quick as you can make it."

The man nodded, and took a coiled rope and two bridles from the wall. He headed down the hall toward the corral, speaking over his shoulder. "I fed and watered 'em about three hours ago," he said. "They're probably about as ready to hit the road as you are."

Jubal dismounted in front of the Hobnob Saloon a few minutes later. He tied his animals to one of the three hitching rails, surprised that several other saddlers were there so early in the day. He supposed that maybe their riders had drunk heavily last night, and were back this morning trying to ease their aching heads.

After looking at his watch and seeing that it was half past ten, he parted the doors and stepped inside. He lingered at the front of the building till his eyes adjusted, then moved on to the bar.

There were four customers in the establishment at the moment, all of them seated side by side at the bar. Seeing that there was a girl on the floor with little to do, Jubal pointed to a particular table, and spoke to the bartender. "I'm gonna be sitting right over there, Dan. Would you have the girl bring me a pitcher of beer and a glass?" He laid a dime on the bar and headed for the table.

He had barely taken his seat when the young girl arrived with his beer. He laid a dime in her hand, which she dropped into the pocket of her apron. Though she appeared to be no more than fifteen years old, she was nonetheless a pretty thing, with coal-black hair and sky-blue eyes. She stood about five-foot-two and weighed in the neighborhood of a hundred pounds, and her well-developed bosom looked as if it might snap the buttons off her blouse. "Thank you, sir," she said. "If there's anything else I can do for you, please let me know."

Kane fished a dollar out of his pocket and laid it in her hand. "Come to think of it, there is something you can do for me, little girl." He got to his feet and pulled out a chair for her. "Just have a seat, and let's talk a minute."

She looked the coin over, turning it from one side to the other. "A dollar?" she asked, seating herself in the chair. "Just for talking?"

"Well, yes," he said. "That's all I want you to do: just talk." He sat thoughtful for a moment, then asked, "Do you know how to read, miss?"

"Of course," she answered. "I read very well, and my name is Katie."

"All right, Katie," he said. "My name is Jubal, and I've got something I need you to help me with." He handed her the seven-year-old newspaper clipping. "Whenever I give you the word, all I want you to do is stand over there beside the bar and read this loudly and clearly. Make sure everybody in the building hears it. Can you handle that?"

She smiled broadly. "You bet. And I get paid a dollar just for doing that?"

"No," Jubal said, laying another coin in her hand. "You get two dollars. Just put the clipping in your pocket, and don't mention it to anybody till I tell you to read it to everybody." He was quiet for a moment, then added, "I guess you'd better get up and go on about your business now, the big boss is liable to come in and catch you sitting at my table."

She rose from the chair. "He don't care," she said. "He don't care what I do as long as I give him all the money."

Jubal shook his head emphatically. "Don't give it to him, Katie."

Though Kane had drunk less than half a glass of beer, he was still sitting at the table with his pitcher, when Leroy Lively arrived. He had changed clothes since Jubal had seen him at the bank. He now wore a brown broadcloth suit and a tan felt hat, and though Kane could not see them from where he was sitting, he had no doubt that the man was standing in a pair of very expensive boots. Lively stood at the door for a few moments, then made a beeline for his office.

Jubal was on his feet now. With his glass in one hand and the pitcher in the other, he walked to the bar. "I just don't feel very thirsty today," he said, when the bartender seemed to take note of the fact that the pitcher was still almost full. Kane filled his glass again so he would appear to have a reason for standing at the bar, then motioned for Wiser to pour the remainder down the drain. "It's done got hot, anyway," he said.

A few minutes later, now coatless, hatless, and with a Colt revolver hanging low on his right leg, Lively walked from the office. Without a word to anyone, he moved behind the bar and began to count the money in the cashbox. He stuffed some of it into his pocket, then stepped out into the aisle, less than thirty feet from where Kane stood.

Now was the time, Jubal decided quickly. He banged his fist against the bar for attention. "Listen up, everbody!" he shouted. "Listen up! Katie's gonna read us a clipping from a newspaper printed on August eighth, eighteen sixty-eight." He motioned for the girl to start reading, then made eye contact with Lively. "Listen up now," he said. "This concerns you."

The room had grown eerily quiet, and all eyes were on the girl as she began to read. She spoke slowly and clearly, so that no man present could misunderstand her words.

Though Lively's eyes were on the girl, Jubal's eyes were on Lively, noting that the man's facial expression had suddenly turned to granite. With his feet spread apart and his body leaning slightly forward, Kane continued to watch the man so closely that he could have counted the batting of his eyelashes.

When the girl finished reading, Lively turned toward Kane with a smirk. "What makes you think all that concerns me, fellow?"

Jubal was leaning forward even more now. "It concerns you because you're the son of a bitch who murdered my ma, Lively! I lay in that loft watching while you, Calvin Mitchell, and a beaky-nosed bastard whose name I don't know, killed both of my parents." He was in a crouch now. "Who was that third man, Lively?"

There was an indistinguishable blur, then Kane's right fist appeared to be spitting flame. He had moved at the crucial moment, for Lively's answer to the question had been to go for his gun. And though Lively's draw had been anything but slow, he took a shot in the mouth just as he cleared his holster. Jubal shot him a second time as he was falling, then walked over and toed his body with a boot to make sure he was dead.

None of the men at the bar had moved or spoken, and the young waitress stood leaning against a post with her mouth open. Kane stood in the aisle looking at her for a moment. "Thank you, Katie," he said. Then he shifted his eyes to the bartender. "Good luck to you, Dan." He walked sideways to the front of the saloon, then holstered his weapon and stepped through the doorway. He mounted the gray and rode east as far as the livery stable, then turned north and headed cross-country. A few minutes later, he was out of sight.

27

★

The distance from Roma to Nacogdoches was five hundred miles, and Kane had been traveling steadily for the past seventeen days. Tonight, he sat beside a campfire a few miles southwest of the Neches River. He would ford the Angelina sometime tomorrow afternoon, then he would be home.

Although it was against his policy to sit in the glow of a campfire, tonight he had made an exception, for he had been cold all day long. The weather had cooled down as soon as he left the lower Rio Grande Valley, then turned downright cold as he rode farther north. He had stopped in the relatively new town of Cuero and bought a quilt and two blankets, for the covering he normally carried had become woefully inadequate.

He had build his fire beside a large boulder, knowing that the rock would deflect the heat back to his body. He did not need the fire for cooking, for he had already eaten a cold supper. He turned his body back and forth in front of the blaze till he began to feel like his bones had thawed out, then poured a coffeepotful of water on the fire. Moments later, he stretched out on the opposite side of the rock, with four blankets and a quilt atop his bedroll. Although the temperature would get below freezing before morning, he would be warm enough as long as he stayed under so much covering.

With his blankets pulled up under his chin, he lay thinking about his recent past, and contemplating his future. The thing with Mitchell and Lively was done, and he expected to hear no more about it. The identity and the whereabouts of the Third Man, however, might forever remain a mystery. The man could literally be anywhere, and with no name and no starting place, finding him would be next to impossible. Therefore, Jubal had decided that he would no longer be a manhunter, but a cattle rancher.

Though it would be several weeks yet before Grandpa took delivery of the Herefords, there was much to be done in the meantime. Turning a grain-and-hay farm into a cattle ranch not only involved a great deal of thinking, but also a lot of hard work. A rancher needed a vast number of things that a farmer had no use for, and most of them were acquired by the sweat of the brow.

Grandpa had said that he would keep as many of his farmers as he could turn into ranch hands, and Jubal had liked the idea. Both he and his grandfather already knew that the farmers would deliver an honest day's work for a dollar, and that they could very easily learn everything they needed to know as they went along. Besides, there was certainly nothing complicated about being a ranch hand, although it did involve a lot of hard work.

Jubal had long since decided that farming was harder work than ranching, however, and he was well experienced at both. Though he had been raised on a farm, he had hired out for three summers in a row to a Nacogdoches County cattle rancher, starting the year he was sixteen. Grandpa had not needed Jubal's help anyway, and had suggested that he accept the ranch work for both the money and the experience.

Jubal had even been involved in a three-hundred-mile cattle drive, which had left him with no desire to follow a herd all the way to Kansas. The forty-day round trip had been enough to rid him of any hankerings he might have had about pushing a herd north to the rails. Even when the day came that he had a herd of his own for sale, he expected to turn over the job of getting it to Kansas to a trail boss with a good reputation. Though such men did not come cheap, ranchers were nonetheless wise to hire them, for some of them knew the treacherous country between Texas and Kansas like the backs of their hands. They also knew cattle, and they knew how to dicker with buyers once they got a herd to the rails.

Kane turned on his side and pushed the matter out of his mind. He would have to grow a damned herd before he could sell it, and that took time, more than enough time to figure out who would be taking it to Kansas. He pulled the cover up over his stinging right ear, then went to sleep.

For the first time in several days, he saw the sun when he opened his eyes next morning. And though it was cold at the moment, he believed it might even become pleasant as the day wore on. He pulled on his boots, then got to his feet and buckled on his gunbelt. Using the dead grass and twigs he had gathered up the night before, he soon had a fire going.

He filled his coffeepot and set it on the fire, then led his horses into camp. He tied on their nosebags, then saddled the gray and buckled the packsaddle on the black while the animals ate.

When the coffeepot came to a boil, he set it on a rock and extinguished the fire with several handfuls of dirt. Then he dug Bologna sausage, cheese, and a tin of fish out of his pack and ate a cold breakfast, washing it down with three cups of strong coffee.

He was in the saddle ten minutes later, headed in a northeasterly direction. His long journey was about to come to an end, for he was now no more than twenty miles from the Angelina River. He would get a far-off look at his new home before he even reached the river, and he was more than a little anxious to see it. The house would not yet be ready to live in, of course, for such things took time, even for a master builder like Jesse Harper.

He forded the Neches River two hours later, then continued on at a steady pace. He had jumped more rabbits than he could count this morning, along with several white-tailed deer. Maybe the animals were as appreciative of this warming trend in the weather as he was, for they had seemed to be hopping along playfully instead of running for their lives.

Jubal saw the house from almost a mile away. He halted his animals and sat his saddle for a while, feasting his eyes on the place that he would most likely call home for the rest of his life. Perched atop Cedar Ridge, he could see that it was a two-story house, as he had requested, but none of the details was clear from this distance. He kicked the gray toward the river at a trot.

He was in the yard a few minutes later, circling the house. The builders had no doubt proved him wrong, for, from all appearances, they had already done their job and left the premises. They had not only finished building the house, but had painted it. Jubal had never even given a thought to what color he wanted, but the white with green trim looked beautiful, and could be seen from a long distance away. And though he had not mentioned it to his grandfather, the tin roof was exactly what he wanted. The day of the shingled roof had come and gone, Jubal believed. Tin did not leak, and it would last a long time.

Finally, he dismounted and tied his animals at the hitching rail some nice fellow had remembered to erect, then walked around the building, peeking through the windows. He tried both the front and the rear doors, only to find them locked, then walked several yards up the slope for a more commanding view. There were four large rooms on the ground floor, and he assumed that there were three or four smaller ones on the second story. He would have no way of knowing what was up there till he climbed the stairs.

Knowing that with no more than normal upkeep the house would last a man a lifetime, he was wondering how much money it had cost to build it. For no other reason than that his name was Jubal Kane, he himself now owned it free and clear, and the thought put a lump in his throat. He stood looking at the house for a long time, and though few of his friends would have considered him an emotional man, wiped a tear off his cheek as he walked back down the slope.

He untied his animals and mounted, then sat his saddle a few minutes longer, amazed at what the builders had accomplished in such a short time. Although the barn he would eventually need was yet to be built, a shed with a few stables and a pole corral had been erected. The well had been dug exactly where he had driven his stake, and the curb painted white.

Jubal smiled broadly when he noticed how Jesse Harper or some of his workers had solved the problem of getting water down to the animals. One-by-ten boards had been nailed together so that they formed a V, then dozens of them placed end to end, much like clapboarding, all the way down the slope to a large watering trough. There would be no carrying water to the horses in buckets. A man could stand right at the well and send any measure of it down to the corral without taking a step.

Well-pleased, Jubal kneed the gray down the hill toward the main road. A short time later, he rode into his grandfather's yard and dismounted. Frank Opal was quickly beside him, his right hand extended for a shake, while he gripped Jubal's shoulder with his left. "Best-looking fellow I ever laid eyes on," he said, pumping Jubal's hand a few times then releasing it. "I can't tell you how happy I am to see you, young man. Mr. and Mrs. Kane are gonna be happier'n that, just as soon as they get back." He pointed up the road. "They took the buggy and went into town about three hours ago."

Jubal smiled. "It's good to hear that," he said. "I mean, I'm happy to know that they're out doing a few things for themselves." He began to lead his horses toward the barn, and Opal walked alongside him. Jubal continued to talk. "I think Grandpa and Grandma ought to get out of that house and do something every day, Frank. I believe it'll make them feel younger, and it might even help them live a little longer. I've been after Grandma for years to take a long walk once in a while, anything besides staying cooped up all day."

Opal was now busy taking the load off the packhorse. "They must have paid a little bit of attention to you, then, Jubal," he said. "Both of 'em get out of the house pretty regular nowadays, setting out fruit trees or piddling around at something else. One time they were gone all morning. When they came back, they said they had walked more than ten miles."

"Ten miles," Jubal repeated, a look of satisfaction on his face.

A few minutes later, he walked into what had been his bedroom since he was fifteen years old. He took off his fleece-lined coat and draped it across the back of a chair, then stood for a while, taking stock. Every item in the room was lying exactly where he had left it. His grandmother surely dusted the room occasionally, he was thinking, but obviously took great pains to leave things the way she found them. He shook his head a few times, then sat down on the bed and took off his boots. He crawled under a thick quilt and fluffed up the pillow, then went to sleep.

The moment he opened his eyes, he knew that he had slept longer than he had intended to. His bedroom was on the west side of the house, and he could see through the window that the sun was already hanging low over the horizon. He quickly pulled on his boots, then got to his feet.

He walked down the hall and entered the living room just as Silas Kane was adding a thick chunk of wood to the fire in the fireplace. When he saw Jubal, he dropped the log in a shower of sparks, and quickly crossed the room. "Frank said you got back," he said, hugging his grandson. "We didn't want to wake you up, 'cause we figured you might need that sleep pretty bad."

Jubal returned the hug. "I guess I've been getting as much sleep as a man needs," he said. "It's just that I'd been cold all day, and that bed looked warm and inviting."

"Well, anyway, it's good to have you home again. Did you find your man?"

"Yes, sir. I found him in a little south Texas town called Roma. His name was Leroy Lively, and he won't be murdering anybody else's ma."

"I'm glad of that," the elder Kane said, pointing to a chair and motioning for Jubal to seat himself. "But mostly I'm just glad you're gonna be home from now on." He was quiet for a while, then added, "You are gonna be home, ain't you?"

Jubal nodded, then sat down. "I never could get a lead on the Third Man, Grandpa. Both of the men that I did find, refused to tell me anything at all about him. I don't even know his name, much less where he might be, so I guess the manhunt's over. Anyway, Ma and Pa were both already dead when he shot them."

Silas poked at the fire. "Did you look your new home over?" he asked.

"I sure did, and it looks like you outdid yourself. I can't think of anything I've ever done to deserve it, but I certainly won't forget that you did it." He sat quietly for a moment, then added, "I'll be moving a wife into the house pretty soon, Grandpa."

"A wife?" Silas asked excitedly. "You already got one picked out? Is it that girl in Bandera?"

Jubal nodded. "Yes," he said. "Yes, to all three questions. I'll take a wagon out there and get her after everything gets squared away here. We'll be married in her church, at Bandera."

"Well, I'll be," the old man said. "I bet she's a pretty one, too. Does she want to have children?"

"About six, is what she told me."

"Six!" Silas repeated loudly. "Six great-grandchildren." He got to his feet hurriedly, then turned toward the door. "Let me go tell your grandma about this. Don't know what's keeping her, she went to the chickenhouse to get the eggs quite a while ago."

At that moment, Estelle Kane stepped through the doorway, almost running into her husband. Bundled up against the cold, she set her basket of eggs on the floor and rushed into Jubal's open arms. "I prayed every day that you'd be all right," she said, hugging him as tightly as she could. "And it looks like you are." She pushed herself away and began to pinch his shoulder and his arm with a thumb and forefinger. "I do believe you've fell off a lot, though."

Jubal chuckled. "Maybe so," he said. "It's not just anywhere that a man can find cooking like yours, Grandma."

She hugged him again, then turned toward the kitchen. "We'll put that flesh right back on them bones," she said. Although she had by now disappeared into the kitchen, she was still within earshot. "Won't take me long to do it, either," she added.

Jubal walked down the hall to his bedroom, then returned with his heavy coat buttoned up under his chin. "I'm gonna walk up to the cemetery, Grandpa. I won't be gone long."

Silas nodded. "Want me to go with you?"

Jubal shook his head. "No, sir," he said. "I think I should go alone this time."

The old man squeezed Jubal's arm. "I understand," he said.

The cemetery was located atop a small knoll about three hundred yards from the house. Aside from his great-grandparents, both of whom had died before he was born, Bernard and Tess Kane were the only relatives Jubal had there.

When he reached the graveyard, he spoke to his great-grandparents just as if they were alive, then moved on to his parents' tall headstone. He stood between the graves with his hat in his hand for a while, then spoke to the mound of earth covering the remains of Bernard Kane: "I kept my promise to you, Pa. I finally found the man who shot you, and I did the same to him." Then he turned to

Tess Kane's mound. "The man who shot you won't be hurting anybody else, either, Ma."

He stood quietly between the mounds for several minutes, then finally spoke to both graves again. "Ma, Pa, I don't know much about the hereafter, and I never asked any of the preachers because I don't believe they know any more about it than I do. But I do know that most folks think there's life after death, and I've even heard that people get some kind of special powers after they die. Now, if that's so, I'm asking you to lead me to the Third Man. Otherwise, I'm gonna have to give up the hunt, because it's like looking for a needle in a haystack." He put on his hat and turned to leave, then as an afterthought, added, "I'll have a wife before long, and then I'll bring her by and let you see how pretty she is." Then he was gone.

Along with Frank Opal, Silas had hung on to six of his workers, four of them not yet out of their teens. Each of the youngsters, besides having youth and vitality on his side, had professed to have a sincere desire to be a cowboy, and all four had long since proved themselves to be good workers.

Fred Mayhue was a thirty-five-year-old jack-of-all-trades who could fix anything with moving parts. He was also the farm blacksmith, and had even been known to pick up a hoe if they were short-handed in the fields. Neither married nor showing any inclination to be, he had been on the farm for many years, and more than once Jubal had heard his grandfather refer to him as his right arm. "I believe I'd rather lose my wife than Mayhue," Silas had often joked.

The sixth man was well known for his ability to whip up a good meal out of nothing. He claimed to be the finished product of a cooking school, but most of the men doubted that he had ever attended a school of any kind. Jubal had no way of knowing, nor did he care. The man had certainly learned to cook somewhere, and few restaurants could put together a better cake, pie, or pudding. Now in his early thirties, Bo Rankin had excelled at one of the few occupations open to a man with only one foot. He had lost the lower part of his right leg to a mowing machine when he was twelve years old, and had worn a peg leg ever since. He was well liked by all who knew him, and had agreed to stay on and cook for the ranch hands.

Today Jubal was eating dinner in the cook's quarters with the hands. The four youngsters were all present, telling jokes and laughing as they ate. "Mr. Silas bought the herd with the understanding that the buyer was gonna deliver it," a boy named Russell was saying. "But he says he wants us to go to Waco and ride back with the cattle, so we can get some experience."

"That oughta be fun," a kid name Andy said quickly. "How many days do you think we'll be on the trail?"

When nobody answered the question, Jubal spoke up. "Long enough for the fun part to wear off," he said. The youngsters finished their meal in silence, then left the building, playfully punching at each other as they trotted out of sight.

Bo Rankin poured a cup of coffee and seated himself on the bench beside Jubal. "Damn shame them boys can't bottle all that extra energy and save it till they get old enough to need it," he said.

"They're excited about the fact that they're gonna be trailing cows instead of hanging on to a plow handle," Jubal said. "I can't say that I blame them there, because I never did look forward to a plow or a hoe handle in my hand, either. There's plenty of work involved in trailing cows, though, and they'll find that out soon enough. They think it's gonna be nothing but fun taking part in a cattle drive, but they'll probably change their minds by the time they get through fighting that herd across the Brazos and the Trinity Rivers."

Jubal spent the next day in the saddle. Both the size and the shape of the ranch had changed since his grandfather had bought the two additional sections of land, and Frank Opal had volunteered to show him the boundaries, as well as the line shacks he and the youngsters had built on the four corners. Knowing that they were going to be the ones who lived there, the boys had worked hard and seen to every last detail, Opal said.

At the northeast corner, Jubal spent several minutes inspecting the shack, then commented, "I believe this thing's put together about as well as most people's houses, Frank." Framed with four-by-fours and two-by-fours, the ten- by twelve-foot clapboard shack had a tin roof with a one-foot overhang. A small stove that would also serve as a heater occupied one corner, and a small table and two chairs were closer to the door. Two bunks were snug against the back wall, both of them furnished with blankets and a pillow.

Back outside, Jubal stood looking at a one- by twelve-inch board that had been nailed between two saplings to form a shelf. He pointed to the washpan and the water bucket on the shelf, then motioned toward the shack. "Hell, Frank, I might want to move into this place myself. Are the other three like this?"

Opal nodded. "They're all off of the same pattern," he said. "If you see one, you've seen 'em all."

Jubal stepped into the stirrup and threw his leg over the saddle. "I haven't been in as many line shacks as a lot of men have," he said. "But I can guarantee you that most ranches don't put their line riders up this good. Hell, the line shacks on all three of the ranches I've worked on were falling down. I remember seeing part of the roof missing on one, but they said a fellow was still living in it."

Opal led off toward the northwest corner. "I've been with your granddaddy so long that I just about don't remember how it was on some of the other farms and ranches that I worked on. I do know that the word gets around mighty quick about how a man treats his workers, though. If he treats 'em good, he can find a hand mighty easy when he needs one. Now, take your granddaddy. He wouldn't have no problem stealing help from any ranch in this county, 'cause everybody knows that he treats a man like a man."

By day's end, Jubal had familiarized himself with the north end of the ranch. The more of it he saw, the more impressed he was. His grandfather's purchase of the two additional sections had been a wise investment, for a man would be hard put to find better cattle country. Shade was abundant, and some of the perennial grasses were almost knee-high. Water would never be a problem, for in addition to the Angelina River, which bordered the property on the west, several springs dotted the landscape, and two creeks ran the length of the ranch. Jubal had no doubt whatsoever that the Herefords would thrive on the Circle K.

He loosed the gray in the corral at sunset, then joined his grandparents for supper. Afterward, the three sat around the fireplace, talking. His grandmother was busy knitting Jubal a sweater by lamplight, while Silas was discussing business.

"I think you oughta take them boys and go on up to Longview and get them horses, Jubal," the old man was saying. "If we allow them to get used to this place before the cows get here, that's one less problem we'll have."

Jubal nodded. "We've got to have 'em, Grandpa. These plow horses we've got now won't be worth two cents after the cows get here."

"We'll be getting rid of most of them pretty soon," Silas said. "I aim to keep three or four of 'em, though, so we can raise a little hay and plow the garden." He was quiet for a while, then asked, "You remember where Will Granger's place is, don't you?"

"Yes, sir. It's been several years since you and I were up there, but I believe I can ride straight to it."

"All right, then," the old man said. "You do that." He poked at the fire for a while, then continued to talk. "Now, I ain't got nothing in writing, but me and Will never have done business that way nohow. The agreement was that he'd sell me twenty head of well-trained cow horses, all of them ten years old or younger, for five hundred dollars. I'll send him a check for that amount."

Jubal was on his feet. "I guess I'll go to the bunkhouse and talk to our young horse wranglers," he said, chuckling. "I know that all four of 'em are gonna hate the idea of traveling."

Silas laughed aloud. "I'll bet," he said.

28

Next morning at ten, Jubal and the four youngsters, Russell Kemp, Andy Furlo, Jimmy Austin, and Hanson Perry, rode out of the barnyard headed for the town of Longview, which was about eighty miles due north. Jubal was leading the same packhorse that had been following him for more than a year, and Russell Kemp led a big gelding that was fully capable of carrying the heavy load strapped on his back.

The two pack animals carried everything the men were likely to need, and eliminated the bother of taking a wagon. And though a man would have a hard time chasing a wayward animal back into the herd while leading a packhorse, Jubal had no intention of doing any chasing. On the return trip he would lead both pack animals and let the youngsters do the work.

Skirting Nacogdoches on the west, they traveled till an hour before sunset, then halted at a spring just across the

Rusk County line. "All right, boys," Jubal said, dismounting. "You're on your own now, and I'm just along for the ride. I want two of you to see how quick you can get these horses on their picket ropes; and the other two can get a fire going and rustle up some grub." He stripped his saddle and turned the gray's reins over to Hanson Perry, then stretched out on the ground, his head resting on his bedroll.

Even the conversation of the young men a few yards away was not enough to keep him awake. He dozed off quickly, and it was dark when Jimmy Austin woke him. "Supper's ready, Jubal," he said. "Better get it while it's hot."

Kane was soon seated beside the fire, holding a tin plate filled with bacon and fried potatoes. Russell Kemp handed him a cup of steaming coffee. "This might be too strong," he said. "I didn't know exactly how many grounds to put in the pot."

"Don't worry about it," Jubal said. He sipped the bitter liquid without complaining, and after sprinkling a pinch of salt on his potatoes, enjoyed his supper.

None of the boys seemed eager to go to bed after the meal was over. Kemp washed the cooking and eating utensils at the spring, then joined the others around the campfire. "Russell cooked that supper," Andy Furlo informed Jubal. "He's a whole lot better cook than the rest of us."

Jubal took a final sip from his cup, then dashed the remainder of the too-strong coffee into the top of a bush. "Well, I guess Russell would always be the best cook if we let him do all of it, but that's not the way it works. Since nobody's been hired for that specific purpose, the cooking job'll pass from one man to another every day or so." Jubal chuckled, then added, "You're next, Andy. Right after daybreak it'll be your job to put breakfast together. Then around noon, you'll be expected to make a pot of coffee. Somebody else'll cook supper tomorrow night, and we'll just keep on rotating. We should be in Longview two days from now, then I'll buy everybody a restaurant meal."

They reached Longview in the early afternoon two days later, and Jubal kept his promise by leading the boys into the first restaurant he saw. A pretty waitress showed them to a table, then laid a bill of fare in front of each man. "Let me know when you decide," she said, then moved across the room.

Jimmy Austin picked up the menu and stared at it for a few moments, then spoke to Jubal. "I ain't never ate in no restaurant before," he said. "Am I supposed to just pick out what I want and tell her?"

"That's what you do, Jimmy," Kane answered. It was then that he noticed that Hanson Perry had never picked up his menu. Jubal turned it over and pointed. "Look at all the choices you've got, Hanson," he said. "Order anything you want, I'll pay for it."

Perry stared at the table for a moment, then shook his head. "I can't read good enough to make all that out, Jubal."

"Why, we can whip that little problem mighty easy," Kane said softly. He bent closer to the boy and began to read the menu to him. "There," Hanson said, after listening to a few of his choices. "Them stuffed pork chops. I bet they taste good."

"I'm sure they do," Jubal said, returning the menu to the table. "When the girl comes back, just tell her that's what you want."

Within the hour, they had eaten and were back at the hitching rail. "Will Granger's place is about four miles up that road," Jubal said, pointing north. "He won't be expecting us, so we probably won't be getting the horses right away. It's too late to start down the trail with them today anyway, but we'll ride on up and let Granger know we're here." He mounted the gray and headed north, with the young men following close behind.

After three miles or so they came to an intersection, where a narrow wagon road led off to the east. A roadside sign stated that the Lazy G ranch was one mile in that direction, and a large, painted arrow pointed the way. Jubal made the turn, and led his crew toward Will Granger's headquarters.

"Awful lot of grass between these ruts," Perry said after a while. "You reckon these folks don't ever go to town?"

"Sure, they go," Jubal answered. "The reason the grass grows in the middle of the road is because most ranches don't use one-horse wagons very often."

"Oh," Perry said.

The Lazy G ranch had the look of a very successful operation, right down to the peeled poles of near-identical size that made up the fences and corrals. There was a host of barns and other outbuildings, most with tin roofs, and all painted red. The main house was two stories high, with front porches above and below. White with gray trim, the building was considerably larger than most ranch houses, and Jubal thought it might have as many as fifteen rooms.

As Kane and his crew rode abreast of the bunkhouse, a medium-sized man of middle age stepped out the door and into their path, signaling them to halt. Though he said nothing, it was obvious that he expected Kane to state his business.

"Good afternoon," Jubal said, tightening the rein on the prancing gray. "I'm Silas Kane's grandson, and I'm here to pick up the horses he bought from Mr. Granger."

The man's feeble attempt at a smile failed. "Howdy," he said in a deep voice. "Get down and rest yourselves. I reckon you've had a long ride."

The two men were soon shaking hands. "My name's Jeb Granger," the man said, squeezing Kane's hand with a grip that was unnecessarily firm. He finally managed the smile he had attempted earlier, then added, "I'm Will Granger's son, which is probably the only reason I'm the boss around here."

Kane introduced himself and his crew. Each of the boys came away rubbing his right hand after shaking hands with Granger, and Jubal's own fingers had not yet quit aching. He had long wondered why some men were forever trying to show off their strength with a bone-crushing handshake, but it was a fact of life that was not likely to change.

"Pa told me about the deal he made with your grand-daddy," Jeb Granger said. "I've pretty much got the horses picked out already, but it'll take a while to round 'em up." He glanced at the sun. "Don't believe we've got enough daylight left to get it done today, but I can put some men on it first thing in the morning."

"That'll be fine," Kane said. "Now, if you don't mind us camping on your premises, we'll be getting on out of your way."

"Why, you can eat supper with us if you want to," Granger said. "Sleep in the bunkhouse, too. Might not be no empty bunks, but we'll make out somehow."

Jubal shook his head. "We brought everything we need, Mr. Granger. If you'll just point out a place for us to set up camp, we'll get to it."

Granger pointed west. "Hell, just anywhere down there in that pasture'll do. There's a good spring about two hundred yards south of that smallest barn, but it might be half full of horse shit. If it is, just let me know.

I'll give you a coupla buckets, and you can get your water from the well."

"Thank you," Kane said, yanking on his packhorse's lead rope. "We'll see you in the morning." He kneed the gray toward the pasture.

"Pa's gonna be in Dallas all this week," Granger called after him. "I sure hate him not being here when you came for the horses."

Jubal turned in the saddle. "That's all right," he said, chuckling. "I already heard you say that you're the boss, so we can do business without him." He rode out into the pasture, and the young men followed.

As he had done for the entire trip, Jubal left all of the camping chores to the boys. "Ain't no horse shit in that spring," Russell Kemp said, as he dropped an armload of deadwood on the spot he had chosen for his cooking fire. Jubal said nothing, and Kemp knelt to kindle a blaze, adding, "I'll get a little heat going and thaw everybody out, then we'll all feel better. Looks like about two hours till dark, so if I put on a pot of beans now, they oughta be ready by then." He struck a match and blew on the small pile of dead grass and twigs till it caught, then laid on a few larger limbs. "I reckon I oughta make a pot of coffee, too. Everybody I know can handle a cup of that just about any time." He picked up the coffeepot and the boiler, then headed for the spring.

When Austin, Furlo, and Perry returned from staking out the horses, each of them carried an armload of deadwood. "This'll be enough to see us through the night and cook breakfast in the morning," Austin said, adding his wood to the pile. He pointed toward the thicket a hundred yards away. "Been a mighty strong storm through here not too many years ago. The trees we got these dead limbs off of hadn't been cut down; the wind tore 'em out of the ground, roots and all."

"A tornado might have touched down and run along that ridge," Jubal said.

"Had to be something like that," Austin agreed. "Whatever it was, tore them trees all to hell, and there's enough deadwood on the ground to burn a campfire for a lifetime. You don't need an ax to get it, either. The wind's done cut it up for you."

Each of the young men selected a spot and spread his bedroll, then returned to the campfire, where all of them sat around talking and drinking coffee till the sun disappeared. Just as darkness closed in, Kemp pulled the boiler and the iron skillet off the fire. "This stuff's as ready as it's ever gonna get," he said, then stepped back to avoid the rush. All five men were soon eating from plates filled with bacon, beans, and fried potatoes, and sipping coffee from Kemp's second pot of the night.

When the meal was over, Hanson Perry washed all of the utensils without being asked, then returned them to the pack. "Guess it'll be my turn to fix breakfast in the morning, huh?" he asked of no one in particular.

The fact that nobody answered his question was an indication that the matter had been settled.

At sunup next morning, with Jubal and the other three youngsters in the meadow catching up the horses, Hanson Perry was alone in camp. He had just kindled his breakfast fire, when one of Granger's hands showed up with two dozen eggs. "The boss thought you fellows might want these for breakfast," the man said. "We've got more hens around here than you can shake a stick at, so it ain't gonna be putting us out none."

Perry accepted the eggs and thanked the man, then very quickly changed his breakfast plans. By the time the others returned with the horses, their potato-and-scrambled-egg meal was well under way. They saddled their mounts and loaded the pack horses, then seated themselves on the ground to await the breakfast call.

A crowd of men had gathered around the main corral, and when Kane noticed that Granger was among them, he walked over. When Kane offered the help of himself and his crew in rounding up the horses, Granger declined, saying that his crew knew exactly where the animals could be found, and since the men were used to working together, they could do the job quicker by themselves. "The horses'll be in that big corral over there in less than two hours," he said, pointing. "Maybe less than one hour."

Knowing that the man was right, Jubal nodded, then walked back to his camp. "Might as well make another pot of coffee, Hanson," he said. "I think we're gonna have at least a two-hour wait." He glanced at his watch, then took a seat on the ground. He would time the roundup.

The wait was not a long one. One hour and ten minutes later, the twenty horses were trotting around inside the corral. Jubal mounted the gray and trotted over, followed closely by the four mounted youngsters. He slowly walked his horse down the side of the corral, looking the animals over. He liked what he saw.

"I'd give 'em about an hour to settle down if I were you," Granger said. "Nervous as they are, they might be hard to handle if you take 'em out now."

"Yes, sir," Kane said. "We'll do that." He handed over Silas Kane's check. "I guess this'll square things up."

Granger looked at the check thoughtfully for a few moments. "Five hundred dollars?" he asked finally.

"That's what Grandpa said the agreement called for," Jubal said. "Were you expecting more?"

Granger shook his head. "Hell, no," he said. "I was expecting less. I reckon by God Pa's a better horse trader than I am." He motioned toward the animals. "Not that these ain't good horses, mind you, 'cause they are. It's just that the price of horseflesh is way down nowadays." He folded the check and shoved it into his pocket.

Once the animals were in the corral, the Lazy G crew's work was done, and the men disappeared soon after. Granger and Kane continued to lean against corral posts, watching the horses. "You can see how much they've settled down," Granger was saying, "and they ain't been in there more'n half an hour."

"I like that," Kane said. "I don't want to have to chase them all day."

"You won't have to chase 'em at all if you handle it right," Granger said. "You ever done much horse wrangling?"

"No," Kane answered.

"Well, in that case, let me tell you a few of the tricks. One of 'em is, to never let the animals get started running. Of course, my boys were running 'em a little while ago, but that's 'cause the horses already knew where they were going." He chuckled, then added, "Getting this bunch to Nacogdoches is gonna be about as easy as falling off a log." He pointed to a big white mare with a flowing mane. "If you put a rope on her and let one of them boys lead her up front, the rest of these horses'll follow her to hell and back. You can take 'em right down the middle of the road for most of the way. Ain't much wagon traffic on that route nohow."

Half an hour later, Kane learned that Granger knew what he was talking about. When Russell Kemp led the white mare through the corral gate, the other horses followed of their own accord. When Kemp circled the corral and headed for the main road, the entire herd, with just a little harassment by the riders, fell in behind the mare. With one of the youngsters on each side of the herd and another riding drag, they soon disappeared up the road.

Bringing up the rear and leading both of the packhorses, Kane waved good-bye to Granger just before he rode out of sight.

Granger had said that all of the horses had trailed before. The truth of that statement became apparent early on, for after jostling one another for a while, each of the animals finally settled on a particular position in line and held it. As Jeb Granger had predicted, there was little driving involved. Even when Kemp circled around the town of Longview, the herd voluntarily left the road and stayed on the mare's heels.

29

★

They continued to travel steadily south, usually making at least twenty miles a day. The weather had turned unseasonably warm, and every man had shucked his coat and tied it behind his saddle. Even at night, when each man took his two-hour turn at guard duty, a coat was unnecessary.

The trip was uneventful, and they reached Nacogdoches an hour before noon on the fourth day. Kane turned the reins of the packhorses over to Hanson Perry, then sat his saddle, watching as Russell Kemp led the herd cross-country to skirt the town. Jubal had told the boys around the campfire last night that he would leave them here, for he had business to take care of. "Just tell Grandpa that I've got to talk a little business with the hardware and the furniture store," he had said to Perry when he handed him the reins. "Tell him I plan to be home before dark."

Jubal sat in the road watching till the herd disappeared, then he kneed the gray toward town at a canter.

He would do no buying today, for he had long since decided to let Jenny Hilton pick out her own furnishings. He would look over the selection in both of the town's furniture stores, however, so he would at least have some idea of what was to be had.

Maybe he would talk stoves and prices with Jeremy Gooding at the hardware store, but since Jenny would be the one to use it, in the end that choice would also be hers. He had already made an estimate as to what it would cost to furnish his home, but if he had to pay more, so be it. He certainly wanted quality goods that would not fall apart the first year.

Jubal had also decided not to tarry any longer before going after Jenny. Now that he would not be spending his time searching for the Third Man, he saw no compelling reason why he should not hitch up a team and leave for Bandera right away. There was no doubt in his mind that Jenny would marry him on any date he chose, so why wait till spring? Even Grandpa had asked why he did not get married in the wintertime, when there was nothing else to do.

By the time he reached town, Kane had made a decision to head for Bandera the day after tomorrow. He had also rethought the matter and decided that he would ask no questions about stoves or furniture. Just by looking in the stores, he could tell whether or not they had the things he was going to need.

He rode by Gooding's hardware first, and did not even have to dismount. A four-burner cast-iron stove with a large oven and hot-water reservoir was on display in front of the store. He could not read the tag from where he sat, but he knew that he would pay the asking price if Jenny wanted the stove.

He did dismount at the furniture store, but did not go inside. Standing on the boardwalk looking through the window, he could see that the store had a wide variety of pretty things for his bride to choose from. The large showroom was filled with furniture of every description. They could please his Jenny, all right.

He remounted and rode down the street at a trot, nodding or waving to one acquaintance after another. A short time later, he tied the gray at the bank's hitching rail, then stepped up onto the boardwalk. Just as he reached for the knob, the door opened from the inside, and Kane was suddenly face-to-face with Sheriff Pat Patterson for the first time in many years.

"Jubal Kane," the lawman said, beaming. "I've been aiming to get in touch with you, but I figured you were still off hunting the men who gunned down Tess and Bernard." He did not extend his right hand, probably because he doubted that Kane would accept it. He moved to the side of the door, and Kane did likewise. "I want to apologize for the way I treated you back then, Jubal," Patterson said. "My only excuse is that I couldn't find any evidence to support your claim.

"I believe every word of your story now, though. You see, I had a long talk with Warden Brady when I took a prisoner down to the state pen a while back. He told me how Sheriff Randy Bacon had vouched for you, and how you identified two of the killers from pictures in his files. Brady said you left Huntsville on the trail of two men named Mitchell and Lively. Did you ever find them?"

Kane stood thoughtfully for a few moments. "I heard that somebody killed both of them," he said finally.

Patterson chuckled. "I take that to mean you found them," he said. "You said there were three men in the barn that morning. Do you know who the third man is?"

Kane shook his head. "Never have been able to find out. I know what he looks like and what he sounds like, but I have no idea where he lives or what his name is."

The sheriff finally offered a handshake, and Kane went along. "This makes me feel a lot better," Patterson said, "and I'm hoping we can be friends from now on." He released Kane's hand and took a step backward, then added, "Here's something to think about, Jubal. We know for sure that the third man has been in this area at least once, so who's to say that he won't come around here again? I'll tell you this right now: If you ever see him in this county, plant the son of a bitch. I damn sure won't be asking you no questions if you do." He spun on his heel, and walked down the street.

Even after the lawman had disappeared into a dry-goods store, Kane still stood on the street, wondering about the man. Had Patterson apologized for his earlier actions because he was truly sorry? Or had he done so only because Jubal was now old enough to vote? Kane was inclined to believe the latter, for a skunk did not change its stripes. One thing Patterson had said that Jubal did believe, however, was that he would ask no questions if Kane happened to spot the third man in Nacogdoches County. Small chance, Jubal was thinking, as he pushed the door open and entered the bank.

Although he doubted that he would need anything close to two hundred dollars for his trip to Bandera, he withdrew that amount from his account. A man never knew what he might run into, and it was wise to be prepared. He said hello to a female teller that he had gone to school with, then left the building.

He did not remount, but led the gray across the street and tied him at one of Toot Brewster's hitching rails. Then he entered the saloon. Standing just inside the doorway, he could see at a glance that the establishment was much busier than usual. Several drinkers sat around tables, and at least two poker games were in progress. A waitress was on the floor, and Brewster himself was behind the bar.

Kane stepped forward and pulled out a barstool. "I stopped in for a beer or two or three, Toot," he said, pushing his right hand across the bar for a shake.

Brewster pumped the hand a few times and released it. "Good to see you, Jubal." He turned to draw the beer. A moment later, he set the mug at Kane's elbow, then wiped the bar. "This one's on me," he said. "Maybe you'll come around a little more often if you don't have to pay for anything."

Brewster was a big man, not quite as tall as Kane, but both wider and thicker. About thirty years old, with thinning brown hair and brown eyes, he was the younger of the two brothers who had erected the building half a dozen years ago. The only sons of Elwood Brewster, a wealthy cattleman in the northern part of the county, the young men had been staked and encouraged to go into business by their father.

The establishment had originally been a restaurant, but because most diners had ignored it, a few modifications had eventually turned it into a saloon. Elwood Jr. had finally sold his interest to his younger brother Toot, and had rejoined his father in the cattle business. The saloon had immediately begun to prosper after Elwood Jr.'s departure, leading Jubal to think that the elder brother might have been the problem right from the start.

Kane jerked his head toward the back of the room. "Looks like business is a whole lot better than it used to be, Toot. Are you giving free beer to everybody?"

Brewster chuckled, and shook his head. "Not very often," he said. "Business picked up right after I bought my brother out. A few men have told me that they hadn't used to come in here on account of him, so I guess maybe that's part of it. All I know for sure is that I sell a hell of a lot more whiskey than I did when I had a partner, so I intend to go it alone."

Kane took a sip of his beer, then changed the subject. "Where'd you get her?" he asked, indicating the waitress with a shift of his eyes.

"Oh," Brewster said, smiling from only one corner of his mouth. "She's from Longview." He refilled Kane's mug, then continued. "Her name is Lily, and she used to work at a restaurant up in Longview. I was eating there one day, and when she found out that I owned a saloon, she came right to my table and asked me if it was true that some saloon waitresses earned as much as two dollars a night in gratuities. When I told her it was, she asked me for a job right on the spot."

"Did you hire her right on the spot?" Jubal asked.

"No," Brewster said, the smile constant. "The man who owns that restaurant is a friend of mine, and I wouldn't do that to a friend." He laughed aloud. "All I did was tell her that if she quit and came to Nacogdoches, I'd hire her after she got here. A week later, she walked through the front door."

"Well, she's damn sure a looker," Jubal said.

Brewster nodded. "She's getting her two dollars a day, too."

The saloon became more crowded as the afternoon wore on, and Brewster had less time to talk. Jubal had refused a refill the last time Toot walked by, for he had reached his three-beer limit, and was about to vacate the premises.

He had just slid off his stool and tilted his beer mug to empty it, when he heard a sound that had haunted him in his dreams: "That's my queen right there!" a squeaky voice shouted at a nearby poker table. Jubal's hand froze in midair.

The Third Man! There was no mistaking the voice, and Kane knew what he would see even before he turned his head to look. He set his mug down quietly, then slowly turned around and leaned against the bar. The speaker was on his feet pointing to a pile of cards on the table. "The queen of clubs!" he was shouting. "That's the first card I drawed right off'n the top of the deck!"

Kane continued to stare, amazed at how little the man had changed. The sandy-colored hair, the beak-shaped nose, and the long lower jaw looked just as they had in the barn that morning more than seven years ago. And that squeaky voice was surely one of a kind. He was as short and skinny as Jubal remembered, and now appeared to be about thirty years old.

Kane was relieved to see that the man had a gunbelt around his waist and a six-gun hanging on his right leg, for that meant Jubal could challenge him openly. Though two of the gamblers had gotten to their feet and moved away, the other two had kept their seats. The Third Man was still standing beside the poker table arguing, when Jubal decided that the time had come.

He jiggled his Peacemaker up and down a few times to make sure it was riding easy in its holster, then moved away from the bar. He was at the table quickly. He spoke to the men who were still seated, though his eyes were on the Third Man. "I'd appreciate it if you men would move away from the table," he said. "I've got some business with this man who's doing all the talking." The men got to their feet and scampered away.

"Wha—what do you mean, fella?" the Third Man asked. "I never saw you before in my life!"

Jubal was already in his gunfighter's crouch. "I know you haven't seen me before, but I've damn sure seen you!

Seven years ago, I lay in a barn loft not ten miles from here and watched you put a bullet into my dead ma and another one into my pa. Of course, your friends Mitchell and Lively had already killed both of them, but you didn't know that. You put a bullet in each one of them just to make sure." Kane pointed at the man with the forefinger of his left hand. "Mitchell and Lively are both dead, you son of a bitch, and you're next!"

Three shots rang out so quickly that they sounded almost like one, then the Third Man was on the floor. He had never fired his weapon, for Kane's first shot had taken him in the right shoulder and paralyzed his shooting arm. Jubal had placed his second and third shots just below the man's belt.

When Kane stepped forward to look the man over, one glance told him all he needed to know. He holstered his weapon and walked to the bar, where Toot Brewster stood with his mouth open. "He was one of the three men who murdered my parents, Toot," Jubal said.

"Well, I'll be damned!" Brewster said loudly.

Kane took an eagle from his pocket and laid it on the bar. "Give this to the undertaker. If it costs more, tell him to send me a bill." He took several long strides, and was quickly out the front door.

He rode to the top of the hill, then halted. He twisted his body in the saddle and sat gazing down into the little community. It was probably the last town on earth in which he would have expected to find the Third Man. With all the bigger and richer places Texas had to offer, what would bring him to Nacogdoches? A slight chill ran through Jubal's body when he suddenly remembered that only a few days ago he had asked his parents to lead him to the Third Man. Was that it? Had Ma and Pa arranged the meeting? He would never know.

He turned in the saddle and headed for home. Some big changes were about to take place in his life. His man-hunting days were over, and he would soon have a wife, then children. And he had some cattle to raise. He kicked the gray to a canter, then disappeared over the hill.